THE COMPLETE HOLLY WRAITHS
2023 Edition

Ghost Stories and Dark Tales for Christmas
on British Radio and Television

THE COMPLETE HOLLY WRAITHS

By Jack L. Hughes

Ghost stories and Dark Tales for Christmas on British Radio and Television

Other books by Jack L. Hughes:

Holly Wraiths
Ghost Stories for Christmas on British Radio & Television

Holly Terrors
Dark Tales for Christmas on British Radio & Television

Target Books: Adventures Without the Doctor
A survey of 200 non-Doctor Who Target Books

Nosferatu: A Fairy Tale

The Complete Holly Wraiths: 2023 Edition
© Jack L. Hughes & Tristan Sargent 2023

All Rights Reserved

Contents

Introduction 25
THE AFFAIR AT GROVER STATION 29
AFTER SUPPER GHOST STORIES 30
A.J. ALAN'S GHOST STORIES 31
ALAS, POOR GHOST! 32
AND THEN THERE WERE NONE 33
ANGELS AT PARTRIDGE COTTAGE 34
THE ASH TREE (1975) 35
THE BALLAD OF COCK LANE 36
BELL, BOOK AND CANDLE 37
THE BELLS OF ASTERCOTE 37
BEOWULF 39
BERGERAC: FIRES IN THE FALL 40
THE BEST OF BIERCE 41
BLACK CHRISTMAS (1993) 41
BLACK NARCISSUS (2020) 42
BLIND MAN'S HOOD 44
BLITHE SPIRIT 45
    Blithe Spirit (1954) 45

    Blithe Spirit (1983) 45

    Blithe Spirit (2008) 46

    Blithe Spirit (2014) 46

THE BLUE BOY 47

THE BOARDED WINDOW 48

THE BOOK PROGRAMME: TALES OF HORROR 48

BUMP IN THE NIGHT 49

BWGANOD 49

THE CABARET OF DOCTOR CALIGARI: THE BODY POLITIC .. 50

CABIN B-13 51

THE CAMP OF THE DOG 52

A CANDLE FOR CASEY 53

THE CANTERVILLE GHOST 53

    The Canterville Ghost (1962) 53

    The Canterville Ghost (1974) 54

    The Canterville Ghost (1992) 54

    Theatre Royal: The Canterville Ghost (1953) 54

    The Canterville Ghost (1997) 55

    The Canterville Ghost (2004) 55

    The Canterville Ghost (2021) 55

THE CASK OF AMONTILLADO (1995) 55

CAUSING A SCENE: GHOSTS (2022) 57

THE CAVE OF HARMONY (2000) 57

THE CHANNEL 4 SILENT 58

THE CHILD AND THE MAN 59

THE CHILDREN OF GREEN KNOWE 59

    Jackanory - The Children of Green Knowe (1966) 60

The Children of Green Knowe (1989)	60
The Children of Green Knowe (1999)	61
A CHILD'S VOICE	62
THE CHIMES	64
The Chimes (1944)	65
The Chimes (1961)	65
The Chimes (2003)	66
A CHRISTMAS CAROL	66
Scholars' Half-Hour: A Short Talk on Dickens's Christmas Carol	66
A Christmas Carol (1924)	67
A Christmas Carol (1926)	67
A Christmas Carol (1926)	67
Scrooge (1928)	67
A Christmas Carol (1929)	67
Scrooge (1932)	68
A Christmas Carol (1933)	68
A Christmas Carol (1935)	69
A Christmas Carol (1936)	69
Children's Hour: A Christmas Carol	69
A Christmas Carol (1942)	70
A Christmas Carol (1943)	70
A Christmas Carol (1947)	71
A Christmas Carol (1948)	71
A Christmas Carol (1950, Radio)	71
A Christmas Carol (1950, TV)	71
A Christmas Carol (1951, Radio)	72
Scrooge (1951, Radio)	72

Solo Performance (1952) 72

Theatre Royal: A Christmas Carol (1953) 73

A Christmas Carol (1955) 73

A Christmas Carol (1962) 73

Sunday Story: A Christmas Carol (1963) 74

A Christmas Carol (1965) 74

A Christmas Carol (1966) 74

Mr Scrooge (1967) 75

Characters from Dickens: Ebenezer Scrooge 75

A Christmas Carol (1970) 75

A Christmas Carol (1971) 76

A Christmas Carol (1974) 77

Marcel Marceau presents A Christmas Carol 77

A Christmas Carol (1977) 78

A Christmas Carol (1978) 79

A Christmas Carol (1982) 79

A Christmas Carol (1982) 79

A Book at Bedtime - A Christmas Carol (1985) 80

Humbug! 80

Saturday Playhouse - A Christmas Carol (1990) 80

A Christmas Carol (1993) 81

Scrooge – The Musical (1995) 81

A Christmas Carol (1995) 81

An Audience with Charles Dickens (1996) 82

A Christmas Carol (2000) 82

A Christmas Carol (2005) 83

A Christmas Carol (2006) 83

A Book at Bedtime - A Christmas Carol (2008) 83

Saturday Drama - A Christmas Carol (2014) 84

Archive on 4 – The Many Faces of Ebenezer Scrooge 84

Friday Night is Music Night – A Christmas Carol (2016) 85

A Christmas Carol (2018) 85

A Christmas Carol (2019) 86

A Christmas Carol (2021) 87

A Christmas Carol: A Ghost Story (2022) 87

CHRISTMAS CHILLS 87

A CHRISTMAS GHOST STORY 88

CHRISTMAS SPIRITS (1981) 88

CHRISTMAS SPIRITS (1992) 89

CHRISTMAS SPIRITS (2003) 90

CHRISTOPHER LEE'S FIRESIDE TALES 90

CHRISTOPHER LEE'S GHOST STORIES FOR CHRISTMAS 91

CLASSIC GHOST STORIES (1986) 92

CLASSIC STORIES: STORIES FOR CHRISTMAS (2018) 93

COUNT DRACULA 95

DAEMON 100

THE DARKEST ROOM 101

DARK MATTER 101

DEAD OF NIGHT: THE EXORCISM 102

THE DEAD ROOM 104

THE DEMON CAKESTAND OF BEESTLEY CHASE 105

THE DEMON KING 106

THE DEMON OF TIDWORTH 107

DETECTORISTS: 2015 CHRISTMAS SPECIAL 107

THE DEVIL'S CHRISTMAS	109
THE DICK POWELL SHOW PRESENTS: THE CLOCKS	110
DOCTOR WHO: THE CHIMES OF MIDNIGHT	111
DOCTOR WHO AND THE DAEMONS	111
DOCTOR WHO: THE UNQUIET DEAD	113
THE DOG	114
DON'T LOOK NOW	114
DO YOU BELIEVE IN GHOSTS?	115
DRACULA (1975)	116
DRACULA (1991)	117
DRACULA (BBC World Service, 2006)	118
DRACULA (BBC1, 2006)	120
DRACULA (2012)	121
DRACULA (2020)	122
DRACULA'S GUEST	124
DRACULA RE-VISITED	125
THE DRACULA TOUR	125
THE DROVER'S PATH	125
DUNWORTHY 13	126
ECHOES	126
ECHOES FROM THE ABBEY	127
EDGAR ALLAN POE'S GOTHIC TALES	127
EMILY'S GHOST	128
THE EMPTY HOUSE	129
THE EMPTY SLEEVE	129
THE ENFIELD POLTERGEIST	130
ENOCH SOAMES	131

THE EXORCISM	131
FAMOUS GHOSTS	132
FANTASTIC TALES	132
FEAR ON FOUR	133
Gobble Gobble	133
The Horn	134
The Snowman Killing	135
THE FEMALE GHOST	135
THE FIDDLER	136
FIVE DAHLS	136
THE FLIES OF ISIS	137
FORGET TOMORROW'S MONDAY	138
FOUR ROUND A FIRE	138
FRANKENSTEIN (1984)	139
FRANKENSTEIN (2012)	140
FRANKENSTEIN, OR THE MODERN PROMETHEUS (1972)	141
FRANKENSTEIN - THE REAL STORY	141
FRANKENSTEIN: THE TRUE STORY	142
FRANKENSTEIN (2004)	144
FROM UNQUIET REST	144
THE FURTHER REALM	144
THE GHOST OF CHRISTMAS TURKEY PAST	145
THE GHOST DOWNSTAIRS	145
A GHOST FOR CHRISTMAS	146
THE GHOST HUNTERS	147
GHOST IN THE WATER	148
A GHOST IN THE NIGHT	149

THE GHOST IN YOUR HOUSE 149
THE GHOST OF JERRY BUNDLER 149
THE GHOST AND MRS MUIR... 150
GHOST POEMS – VOICES IN AN EMPTY ROOM 150
GHOSTS FROM THE ARCHIVES... 151
GHOSTS IN THE MACHINE... 151
THE GHOSTS OF FRANGOCASTELLA... 151
THE GHOSTS OF MOTLEY HALL... 152
   The Christmas Spirit 152
   Phantomime 153
THE GHOSTS OF M.R. JAMES 153
GHOSTS (1926) 154
GHOSTS (1928) 154
GHOSTS (1949) 155
GHOSTS! (1950) 155
GHOSTS AND APPARITIONS 156
GHOSTLY EXPERIENCES.. 156
GHOST STORIES 156
GHOST STORIES AT CHRISTMAS 157
GHOST STORIES FROM AMBRIDGE.. 158
GHOST STORIES FROM THEATRELAND 159
GHOST STORIES OF WALTER DE LA MARE 159
A GHOST STORY: THE CREEPING HORROR ON CHRISTMAS EVE 160
GHOST STORY 160
A GHOST STORY FOR CHRISTMAS... 161
THE GHOST TRAIN... 164

    The Ghost Train (1937) 165
    The Ghost Train (1969) 165
    The Ghost Train (1998) 165
GHOST TRILOGY 166
THE GIANT UNDER THE SNOW 166
GIDEON COE'S A GHOST STORY FOR CHRISTMAS 167
    The Hospice, by Robert Aickman (2016) 167
    The Girl I Left Behind Me, by Muriel Spark (2018) 168
THE GIRL BEFORE 168
THE GOBLINS WHO STOLE A SEXTON 169
    The Goblins Who Stole a Sexton (1962) 169
    The Goblins Who Stole a Sexton (1984) 170
    The Goblins Who Stole a Sexton (1997) 170
THE GOTHIC IMAGINATION 170
THE GREEN MAN 171
THE GREEN MAN REVISITED 172
GREY CLAY DOLLS 174
GUINEAS FOR THE GHOST 174
HAIL, HORRORS, HAIL 175
HARRY PRICE: GHOST HUNTER (2015) 175
HAUNTED: THE FERRYMAN 176
HAUNTED: POOR GIRL 177
THE HAUNTED AIRMAN 178
HAUNTED HOGMANAY 179
THE HAUNTED HOTEL 180
THE HAUNTED HOUR 181
THE HAUNTED MAN AND THE GHOST'S BARGAIN 181

HAUNTERS OF THE DEEP	182
A HAUNTING	182
A HAUNTING HARMONY	183
THE HAUNTING OF HELEN WALKER	184
THE HAUNTING OF M.R. JAMES [Series]	185
THE HAUNTING OF M.R. JAMES [Drama]	186
THE HAUNTING OF RADCLIFFE HOUSE	186
HAUNTING WOMEN	187
HERE AM I, WHERE ARE YOU?	188
THE HEX	188
A HISTORY OF HORROR	190
THE HORSEMAN	191
THE HOUND OF THE BASKERVILLES	191
The Hound of the Baskervilles (Granada, 1988)	191
The Hound of the Baskervilles (BBC Radio, 1988)	192
The Hound of the Baskervilles 2002)	193
THE HOUSE AT WORLD'S END	194
HUNTING GHOSTS WITH GATISS AND COLES	195
HURST OF HURSTCOTE	196
THE ICE HOUSE (1978)	196
THE IMP OF THE PERVERSE	197
THE INEXPERIENCED GHOST	198
THE INFINITE MONKEY CAGE: CHRISTMAS SPECIAL 2016	198
THE INGOLDSBY LEGENDS	199
THE INN	200
IN SEARCH OF DRACULA WITH MARK GATISS	202
INSIDE NO. 9: CHRISTMAS SPECIALS	202

The Devil of Christmas (2016) 203
The Bones of St. Nicholas (2022) 204
IS ANYBODY THERE? 205
IT WAS A DARK AND STORMY NIGHT ON *BOOKSHELF* 206
JAMES STEWART 206
JONAS 207
JONATHAN CREEK 208
Jonathan Creek: Black Canary (1998) 209
Jonathan Creek: Satan's Chimney (2001) 209
Jonathan Creek: The Grinning Man (2009) 210
Jonathan Creek: The Judas Tree (2010) 210
Jonathan Creek: Daemon's Roost (2016) 211
K9 & COMPANY 211
KALEIDOSCOPE: COME BECK'NING GHOST 212
KISS KISS 213
LADY WITH POMEGRANATE 214
THE LAST VAMPYRE 214
THE LATE ARRIVALS 215
LATE NIGHT STORY 215
LAYING A GHOST 216
THE LEAGUE OF GENTLEMEN: CHRISTMAS SPECIAL 216
THE LEAGUE OF GENTLEMEN'S GHOST CHASE 218
LEAVING LILY 219
THE LEGEND OF SLEEPY HOLLOW (1980) 220
THE LEGEND OF SLEEPY HOLLOW (2005) 220
THE LINTEL 221
THE LOOKING GLASS 222

LITTLE HORRORS	222
A LITTLE TWIST OF DAHL	223
LOSING CONTACT	223
THE LOST GHOST STORY	224
LOST HEARTS (1957)	224
LOST HEARTS (1973)	225
MACABRE	226
MARKHEIM	227
Markheim (1952)	227
Markheim (1971)	228
Markheim (1974)	228
10 x 10: Markheim (1990)	228
MARK TWAIN STORIES: A GHOST STORY	228
MARTIN'S CLOSE	229
THE MASQUE OF THE RED DEATH	230
MCLEVY: CHRISTMAS SPECIAL	230
MEDIAEVAL GHOST STORIES	231
THE MEZZOTINT	231
MIDNIGHT TALES	232
MIKE RAVEN'S GHOST SHOW	233
THE MONK	234
THE MONKEY'S PAW	234
MORE GHOST STORIES	235
THE MOONSTONE	235
The Moonstone (1996)	236
The Moonstone (2016)	237
M.R. JAMES: THE CORNER OF THE RETINA	237

M.R. JAMES AT CHRISTMAS 238
M.R. JAMES: GHOST WRITER 239
MRS OSBORNE'S STORY 240
MURDER ROOMS 240
THE MUSIC ON THE HILL 242
MY CHRISTMAS GHOSTS 243
MY CHRISTMAS GHOST STORY 243
THE MYSTERIES OF UDOLPHO 243
THE MYSTERIOUS HORSEMAN 244
THE NEED FOR NIGHTMARE 244
THE NEMESIS OF FIRE 245
A NEW YEAR GHOST STORY 246
NIGHT OF THE WOLF 246
NIGHTMARE THE BIRTH OF HORROR 247
NOT ONE RETURNS TO TELL (1937) 248
NOT ONE RETURNS TO TELL (2017) 250
NUMBER 13 (2006) 251
THE OCCUPANT OF THE ROOM 252
OF THIS AND THAT BUT MAINLY ABOUT GHOSTS 252
OH, WHISTLE AND I'LL COME TO YOU 253
OPEN BOOK – M.R. JAMES 253
A PATTERN OF ROSES 254
THE PERIWIG MAKER 255
THE PHANTOM OF THE OPERA (2007) 255
THE PHANTOM OF THE OPERA: BEHIND THE MASK 256
THE PICTURE OF DORIAN GRAY 257
PLAYING WITH DRACULA 258

A PLEASING TERROR – THE LIFE & GHOSTS OF M.R. JAMES . 259
THE PRICE OF FEAR (1978) 259
QUATERMASS AND THE PIT 260
REBECCA (1976 & 1989) 262
THE RED ROOM (1977) 263
THE RED ROOM (2000) 263
THE RIME OF THE ANCIENT MARINER 265
SALEM'S LOT 266
SCARRA ROCK 267
SCHALCKEN THE PAINTER 268
SCHALKEN THE PAINTER 269
SCREENSHOT: CHRISTMAS TV TRADITIONS 270
THE SECOND PAN BOOK OF HORROR STORIES 270
SEE HEAR! A Christmas Carol & The Monkey's Paw 271
SHAKESPEARE, THE ANIMATED TALES: HAMLET 272
THE SHEPHERD 273
   The Shepherd (1983) 274
   The Shepherd (2016) 274
SHERLOCK: THE ABOMINABLE BRIDE 274
SHERLOCK HOLMES & THE CASE OF THE SILK STOCKING .. 276
SHERLOCK HOLMES VS DRACULA 277
A SHORT HISTORY OF VAMPIRES 278
A SHORT SEASON OF GHOST FILMS 278
A SHORT HISTORY OF GOTHIC 279
SHORT SHOCKS: FOUR WEIRD TALES 280
THE SIGNALMAN 280
   The Signalman (1940) 281

The Signalman (1956)	281
The Signalman (1958)	282
The Signalman (1976)	283
The Signalman (2022)	284
SIX GHOST STORIES	285
A SLIP IN TIME	286
THE SMALL HAND	286
SOME GHOST STORIES	286
SOME GHOST STORIES OF THE MIDLANDS	286
SOMETHING FROM THE DARK	287
SOMEONE LIKE YOU	287
THE SPECKLED BAND	288
The Speckled Band (1948)	289
The Speckled Band (1962)	289
The Speckled Band (1984)	289
SPINE CHILLERS	290
A SPIRIT ELOPEMENT	292
THE SPIRIT OF THE HOUSE	293
STAG	293
THE STALLS OF BARCHESTER	295
STIGMA	295
A STING IN THE TALE: NO CONFERRING	297
THE STONE TAPE	297
A STORY FOR CHRISTMAS: THE VISITOR'S BOOK	299
THE STORY OF THE GHOST STORY	299
THE STRANGE CASE OF DR JEKYLL AND MR HYDE (1973)	300
THE STRANGE CASE OF DR JEKYLL AND MR HYDE (1993)	301

THE STRANGE CASE OF EDGAR ALLAN POE	302
STRANGE STORIES	303
STUDY ON 3 - THE HORROR STORY	303
SUSAN HILL'S GHOST STORY	305
SWEET CHARIOT	306
TAKE THE HIGH ROAD: MILLENIUM SPECIAL	307
TALES OF THE SUPERNATURAL (1980)	307
TALES OF THE SUPERNATURAL (2016)	308
TALES OF THE UNCANNY AND SUPERNATURAL	308
THE TEETH OF ABBOT THOMAS	309
TELLING TALES: JEREMY DYSON	310
THINGS THAT GO BUMP IN THE NIGHT	310
THE THIRTEENTH TALE	310
THREE JAPANESE GOTHIC TALES	311
THREE STORIES	312
TO BUILD A FIRE	312
THE TRACTATE MIDDOTH	314
TRANSYLVANIA BABYLON	315
THE TREASURE OF ABBOT THOMAS (1974)	315
TUESDAY CALL	316
Benjamin Britten's The Turn of the Screw (1959)	318
The Turn of the Screw (1977)	318
Benjamin Britten's The Turn of the Screw (1982)	318
The Turn of the Screw (1993)	319
The Turn of the Screw (1999)	319
The Turn of the Screw (2009)	320
The Turn of the Screw (2018)	320

TURN, TURN, TURN 321
TWO AMERICAN GHOST STORIES... 321
UNCANNY 322
   Uncanny: Christmas Special 322
   Uncanny Live with Mark Gatiss.. 322
UNIVERSAL HORROR 323
THE UNSETTLED DUST: THE STRANGE STORIES OF ROBERT AICKMAN 324
THE VAMPYR – A SOAP OPERA 324
A VIEW FROM A HILL (2005) 325
VIOLENCE 327
THE VISITOR'S BOOK 327
THE VOICE OF MICHAEL VANE 327
A WARNING TO THE CURIOUS (1954).. 328
A WARNING TO THE CURIOUS (1972).. 328
A WARNING TO THE FURIOUS 330
THE WATCH HOUSE.. 330
WATERSHIP DOWN (1978) 332
THE WAY YOU LOOK AT IT: GHOSTS (1945) 333
THE WEIR 334
WELSH GHOST STORIES 335
THE WEREWOLF... 335
WHEN STANDING STONES COME DOWN TO DRINK 336
WHISTLE AND I'LL COME TO YOU (1968) 336
WHISTLE AND I'LL COME TO YOU (2010) 337
WILLIAM WILSON 339
THE WILLOWS 339

THE WITHERED ARM 340
WITH INTENT TO STEAL 341
THE WOLVES OF WILLOUGHBY CHASE (1994) 341
THE WOMAN IN BLACK 342
    The Woman in Black (1984) 343
    The Woman in Black (1989) 343
    The Woman in Black (1993) 345
THE WOMAN IN WHITE (1997) 347
THE WOMAN'S GHOST STORY 348
A WORLD OF SOUND: A GHOST FOR BREAKFAST 348
THE WYVERN MYSTERY 348
THE YELLOW WALLPAPER 350
YESTERDAY – ONCE MORE 350
YOU THE JURY: "Today's proposition: Ghosts Exist" 351

Introduction

Ghost Stories for Christmas didn't start in the 1970s of course, and they certainly didn't start with the arrival of television or radio. However, with respect to ghost stories and tales of horror on British broadcast media, the tradition is as old as the BBC itself.

This book covers ghost stories broadcast at Christmas, albeit the definition is liberally interpreted at times (there is no ghost in The Ice House – but it's still considered A Ghost Story for Christmas). It also covers programmes *about* ghost stories.

The extent to which it has been possible to comment on all of the programmes listed is very variable; in some instances, the only information available has been the transmission date and the title.

Inevitably this has been an arbitrary exercise, and while I worked to a set of rules when compiling this text, I have freely broken them when it seemed appropriate. I have tended to include programmes broadcast no earlier than the tenth of December, and no later than the 3rd of January – but exceptions have been made, including one or two items that have never been broadcast at Christmas at all.

In general, feature films shown at Christmas are *not* included, unless there is something particularly televisual about their broadcast – for example, if a TV channel had a special season of horror films for the holidays.

A good many of these programmes shown at Christmas had already been broadcast at other times of year, especially Halloween. Some may feel that a Christmas ghost story only qualifies as such if it was specifically made for Christmas broadcast – but it's worth remembering that Jonathan Miller's much-celebrated **Whistle and I'll Come to You** was not only not made for Christmas, but it wasn't broadcast at Christmas until more than thirty years after it was made, and nobody ever quarrels with its inclusion on the BFI **Ghost Stories for Christmas** DVD boxed set.

All of the transmission dates herein refer to the day, rather than the date, of broadcast. That is, a programme that you had to stay up past midnight on Christmas Day to watch is listed as having been broadcast on the 25th, not on the 26th December.

While this may be technically inaccurate, it corresponds to the way in which TV schedules have generally been organised, and the distinction will be crucial if you ever find yourself doing your own research, looking through old scans of the Radio Times... not that I recommend it.

- J.L.H.

James McBryde's illustration for M.R. James's story
Oh, Whistle and I'll Come to You, My Lad.

THE AFFAIR AT GROVER STATION

Drama | Radio | 90 mins

TX: 27/12/1997, Radio 4

A love rivalry escalates into murder in Jonathan Holloway's supernatural drama, adapted from Willa Cather's short story.

Two old acquaintances, Will Carter and Arnold Rodgers, meet, talk, and spend time together. Carter (unnamed in the original story, evidently named after the author here), asks Rodgers to tell him about the recent death of his friend Larry, the station agent. The mystery of his friend's misfortune was resolved by Rodgers through events that are painful and disturbing for him to relate – and, ultimately, for Carter to hear.

This play has a solid cast, led by British radio's busiest American accents Kerry Shale and Stuart Milligan, and it benefits greatly from eerie sound design and urgent, discordant music. Jonathan Holloway's adaptation also plays to the strengths of the medium, having the tale emerge from the conversation between the two leads. Their interaction is more than an incidental framing, allowing us to perceive the aftermath of Carter's tale before he has told it, and giving the ghost story an extra layer. It's worth saying that the original story is comparatively slight, but its expansion here to feature-length does not feel drawn out.

Tom Watt's performance as the villain of the piece, Mr. Freymark, is also worthy of note. Among the most flesh-crawling antagonists I've ever heard in a radio drama, Freymark is an outsider working hard to carve a dishonest place for himself in the world. Widely disliked, he is the subject of racist gossip and banter, but any sympathy we feel for him on that count fails to mitigate our keen sense of his coldness and emptiness as a person.

If anything, the prejudice directed at Freymark (which is depicted by the adaptation but not endorsed by it) simply makes it harder to truly like any of the characters in this deeply uncomfortable tale.

AFTER SUPPER GHOST STORIES

Drama | Radio | 45 mins

TX: 26/12/1992, Radio 4
 25/12/2016, Radio 4 Extra
 26/12/2021, Radio 4 Extra

Originally appearing in 1891 under the title *Told After Supper*, Jerome K. Jerome's collection of ghost stories also serves as a commentary upon the act of tale-telling, and its importance to Christmas celebrations. As such, it contains as much musing upon the nature of good company as it does contemplation of the conventions and narrative inevitabilities of the ghost story – and all in a spirit of good humour.

Paul Wetherby's adaptation of the book condenses it into a very pleasant 45 minutes, enlivened by songs with piano accompaniment. It's a successful exercise in conjuring the atmosphere of a family gathering on Christmas Eve, and while it isn't going to freeze anybody's blood, nor is it attempting to. It's likely to raise a few smiles, though.

In this respect, the piece is aided greatly by that piano music, provided by composer and dramatist Neil Brand. Brand would return to BBC radio in ghostly company years later, with his own adaptation of **A Christmas Carol**, and his series of dramas **The Haunting of M.R. James**.

A.J. ALAN'S GHOST STORIES

Readings | Radio | 15 mins

Leslie Harrison Lambert was a magician and government official who fell into broadcasting when he wrote to the BBC (then still a company rather than a corporation), suggesting that he might read one of his stories on the radio. When his offer was accepted, his first reading in January 1924 was a success; under the pseudonym A.J. Alan, he quickly became one of the most popular broadcasters of the early days of British radio.

Although the stories were a side-line for Lambert, he was painstaking in the writing of them, and in the preparation of their performance. Nonetheless, he relied upon an anecdotal style of storytelling that lent his tales a sense of the real and the personal; the popularity of his stories meant that they were later published in a two-volume collection, and some of them were subsequently included in later anthologies.

In fact, most of Alan's stories were not about supernatural experiences– though many of them were and these seem to be the best-remembered.

On at least four occasions he was called on to deliver a ghost story to the nation at Christmas, according to the Radio Times listings:

A.J. "Alan Telling a Ghost Story"
TX: 25/12/1925, 5WA Cardiff

A.J. "Alan Will Tell a Christmas Ghost Story"
TX: 26/12/1924, 2LO London

The Diver, a ghost story by A. J. Alan
TX: 25/12/1925, 2LO London, 5WA Cardiff

The Visitor's Book, a ghost story by A. J. Alan
TX: 21/12/1927, 2LO London, 5XX Daventry

Alan's stories had a bit of a revival on the BBC in the late 1960s and early 1970s when new readings were broadcast on the radio, including two in the week before Christmas 1969 (**The Visitor's Book**, and **A Christmas Ghost Story**), and on television in 1974 (**A Story for Christmas**)

There are no complete recordings of Alan reading one of his ghost stories - however, a full reading of *The Diver*, performed in a charming homage to Alan's style, can be heard on the **EnCrypted Classic Horror** YouTube channel.

ALAS, POOR GHOST!

Reading | Radio | 30 mins

TX: 24/12/1938, BBC Regional Programme

Taking its name from Hamlet's exclamation on witnessing the spectre of his father, this ghostly anthology features verse by Thomas Hardy, Walter de la Mare, Edith Sitwell, A.E. Housman, Rudyard Kipling, Christina Rossetti, and Thomas Campion

Sadly, records don't indicate which poems were chosen, though it seems very likely that Rossetti's Poor Ghost was included. The readers were John Abbott, Nancy Brown, Lilian Harrison, and Hubert Gregg.

A second programme of supernaturally-themed verse and prose under this title followed in August 1941.

AND THEN THERE WERE NONE

Drama | TV | 3 x 60 mins

TX: 26/12/2015 - 28/12/2015, BBC1

Some might feel that adaptations of Agatha Christie's mystery novels have tended toward a certain cosiness, with acts of murder playing out like a high-stakes parlour-game for the upper classes. If this was ever true, then the BBCs 2015 serial of **And Then There Were None** does much to correct things, mining the seam of hard darkness found in Christie's story. There is a real sense of evil, of horror, in this adaptation.

And Then There Were None sometimes feels like it anticipates the more modern crime-horrors about serial killers following elaborate themes or creating fiendish patterns that trap the hapless and innocent. The victims in this story are all killed in ways suggested by the lines of a poem; each of them has a secret guilt to face, and accompanying that secret is the dread suspicion that perhaps, after all, they deserve their fate.

At the story's outset a group of strangers is lured to a remote island, where they find that they have attracted the attention of somebody with vengeful intent. For each of them, their anonymous host claims, has committed a murder but escaped punishment. Now, here on the island, justice will be done and there will be no escape.

Earlier adaptations of the novel contrived a change to the ending which compromised the darkest parts of the story. However, they survive intact in this version, and it has a somewhat hellish streak as a result. As the characters inevitably come to realise that they are trapped on the island, with nothing to do but ruminate upon their guilt and their impending murders, they begin to let go of hope and sanity and it becomes difficult to imagine any kind of happy ending for any of them.

A really excellent ensemble cast includes Charles Dance, Miranda Richardson, Toby Stephens, Aidan Turner, Burn Gorman, Douglas Booth, and Sam Neill. The heroine, Vera Claythorne, is played by Maeve Dermody who is less of a household name than her co-stars, but she's excellent here as the former governess whose young charge tragically drowned despite her best efforts. Now it seems that the mastermind of this cruel game has decided she's responsible for the child's death and must be punished for it.

How could anybody think that of so beguiling a young woman? What motive could she possibly have had to do such a terrible thing? Dermody's spirited mix of innocence and ambiguity makes for an excellent protagonist in this particularly unsettling variation on the period murder mystery.

ANGELS AT PARTRIDGE COTTAGE

Drama | Radio | 60 mins

TX: 22/12/1988, Radio 4
     20/12/1990, Radio 4
     18/12/2016, Radio 4 Extra
     25/12/2020, Radio 4 Extra

An early work by Lucy Gannon, this play makes good use of the familiar idea of a house haunted by comfortingly benign ghosts who befriend the latest mortal inhabitants.

As in other popular examples of this conceit, the phantoms inhabiting the old building are a mix-and-match makeshift family of souls from very different historical eras. It's a family unit under stress, however – not least because of the latest arrival, a 1970s motorcycle crash casualty called Gary, who finds his afterlife tedious and frustrating.

The cottage's new owners are a modern couple, Zoe and Magnus, who decide to spend their Christmas alone in their cottage, without company and without any of the traditional pressures and affectations of Christmas. The ghosts are looking forward to Christmas, and are disappointed by the lack of proper celebration or decoration...

THE ASH TREE (1975)

Drama | TV | 32 mins

TX: 23/12/1975, BBC1
       18/12/2005, BBC4
       24/12/2018, BBC4
       29/11/2021, BBC4

The Ash Tree was the last of the M.R. James adaptations directed by Lawrence Gordon Clark for the BBC, and his penultimate contribution to **A Ghost Story for Christmas**.

David Rudkin's adaptation skilfully rearranges the ingredients found in James's story, and it's striking just how well **The Ash Tree** fits into the genre that we're happy to call folk horror these days. The trial and execution of Anne Mothersole (Barbara Ewing), accused of witchcraft, is given greater prominence, and the motives of Sir Matthew Fell (Edward Petherbridge) in accusing her seem to be grubbier, more ambiguous.

These events cast a long shadow, and only find resolution years later when Matthew's grandson Sir Richard (also played by Petherbridge) takes up residence at the hall.

For much of the story, the sense of horror comes from the barbarity of the torture and execution meted out to those accused of witchcraft, but with Anne Mothersole's curse spoken from the gallows the drama takes a sharp turn for the weird.

Perhaps the final supernatural manifestation is necessarily too explicit for some – no half-glimpsed shadowy figures here – and perhaps this is part of the reason why **The Ash Tree** is rarely the first of the 1970s James adaptations to be cited or celebrated. Nonetheless, there is something truly disturbing in the sight of the clustering, mewling 'children' who come out of the Ash Tree...

THE BALLAD OF COCK LANE

Drama | Radio | 90 mins

TX: 17/12/1973, Radio 4 (The Monday Play)
        23/12/1973, Radio 4 (Afternoon Theatre)

Billed as a 'ghost mystery', this play by David Buck dramatizes a well-documented cause celebre of the 1760s, an alleged haunting at Cock Lane in London. Later declared to be a fraud – one of the perpetrators was tried and punished for his part in it – it attracted significant public attention, including from figures as notable as Samuel Johnson.

The haunting led to séances and investigations by various parties, and it even figured in contemporary theological discussion of ghosts and the survival of the soul. Largely forgotten today, the events nonetheless left their mark in popular culture; Dickens refers to 'the cock lane ghost' several times in his work, for example.

BELL, BOOK AND CANDLE

Drama | Radio | 90 mins

TX: 01/01/1997, Radio 4
     20/12/1997, Radio 4

John Van Drutten's 1950 play is likely best-known today for its film adaptation starring Kim Novak and James Stewart; a romantic comedy commencing on Christmas Eve, it concerns a beautiful young witch who has designs on the publisher who lives upstairs. She resorts to sorcery to secure his interest.

There was also a UK production of the play in 1954; this relocated the story to Knightsbridge in London, and changed a few details including the name of the male lead from Shep to Anthony.

It was this UK-set version of the play that Radio 4 adapted in 1997; Beatie Edney makes a worthy Gillian, and Stephen Moore's placid, good-natured tones are well suited to the role of Anthony.

THE BELLS OF ASTERCOTE

Drama | TV | 60 mins

TX: 23/12/1980, BBC1

Penelope Lively was a successful writer of fiction for readers both young and old, winning both the Carnegie Medal and the Booker Prize during her career. Her first novel, *Astercote*, was for children and although critics have argued that it isn't particularly innovative, it was consistently available in print for more than thirty years. In 1980 it was adapted for BBC children's television as **The Bells of Astercote**.

In fact, **The Bells of Astercote** is as much about a clash of rationalism and superstition as it is about supernatural manifestations per se – but it is the haunting mood of the piece that became lodged in the imagination of many a young viewer whose Christmas was ushered in by this special one-off drama on the last day of school.

Aptly enough, there is a strongly Jamesian feel to **Bells...** in that the plot revolves around a medieval treasure hidden in a forbidden patch of land, and the belief that a curse will descend if it is ever found and removed.

The treasure is a chalice rather than an Anglo-Saxon crown, however, and the forbidden land is a section of woodland containing the last ruins of the village of Astercote. The entire population of the village was wiped out by the plague centuries before, and a local belief emerged that should the chalice hidden in the ruins ever be stolen, the terrible plague would return.

Two children new to the area befriend a strange man who inhabits the woodland, and the chalice disappears soon after. Then, local people start to fall sick...

Although the story seeks to weigh the old against the new, rational modernity against irrational tradition, it never quite comes down entirely on the side of the rational. No rational explanations are given for how the young heroine can hear the ringing of distant church bells when there has been no church since the death of Astercote, nor why she experiences a bleak, terrifying vision of the corpse-strewn village when she first walks into the woodland. Quite right too; we can have our rational explanations, but sometimes it can be nice to hang on to our nightmares as well.

BEOWULF

Drama | TV | 30 mins

TX: 23/12/19987, BBC2

It can't be a coincidence that **Beowulf** was produced by Christmas Films and broadcast on the 23rd of December - evidently this adaptation of the tale was always meant to be watched on a dark evening. Perhaps it's also telling that this, among the oldest known examples of English literature, is a story of creeping horror and a confrontation with dark forces harboured by the implacable landscape.

Beowulf is at first the story of the misfortunes of the Danish King Hrothgar, whose mead-hall is visited in the night by a terrible creature emerged from the fens named Grendel. Enraged by the sounds of celebration coming from the hall, Grendel slaughters the king's men and returns, night after night. The beleaguered Hrothgar calls for help, and in answer the warrior Beowulf arrives, intent on ending Grendel's reign of terror.

In the early 1990s the BBC had broadcast two series of **Shakespeare: The Animated Tales**, which had included notable adaptations of **Hamlet** and *Macbeth*; the director of *Macbeth*, Yuri Kulakov, returned to the BBC with this UK-Russian co-production.

As with the Shakespeare animations, this classic tale is economically retold and richly imagined – the butchering of Hrothgar's men is not diluted by the fact we are not shown it directly. The creeping shadow of Grendel, extending its claws Nosferatu-like in the night, is quite enough to convey the violence of the events. The animation is matched by an excellent voice cast including Derek Jacobi and Joseph Fiennes as Beowulf himself.

BERGERAC: FIRES IN THE FALL

Drama | TV | 90 mins

TX: 26/12/1986, BBC1

The adventures of a hard-bitten police detective who has relocated to the mean streets of Jersey (the Channel Island), **Bergerac** ran for ten years on British television, and during its long span it often found the confidence to experiment with its format.

Though a straightforward drama series most of the time, several episodes of **Bergerac** made use of strange or supernatural elements, including an episode broadcast a few days before Halloween, and another in which an archaeological dig appears to stir up ancient, malevolent forces in a manner reminiscent of an M.R. James story.

The special feature-length Christmas episode, **Fires in the Fall**, also uses the supernatural in its plot, which concerns an older lady who has come under the influence of a spiritualist medium. The man claims to have been contacted by the spirit of a little girl who died years earlier, and for whom the elderly Mrs Jardine feels some unexplained responsibility.

Things escalate in the latter parts of the story with the arrival of a vengeful, hooded, monk-like figure.

However, despite being written by Chris Boucher - a veteran of fantasy shows like *Doctor Who* and *Blake's 7* - **Fires in the Fall** uses the supernatural more as a seasoning than a main ingredient, resolving things with prosaic explanations. Happily, the rational is not allowed to entirely hold sway over the narrative's conclusion, though.

THE BEST OF BIERCE

Reading | Radio | 4 x 15 mins

TX: 02/01/1978 - 05/01/1978, BBC Radio 4

Commencing on the New Year Bank Holiday and finishing on Twelfth Night, this little selection of macabre tales by Ambrose Bierce sneaked into the remaining days of the Christmas season.

Read by Robert Lang, the featured stories were:

- A Horseman in the Sky
- The Man and the Snake
- An Occurrence at Owl Creek Bridge
- The Middle Toe of the Right Foot

BLACK CHRISTMAS (1993)

Film seasons were once a commonplace on British television, especially on the BBC channels, and every now and again there would be seasons devoted to the fantastic and the supernatural, exciting parades of genre entertainment that sometimes highlighted the unusual or the little-seen.

While horror films frequently made an appearance in Christmas schedules from at least the 1980s onwards, sometimes the BBC would take the opportunity to celebrate Christmas by gathering together a whole selection box of darker entertainments.

Black Christmas was the least specifically supernatural of these seasons, but it was billed as 'a short, dark festive season of madness, murder and dark humour', so I feel it deserves a mention here.

This season comprised the following films:

- *The Fly* (1958) TX: 24/12/93, BBC2
- *Hangover Square* (1945) TX: 25/12/93, BBC2
- *The Honeymoon Killers* (1970) TX: 27/12/93, BBC2
- *The Hospital* (1971) TX: 28/12/93, BBC2
- *Mad Love* (1935) TX: 29/12/93, BBC2
- *Crimewave* (1985) TX: 30/12/93, BBC2

BLACK NARCISSUS (2020)

Drama | TV | 3 x 60 mins

TX: 27/12/2020 - 29/12/2020, BBC1

I'd like to extend my personal thanks to the wits in BBC scheduling who decided to place the first episode of their new serialisation of **Black Narcissus** just a few short hours after an afternoon-spanning broadcast of *The Sound of Music* on the same channel.

The amusing juxtaposition of nuns going loopy halfway up a mountain aside, **Black Narcissus (2020)** is a good example of the kind of lavish but dark Christmas drama that BBC1 has tended to broadcast in recent years. One Christmas it was a very dark version of *Great Expectations*, another year a paranoid thriller called *Restless*, and in another year *Pride & Prejudice* got a murder mystery sequel with *Death Comes to Pemberley*. **Black Narcissus** is a perfect addition to this trend.

Gemma Arterton stars as Sister Clodagh, the inexperienced leader of a convent who brings her nuns to an isolated, abandoned Indian palace in the Himalayas. The palace once housed a harem, and the juxtaposition of former carnality and present chastity underpins the tensions of this story. Quickly, the place becomes a cauldron of repressions and obsessions that threaten to boil over, raising shadows of the past.

Black Narcissus is certainly a dark and compelling tale that never quite steps over the line into explicitly supernatural territory, and perhaps it's all the more effective for that. There is quite enough haunting going on in the palace, in the minds of the nuns living there, without any direct, spectral assistance.

Some may reasonably feel that the greatest shadow of the past in the whole exercise is that of the 1947 film adaptation starring Deborah Kerr, but this does not prevent the new production from doing a fair job with the material. Moreover, the cast includes actors of proven strength and reliability, like Rosie Cavaliero, Gina McKee, and Jim Broadbent, not to mention a brief appearance by Diana Rigg in the role of Mother Dorothea, Clodagh's superior.

Godden's story has proved surprisingly popular and persistent as a fixture in the BBCs December schedules. As early as 1955 the book was read in daily instalments on Woman's Hour during December, and a feature-length radio adaptation appeared a couple of weeks before

Christmas in 1997. Even the Powell & Pressburger film was Christmas Eve viewing on BBC2 in 2000 and 2005.

BLIND MAN'S HOOD

Drama | Radio | 30 mins

TX: 24/12/2022, BBC Radio 4 Extra
     25/12/2022, BBC Radio 4 Extra

One of Michael and Mollie Hardwick's many radio adaptations that you'll find in these pages, this 1963 play is certainly a ghost story for Christmas, but it was nonetheless originally broadcast in April. It finally took its rightful place in the Christmas schedules when it was repeated in 2022. Strictly speaking it was broadcast twice on Christmas Day, but since the first of these was at Midnight, it will have been the conclusion of Christmas Eve listening for many – and appropriately so.

The play is based on a story by John Dickson Carr, which was originally published in the 1937 Christmas edition of *The Sketch*. The action of the story takes place on Christmas Eve, at a lonely old house in Kent. At the story's outset a young couple take refuge in the apparently empty house, but are met by a young woman who explains that the occupants always find a reason to be out of the house at this particular hour on Christmas Eve every year. She then proceeds to relate past events that took place in the house: the horrific murder of a young woman inside the house while all of the doors and windows were locked... and then subsequent (apparently related) events of an equally sinister but even more inexplicable character.

BLITHE SPIRIT

Noël Coward's takes of an author plagued by the ghost of his first wife has been a popular play since it was first performed in 1941, and in British Broadcasting it has proved a common choice of Christmas entertainment.

The play's protagonist, Charles Condomine, engages the services of a medium, Madame Arcati, to hold a séance at his house. Charles is researching the occult for a novel he is writing, but he does not expect that the séance will summon the spirit of his wife Elvira, seven years dead. Elvira is not amused to find that her husband has since remarried...

Blithe Spirit (1954)
Drama | Radio | 90 mins
TX: 22/12/1954, Light Programme
　　 28/12/1954, Light Programme
　　 25/12/1972, Radio 4

Michael Denison and Dulcie Gray star as Charles and Elvira in this radio adaptation, with Thelma Scott as Ruth, Charles's second wife.

Blithe Spirit (1983)
Drama | Radio | 90 mins
TX: 27/12/1983, Radio 4
　　 01/01/1984, Radio 4
　　 29/12/1992, Radio 4 (as part of the **Christmas Spirits** season)

Paul Eddington and Anna Massey take the roles of Charles and Elvira in this new production of Coward's play, with Julia McKenzie as Ruth and Peggy Mount as Madame Arcati.

This radio play was directed by Glyn Dearman, a former child actor best-known for having played Tiny Tim opposite Alastair Sim's Scrooge in the 1951 film version of **A Christmas Carol**.

Blithe Spirit (2008)
Drama | Radio | 90 mins
TX: 13/12/2008, Radio 4

Roger Allam and Zoe Waites star as Charles and Elvira, with Maggie Steed as Madame Arcati and Hermione Gulliford as Ruth in this adaptation by Bert Coules.

Blithe Spirit (2014)
Drama | Radio | 90 mins
TX: 26/12/2014, Radio 4

It's now a tradition that the characters in Radio 4's daily soap opera The Archers are roped into an annual amateur dramatic production for Christmas by Lynda Snell, the local busybody and llama-enthusiast. Radio 4 listeners are then treated to the resulting production as a stand-alone drama, albeit with the added conceit that the cast are playing their Archers characters who are in turn playing the characters in the play.

Blithe Spirit got the Archers treatment in 2014, with Julian Rhind-Tutt as Douglas Herrington, playing Charles Condomine; Joanna Van Kampen as Fallon Rogers, playing Elvia, and Louiza Patikas as Helen Archer playing Ruth. Lynda Snell (Carole Boyd) naturally takes the role of Madame Arcati for herself.

THE BLUE BOY

Drama | TV | 60 mins

TX: 02/01/1995, BBC2

Referred to in the Radio Times as 'a ghost story' and 'a haunting tale', **The Blue Boy** is a one-off drama from the old *Screen Two* strand, shown at the tail end of the Christmas holidays. The story itself is set over Christmas, too.

It's a subtle drama, even by the standards of ghost stories, and there are almost no explicit manifestations of the supernatural in the story - though there is plenty of ominous mood. An unidentified first-person-perspective presence prowls through quiet corridors, or watches from among the shadows of thick woodland as two people walk a lonely road...

A young couple - pregnant Marie (Emma Thompson) and philandering Joe (Adrian Dunbar) - go on holiday to a lonely hotel in the Scottish countryside, hoping to leave their troubles behind. Joe has been having an affair but has decided to drop his mistress, Beth, since his wife is now pregnant. Beth is furious, and mounts her own campaign of haunting, sending ominous notes, and making silent phone calls...

Marie suspects, and finds comfort in the company of Christine (Eleanor Bron), a kind local lady who tells her the tale of 'The Blue Boy' - a child who was found drowned in the lake outside the hotel decades earlier.

The drama unfolds cautiously, always holding back from being too obvious or overt. Impatient viewers may complain of the total absence of a ghost - but a haunting is a mood more than it is an image, and **The Blue Boy** delivers that, with great care.

For example, we hear the tale of the drowned boy told, of the wet footprints leading back into the hotel as if the dead child's ghost fled in search of his parents... and later there is a scene that directly recalls **M.R. James** - of fluid bubbling under a locked door to the horror of the room's occupant...

Is the tragic death of so many years past about to repeat itself in the present? That's what seems to happen in ghostly tales of the long-ago drowned, after all...

THE BOARDED WINDOW

Reading | Radio | 15 mins

TX: 20/12/1945, BBC Home Service

Ambrose Bierce's bleak, haunting tale of death and nightmare, read by Felix Aylmer.

THE BOOK PROGRAMME: TALES OF HORROR

Documentary | TV | 25 mins

TX: 16/12/1976, BBC2

The weekly programme about new books devoted its penultimate show of 1976 to the subject of ghost and horror stories, by way of a prelude to Christmas.

Rather tantalisingly (from the point of view of somebody unable to see this programme, though one hopes it's still in the archive), the guests invited on to the show to discuss the subject with presenter Robert Robinson were Jonathan Miller (director of **Whistle and I'll Come to You**) and Nigel Kneale (writer of **Quatermass and the Pit** and **The Stone Tape**, who also adapted **The Woman in Black** for television).

BUMP IN THE NIGHT

Talk | Radio | 15 mins

TX: 20/12/1958, BBC Home Service

Patrick MacNaghten was a fairly prolific broadcaster in the late 1950s, and gave a number of talks on BBC radio, often concerning his experiences with a variety of animals, particularly dogs.

His talk 'Bump in the Night' is primarily about his experience of living in two different haunted houses, though he doesn't claim to have personally seen a ghost. He was, however, sure that his dogs often did – and that the footsteps of a ghostly dog could sometimes be heard...

BWGANOD

Reading | Radio | 30 mins

TX: 01/01/1953, BBC Home Service Welsh
        01/01/1954, BBC Home Service Welsh

A short programme of ghost stories performed in the Welsh language ('Bwganod' simply means 'ghosts'). It's not clear whether these were tales from Welsh folklore specifically, or just Welsh translations of classic tales, but given the cultural remit of the Home Service Welsh radio station, one guesses that it would be the former.

THE CABARET OF DOCTOR CALIGARI: THE BODY POLITIC

Comedy | Radio | 30 mins

TX: 12/12/1991, Radio 5

Broadcast in the early days of Radio 5, when the channel's schedules were full of comedy shows and programming for younger listeners, **The Cabaret of Doctor Caligari** was a six-part comedy anthology series of a macabre bent.

Each week, a newly-deceased sinner would arrive at the cabaret hosted by Doctor Caligari (John Woodvine) and his two demonic lackeys, Snuff and Anthrax (Sylvester McCoy and Victoria Wickes). The guest would then tell his or her story before being consigned by the Doctor to an appropriate torment...

I find **Cabaret...** rather fascinating because it was surprisingly angry for a radio comedy show, even by the standards of its time. It's certainly not unusual for horror stories to work as morality plays in some way, but in **Cabaret**'s case the morality reflected then-current social issues, with each week's guest recognisable as a controversial stereotype of the day. This was comedy that was more than willing to bare its teeth.

For example, in one story the plot of *An American Werewolf in London* is parodied, with a racist comedian substituted for the werewolf: an angry young stand-up is bitten by an 'old school' comedian, and subsequently finds that at the full moon he turns into a creature who sounds very similar to Bernard Manning.

In another episode, a chemical spill transforms a mass of homeless people into a giant monster that threatens to devour London; in another, a man who sells cheap and nasty videos in which young women meet grisly fates finds himself pursued by The Teenage Psycho Chainsaw Bimbos.

The final episode – which even the closing credits admit, is rather lacking in the show's customary sense of humour – was **The Body Politic**, a reworking of the familiar format of **A Christmas Carol**, perhaps in acknowledgement of this episode's mid-December broadcast date.

As in the Dickens tale, a morally dubious individual is shown the past, the present and the future, and the part that he plays in all three. However, in this case, the individual is a government minister (John Shrapnel), and he is shown the horrors that could result from the government's 'reform' of the National Health Service. Hmm.

CABIN B-13

Drama | Radio | 30 mins

TX: 24/12/1952, Light Programme

A young woman boards an ocean liner; she is a newlywed and has embarked on her honeymoon – but her new husband has disappeared on board the ship, and none of the crew believe her story.

A little reminiscent of *The Lady Vanishes*, John Dickson-Carr's radio thriller has an eventful history. It was originally a successful episode in the US anthology series *Suspense* (premiering in 1943), and it was then selected by Carr to air as the first episode in the BBCs own anthology series *Appointment with Fear*, which began later the same year.

A few years later the play was given a special repeat broadcast on Christmas Eve 1952, though not as part of *Appointment with Fear* this time.

The play was subsequently adapted as a feature film called *Dangerous Crossing* (1953) and a much later TV movie *Treacherous Crossing* (1992)

THE CAMP OF THE DOG

Drama | Radio | 45 mins

TX: 28/12/1977, Radio 4

Sheila Hodgson is best known (to ghost story enthusiasts anyway) for a series of radio plays based on ideas recorded but never fully developed by **M.R. James** (described in his piece *Stories I Have Tried to Write*). However, in a similar vein she also adapted four of Algernon Blackwood's tales concerning the psychic investigator, Doctor John Silence.

A follow-up to **The Nemesis of Fire, The Camp of the Dog** sees Malcolm Hayes return to the role of Silence. This time, the doctor is called to a lonely island to investigate the manifestation of a creature that has a form somewhere between a wolf and a hound. What has it to do with a pair of ill-starred lovers, and can Silence bring the matter to a happy conclusion?

A CANDLE FOR CASEY

Drama | Radio | 45 mins

TX: 23/12//2003, Radio 4
       24/12//2016, Radio 4 Extra

Harry Towb's warmly comic ghost story about an old Jewish New Yorker, Israelovitch (Henry Goodman), haunted at Christmas by the ghost of his Christian friend, the Irishman Casey (David Kelly).

In order for him to get to Heaven, a candle must be lit for Casey in the cathedral, and only Israelovitch can do it for him. But Israelovitch isn't enthusiastic about the idea...

THE CANTERVILLE GHOST

Oscar Wilde's humorous tale tells of a venerable ghost, Sir Simon de Canterville, who finds himself vexed and humiliated by an American couple who prove too modern and practically-minded to be alarmed by his efforts at haunting them. Nonetheless, he comes to befriend their young daughter, Virginia, who agrees to help him find peace.

A popular story, **The Canterville Ghost** has been adapted many times in different media, and has been a popular choice for the Christmas schedules over the years:

The Canterville Ghost (1962)
Drama | TV | 55 mins
TX: 23/12//1962, BBC Television

Bernard Cribbins stars as the ghostly Sir Simon, with the young Samantha Eggar as Virginia and Derek Francis as her father, Hiram Otis.

The Canterville Ghost (1974)
Drama | TV | 60 mins
TX: 31/12//1974, ITV
     22/12//1976, ITV

David Niven brings a dry melancholy to the role of Sir Simon in this HTV adaptation; he enjoys rather classy company in a cast that includes Flora Robson, Isla Blair, and Lynne Frederick as Virginia. There's also a lovely score by Carl Davis to enrich the proceedings.

The Canterville Ghost (1992)
Drama | Radio| 90 mins
TX: 31/12//1992, Radio 4

Edward Petherbridge stars as Sir Simon in this feature-length adaptation first broadcast as part of Radio 4's Christmas Spirits season.

Theatre Royal: The Canterville Ghost (1953)
Drama | Radio| 30 mins
TX: 31/12//1996, Radio 2

Broadcast as part of Radio 2's Vintage Christmas season, this 1954 US adaptation of Wilde's tale, part of the *Theatre Royal* anthology series, starred Laurence Olivier in the role of Sir Simon.

The Canterville Ghost (1997)
Drama | TV | 90 mins
TX: 26/12//1997, ITV

Ian Richardson takes his turn as Sir Simon, with a splendid supporting cast that includes Celia Imrie, Ian McNeice, James D'Arcy, Rik Mayall and Pauline Quirke. Donald Sinden is also present, fresh from his role in a US TV adaptation of **The Canterville Ghost** the previous year. Sarah-Jane Potts rounds out the cast as Virginia.

The Canterville Ghost (2004)
Reading | Radio | 3 x 30 mins
TX: 16/12/2004, 17/12/2004, & 20/12/2004, BBC 7
      23/12/2007 - 06/01/2008, BBC 7 (weekly)

Alastair McGowan reads Oscar Wilde's original story in three parts.

The Canterville Ghost (2021)
Drama | TV | 2 x 45 mins
TX: 25/12/2022 - 26/12/2022, Channel 5

Originally broadcast in four parts at Halloween 2021, this serial was repeated on Channel 5 the following year; the episodes were doubled-up and broadcast over two afternoons. Anthony Head starred as the ghost, with Laurel Waghorn as Virginia.

THE CASK OF AMONTILLADO (1995)

Drama | TV | 15 mins

TX: 02/01//1998, BBC2

This short dramatization of a famous Poe story was presented as a bookend to the last part of (the rather intermittently-scheduled) *Clive Barker's A-Z of Horror*, a documentary series that ran throughout Autumn 1998.

Just the thing, a macabre tale squeezed in at the end of a Friday night before everybody has to start a weekend facing the reality of Christmas being over.

Though come to think of it, a story about somebody trapped in an enclosed room after being lured by the promise of alcohol is likely to have been a relatable scenario to the sort of person watching telly at half-past-one in the morning on a Friday night...

In fact, this particular Poe dramatization is not as straightforward as it might appear. It actually began life as part of a television arts documentary series called *American Masters*, made by **PBS**. One of the last episodes of this long running series was entitled *Edgar Allan Poe: Terror of the Soul*, which included this illustrative adaptation of **Cask**, with John Heard and Rene Auberjonois starring as Montresor and Fortunato.

It seems only natural that the adaptation would eventually come to be removed from its documentary context and marketed on its own merits, which is presumably how it came to be in the clutches of **BBC2** – though in fact it has a pretty short running time, likely making it the kind of one-off oddity that BBC2 schedules regularly offered to the discerning/drunk viewer in the good old days.

CAUSING A SCENE: GHOSTS (2022)

Documentary | Radio | 15 mins

TX: 26/12//2000, Radio 4

Causing a Scene was a five-part series presented by the ever-incisive Antonia Quirke, in which she discussed the very particular impact that certain scenes in famous films have had on us, and on popular cultures.

Episode 2, broadcast on Boxing Day, was a brief but rich and engaging discussion of ghosts on film, and included an interview with James Watkins, director of the 2012 film adaptation of *The Woman in Black*.

THE CAVE OF HARMONY (2000)

Drama | Radio | 60 mins

TX: 22/12//2000, Radio 4

Michael Eaton and Neil Brand riff on **A Christmas Carol** in this tale in which Dickens's contemporary and friend, William Makepeace Thackeray is taken back in time by supernatural intercession. He's given a chance to see moments from his sometimes-troubled relationship with Dickens once more, and like Scrooge, he is also given a glimpse of his own passing and what he will leave behind in the world.

Though not quite a ghost story, this melancholy reflection on the lives of two great authors is very atmospheric and makes great use of its borrowed supernatural conceit. It being a Neil Brand play there is also a strong musical component, piano music of the lively and companionable kind that Brand also deployed in the 1992 adaptation of

After Supper Ghost Stories. Brand would later write his own heavily musical adaptation of **A Christmas Carol** which was broadcast on BBC radio in 2014.

THE CHANNEL 4 SILENT

Film | TV | various

TX: 28/12/1996, Channel 4 (The Phantom of the Opera)
02/01/1998, Channel 4 (Nosferatu)

The Channel 4 Silent was a regular feature of the London Film Festival between 1992 and 1997, wherein the television channel (noted for its dedication to the broadcasting of a broad variety of cinema) commissioned the restoration of a classic silent film, including the composition of a brand-new score. This film would then be performed with live orchestral accompaniment as part of the festival, before getting an airing on Channel 4 shortly afterwards.

In 1996 the film chosen for restoration was the original 1925 version of **The Phantom of the Opera** with live score by Carl Davis. This was followed in 1997 by **Nosferatu** (1922). In both cases the films were painstakingly restored, including the crucial colour tinting of the night scenes in **Nosferatu**, and the full-colour masque sequence from **Phantom of the Opera**. The new score for **Phantom** was by Carl Davis, and the score for **Nosferatu** was a very special commission from James Bernard, the composer whose distinctive music had helped to give the Hammer Horror films a crucial part of their identity. His finished score took the musical idioms he had used so often before, transplanting them into a full symphonic context, and is a wonderful synthesis of Hammer nostalgia and the wide-open possibilities offered by the requirements of a seventy-minute soundtrack.

Both films were shown in the afternoon on Channel 4 over the Christmas period. Sadly, this gothic trend in **The Channel 4 Silent** only lasted for its final two years, so there were no more - but while they lasted, they were a memorable feature of the Christmas schedules.

(As it happens, **The Phantom of the Opera** (1922) had also been given a Christmas showing in 1986, as part of BBC2s 'Silent Classics' season; broadcast on the 23rd of December, it was followed on Christmas Eve by *Dr Jekyll and Mr Hyde* (1920), though once again this was no more than a brief, gothic blip in the longer run of silent films)

THE CHILD AND THE MAN

Reading | Radio | 25 mins

TX: 25/12/1962, BBC Light Programme

"A ghost story for Christmas written and read by James Langham"

THE CHILDREN OF GREEN KNOWE

Lucy M. Boston's magical fantasy is 'a winter story about an old house deep in the Fen country', and includes a highly memorable climactic encounter with supernatural evil on Christmas Eve. Adapted by the BBC three times in different formats, it has proved an essential Christmas tale.

Jackanory - The Children of Green Knowe (1966)
Reading| TV | 5 x 15 mins
TX: 19/12/66 - 23/12/66, BBC1

Jackanory was a successful programme that serialised readings of novels and short stories for children, and which ran more than thirty years. Often the stories were read to camera by well-known actors, and in the case of this 1966 reading of **The Children of Green Knowe**, the reader was Susannah York.

The Children of Green Knowe (1989)
Drama | TV | 4 x 30 mins
TX: 26/11/86 - 17/12/86, BBC1 (weekly)
        30/11/86 - 21/12/86, BBC2 (Sunday repeat)

Superficially whimsical, and consistently light and magical throughout, **The Children of Green Knowe** is about a youngster rejoicing in the unusual name 'Tolly' (Alec Christie) who is sent to live in a mysterious new home during the Christmas holidays. It's a familiar set-up for a story, especially to those of us who were raised on the classics of children's fiction from the early 20th century.

Tolly's new home is the great country house of the title, and while there he makes all manner of strange and magical discoveries. He encounters the ghosts of children who lived there centuries before, and like many other spirits in stories of this kind they are quite benign. However, there is another presence abroad within the bounds of Green Knowe.

Hinted at from the earliest scenes when a local woman jokes that Tolly should watch out for 'Old Noah', and referred to by the ghost children as a 'demon tree', Tolly discovers the truth of these stories when walking through the grounds of the house after dark on a blustery Christmas Eve. Old Noah - a twisted old Yew Tree, cursed long years ago - comes to life and pursues Tolly through the night.

While not executed with an overabundance of special effects, the sequence can still seem an alarming one if met with an open imagination, especially if the bizarre idea of an evil, child-killing tree is new to you.

The Children of Green Knowe wasn't director Colin Cant's last frightening contribution to children's television, his eerie and haunting serialisation of Helen Cresswell's *Moondial* appearing a little over a year later. Nor was this the last murderous tree to haunt a BBC Christmas (see **The Green Man**).

The Children of Green Knowe (1999)
Drama | Radio | 90 mins
TX: 18/12/1999, Radio 4

Writer and dramatist Brian Sibley has made a speciality of adapting literary fantasies for the radio, including all of *The Narnia Chronicles* and *The Lord of the Rings*. It was well within his remit, then, to adapt Lucy M. Boston's classic children's novel as a feature-length radio play – though it does of course get overlooked in favour of the earlier television version.

The country house of Green Knowe is a world in and of itself, and perhaps we might compare it a little to Gormenghast in that respect – it would be apt, not least because Brian Sibley also adapted Peake's fantasies for the radio.

There is a good deal more lightness and charm at Green Knowe, of course, and young Tolly's time there is a magical adventure – but nonetheless, it takes a sudden plunge into darkness with Tolly's climactic encounter with the forces of evil.

Tolly's aunt Mrs Oldknow is played here by Patricia Routledge no less, and a very young Nicholas Hoult appears as one of the ghosts.

A CHILD'S VOICE

Drama | TV | 30 mins

TX: 29/12/1980, BBC2
     11/12/1982, BBC2

A short film made in Ireland in 1978, **A Child's Voice** found its way to a BBC broadcast not long after the 1970s Ghost Stories For Christmas had come to an end; some like to think of **Schalcken the Painter** as having picked up that torch in 1979, and we could easily think of **A Child's Voice** as having run the next leg the following year.

Though it does attend to some of the same themes detectable in the M.R. James tales – of pride, isolation, and a downfall of reason – it is placed in a radically different setting. The narration tells us that the story is set, 'in those days' when 'radio was a power and a light in the land' which could be as early as the 1920s - but either way, the story makes much use of the sealed isolation of a recording studio. However basic the technology this feels very 20th Century, and therefore well after the end of the ghost story's customary epoch.

Nor is the protagonist in this story any kind of dusty academic, but rather a self-regarding broadcaster named Ainsley Rupert Macreadie (T.P.

McKenna). He is the writer and reader of chilling tales serialised in late-night radio broadcasts, and his latest tale is to be about a boy who is doomed to be murdered by a wicked magician.

Before he can complete the tale, he begins to receive mysterious telephone calls. From the other end of the line, a child's voice begs him not to finish the story...

Calmly insidious and precisely ambiguous, **A Child's Voice** seems to actively harbour spite towards its own protagonist – no matter how pompous he may be, can Macreadie really be as contemptible as the narrator seems to think?

Perhaps this is itself an articulation of Macreadie's own internal fragility; the narration is provided by none other than Valentine Dyall, an actor well-remembered as 'The Man in Black', presenter of sinister stories on the radio - and therefore very much a real-world equivalent of Macreadie (a fact that was, one supposes, not lost on audiences in 1978). Perhaps the narration is as much the voice of Macreadie's sublimated self-hatred as of any simple exposition?

All of which said, despite Dyall's presence, it seems far more likely that A.R. Macreadie is in some degree based on Leslie Harrison Lambert, a broadcaster who wrote and appeared on the BBC under the name A.J. Alan.

Like Macreadie he wrote and prepared his own stories, and like Macreadie he worked with a lit candle in the room – though where Macreadie wrote his stories by candlelight to create 'atmosphere', Alan had a candle beside him while he read so that if the electric lights failed his broadcast need not be interrupted. Unlike Macreadie he took great trouble over writing his stories, only managing to broadcast a handful in a year.

Lambert, to be clear, seems to have lacked the particular vanity that sets Macreadie up for his fall - however, sadly his broadcasting career was curtailed by a decline into ill health.

This layered aspect of **A Child's Voice** also has an interesting echo in Mark Gatiss's **The Dead Room**, which shares much of its premise with the earlier Irish film. It gains an extra layer, however, when one remembers that the mantle of radio's Man in Black was taken up in the 2000s by none other than... Mark Gatiss...

THE CHIMES

Frank Capra's *It's a Wonderful Life* is often said to have been inspired by Dickens's **A Christmas Carol** - and while that may be so, it's rather striking that the second of Dickens's 'Christmas books', **The Chimes**, is a more exact comparison in terms of its plot.

The story's protagonist, Trotty, has fallen into despair at the world around him, at the poverty and wickedness, and at the hopelessness that he sees as commonplace. On New Year's Eve he is drawn to the sound of the bells at a nearby church, and climbs up the tower.

In the bell chamber he encounters a company of goblins – the spirits of the bells – who reveal to him that he has died. He fell during his climb up the tower, and his corpse lies far below.

Trotty is then given a series of visions showing just how miserable the world would be for those he loves without him in it to make it better – that in fact he had the power to put hope into the world, but was too caught up in his own despair to recognise that fact...

Though certainly not the best-known of Dickens's Christmas Books, The Chimes has nonetheless been adapted for radio multiple times.

The Chimes (1944)
Drama | Radio | 75 mins
TX: 30/12/1944, BBC Home Service

An early work by Joan Littlewood, this adaptation also rejoiced in a musical score composed specially for the play by William Alwyn, who was already a prolific composer of film music by that time.

The Chimes (1961)
Drama | Radio | 60 mins
TX: 30/12/1961, BBC Home Service

Miles Malleson stars as Trotty in Mollie Hardwick's adaptation of the tale.

For producer Charles Lefeaux, this play began something of a Christmas tradition as he followed it in subsequent years with radio adaptations of Dickens's **The Story of the Goblins Who Stole a Sexton (1962)**, Priestley's **The Demon King (1962)**, M.R. James's **Oh, Whistle and I'll Come to You (1963)** and **A Christmas Carol (1965)**.

The Chimes (1968)
Reading | Radio | 10 x 15 mins
TX: 23/12/1968 – 03/01/1969, BBC Radio 4

A daily reading by Gary Watson, broadcast in ten instalments.

The Chimes (2003)
Drama | Radio | 60 mins
TX: 27/12/2003, BBC Radio 4
      31/12/2009, BBC Radio 7
      31/12/2010, BBC Radio 7
      01/01/2015, BBC Radio 4 Extra

Ron Cook takes up the role of Trotty Veck in this third dramatization for BBC radio.

A CHRISTMAS CAROL

Certainly, the most frequently-adapted of Christmas ghost stories, broadcasts based on **A Christmas Carol** are as old as the BBC. In the early days of regional broadcasting, there were sometimes multiple, differing performances and adaptations of Dickens's story each year. In December 1923 there were at least six entirely different adaptations broadcast throughout the UK, for example. There is little information about most of these early performances beyond their times and dates of broadcast, however.

Therefore, the list below is not complete, and I've tended to favour those broadcasts of which there is something that can actually be said.

Scholars' Half-Hour: A Short Talk on Dickens's Christmas Carol
Talk | Radio | 35 mins
TX: 22/12/1923, 5NO Newcastle

A Christmas Carol (1924)
Drama | Radio | 60 mins
TX: 26/12/1924, 6FL Sheffield

A Christmas Carol (1926)
Reading | Radio | 30 mins
TX: 24/12/1926, 2BD Aberdeen

A short reading performed by the Marquis of Aberdeen.

A Christmas Carol (1926)
Reading | Radio | 135 mins
TX: 26/12/1926, 2LO London

A lengthy reading of the story, performed by the noted stage actor Robert Loraine. Loraine was subsequently engaged to star in the 1935 adaptation of the story for BBC radio – but fate intervened...

Scrooge (1928)
Drama | Radio | ?? mins
TX: 24/12/1928, 2ZY Manchester

Adapted by J. C. Buckstone, starring Leo Channing as Scrooge.

A Christmas Carol (1929)
Reading | Radio | 15 mins
TX: 25/12/1929, 2LO London/5XX Daventry
      26/12/1932, 2LO London/5XX Daventry

A short, one-man performance of **A Christmas Carol** by the popular character actor Bransby Williams. Williams specialised in Dickensian performances on stage, film, and radio, and played Scrooge many times.

His solo performance of **A Christmas Carol** was first broadcast on the radio in 1929, though it returned to the BBC in a variety of different forms over the years. In 1950, at the age of eighty, Williams even played Scrooge as part of a live, feature-length television play.

Happily, records of Bransby Williams's **A Christmas Carol** were made commercially available on vinyl for many years, and so it can now be heard online if one looks for it.

Scrooge (1932)
Drama | Radio | 50 mins
TX: 25/12/1932, BBC Regional Programme Midland

Edgar Lane performed a 'dramatic recital in three scenes based on A Christmas Carol.

A Christmas Carol (1933)
Drama | Radio | 75 mins
TX: 18/12/1936, BBC Regional Programme Daventry
      19/12/1936, BBC Regional Programme London

This adaptation had the distinction of featuring Seymour Hicks as Scrooge; Hicks was very well-known for playing the role on stage, and had even played Scrooge on a tour of Australia.

A Christmas Carol (1935)
Drama | Radio | 75 mins
TX: 26/12/1935, BBC Regional Programme London/Western, Northern Ireland
27/12/1935, BBC National Programme Daventry

This full-cast radio dramatization by Max Kester was to have seen actor, aviator, and war hero, Robert Loraine return to the role of Scrooge on the radio – he had performed a reading of the story on Boxing Day almost a decade earlier.

Rather poignantly, Loraine did not get to play Scrooge that Christmas, as he passed away suddenly on the 23rd December, aged only 59. One presumes that the broadcasts went ahead with an understudy in the lead, despite the sad circumstances.

A Christmas Carol (1936)
Drama | Radio | 20 mins
TX: 16/12/1936 (BBC Regional Programme Northern

Adapted by The Huddersfield Jubilee Entertainers.

Children's Hour: A Christmas Carol
Drama | Radio | 45 mins
TX: 25/12/1936, Regional Programme
25/12/1937, Regional Programme
25/12/1940, BBC Home Service
24/12/1944, BBC Home Service
25/12/1949, BBC Home Service

Adapted by and starring Philip Wade, this radio play proved popular and so it was performed again the following year with exactly the same cast.

A third Children's Hour performance followed in in 1940, still with Wade playing Scrooge, but with a new cast that included Patricia Hayes and Laidman Browne. The 1944 production once again featured Wade as Scrooge, and the new cast featured the radio stalwart Carleton Hobbs as one of the ghosts, not to mention a certain Charles Hawtrey as one of the Cratchit children.

Wade's adaptation returned once again in 1949, but this time Wade was replaced in the role of Scrooge by Carleton Hobbs.

A Christmas Carol (1942)
Drama | Radio | 30 mins
TX: 21/12/1942, BBC Home Service

Adapted by Max Kester; starring Sir John Martin-Harvey as Scrooge.

A Christmas Carol (1943)
Drama | Radio | 40 mins
TX: 24/12/1943, BBC Home Service

Adapted by Max Kester; Philip Wade starred as Scrooge in this adaptation, after playing the character in several productions of his own adaptation for BBC radio.

A Christmas Carol (1947)
Drama | Radio | 30 mins
TX: 24/12/1947, BBC Light Programme

Adapted by Max Kester; starring Laidman Browne as Scrooge.

A Christmas Carol (1948)
Reading | Radio | 5 x 15 mins
TX: 20/12/1948 – 24/12/1948, BBC Home Service

An abridged reading broadcast in five daily parts under the Woman's Hour Serial banner, performed by Ronald Simpson.

A Christmas Carol (1950, Radio)
Drama | Radio | 30 mins
TX: 24/12/1950, BBC Home Service

Starring Alec Guinness as Scrooge, with Hamilton Dyce as the Ghost of Jacob Marley.

A Christmas Carol (1950, TV)
Drama | TV | 90 mins
TX: 25/12/1950, BBC Television
    27/12/1950, BBC Television

Bransby Williams returned to the role of Scrooge in this live-broadcast adaptation of Dominic Roche's stage play. Williams was eighty years old at this point, and had played Scrooge many times in various media, including a BBC radio broadcast in 1929.

Though this play does not appear to have been recorded or repeated, Bransby Williams returned to the BBC as Scrooge several times in the next few years.

A Christmas Carol (1951, Radio)
Drama | Radio | 15 mins
TX: 25/12/1951, BBC Home Service West

A year after appearing in a full-length dramatization of A Christmas Carol, Bransby Williams returned as Scrooge once again, this time to the role of Scrooge in this live-broadcast adaptation of Dominic Roche's stage play. Williams was eighty years old at this point, and had played Scrooge many times in various media, including a BBC radio broadcast in 1929.

Scrooge (1951, Radio)
Film | Radio | 60 mins
TX: 26/12/1951, Light Programme
      23/12/1952, Home Service

A curious instance of a film being broadcast on the radio, this was a specially edited, narrated version of the soundtrack to the feature film starring Alastair Sim as Scrooge. The exercise is all the more intriguing given that the film had been released in UK cinemas only a few weeks prior to the first broadcast.

Solo Performance (1952)
Drama | Radio | 20 mins
TX: 24/12/1952, BBC Television

21/12/1953, BBC Television
21/12/1955, BBC Television
24/12/1960, BBC Television

Bransby Williams brought his one-man performance of **A Christmas Carol** to television a year after reprising it on radio. Unlike the 1950 play, this television performance was recorded, and repeated several times in subsequent years – though the programme was billed as 'Bransby Williams' on those occasions.

Theatre Royal: A Christmas Carol (1953)
Drama | Radio | 30 mins
TX: 24/12/1996, Radio 2

An episode of the US NBC Radio series picked up by BBC Radio in 1996 and broadcast late in the evening on Christmas Eve (just before *Carols by Candlelight*). Lawrence Olivier narrated and starred as Scrooge.

A Christmas Carol (1955)
Reading | Radio | 30 mins
TX: 23/12/1955, BBC Home Service

A reading by V. C. Clinton-Baddeley.

A Christmas Carol (1962)
Opera | TV | 60 mins
TX: 24/12/1962, BBC Television

An operatic adaptation of Dickens's story, commissioned by the BBC. Music was by Edwin Coleman, and the libretto by Margaret Burns Harris.

Sunday Story: A Christmas Carol (1963)
Reading | TV | 3 x 5 mins
TX: 15/12/1963 - 29/12/1963, BBC Home Service

Michael Hordern performs perhaps the shortest of all the screen adaptations of **A Christmas Carol**, across three weekly episodes, each one five-minutes in duration.

A Christmas Carol (1965)
Drama | Radio | 55 mins
TX: 25/12/1965, BBC Home Service
       20/12/1974, Radio 4
       26/12/1993, Radio 4

Adapted and produced by Charles Lefeaux, starring Ralph Richardson as Scrooge and the Storyteller.

A Christmas Carol (1966)
Musical | Radio | 60 mins
TX: 21/12/1966, BBC Home Service
       24/12/1967, BBC Radio 4

A musical adaptation by Iwan Williams, starring Wilfrid Brambell as Scrooge.

Mr Scrooge (1967)
Opera | Radio | 120 mins
TX: 21/12/1967, BBC Radio 3

A four-scene opera based on **A Christmas Carol**, sung entirely in Czech. The libretto and music were by Jan Cikker (a fairly eminent Slovakian composer).

Characters from Dickens: Ebenezer Scrooge
Drama | Radio | 30 mins
TX: 22/12/1970

Starring Patrick Magee as Scrooge. **Characters from Dickens** was a series of twelve half-hour plays in the Story Time strand, concentrating on specific characters from the work of Charles Dickens; not all of the characters chosen were among the best-remembered or prominent – clearly this is not true of Scrooge, but he must have been the obvious choice for an episode broadcast at Christmas.

A Christmas Carol (1970)
Reading | TV | 50 mins
TX: 23/12/1970, ITV
    24/12/1970, ITV
    26/12/1970 - 27/12/1970, ITV

The productive team of Paul Honeyman and John Worsley was behind serialised readings of a number of classics for children for Anglia Television. This included memorable adaptations of *The Wind in the Willows*, *The Little Grey Men*, and *The Winter of Enchantment*. Similar to the BBCs *Jackanory* in format, these shows featured Honeyman narrating the story, while the camera tracked across

Worsley's specially-painted illustrations. However, quite unlike Jackanory, these programmes typically featured hundreds of Worsley's illustrations, sometimes only showing them on screen for a few seconds, depending on narrative requirement. Though obviously this is some way short of animation, this was nonetheless quite a dynamic approach to story illustration for the medium (some of Worsley's paintings even featured moving parts)

In 1970, Honeyman and Worsley produced an adaptation of A Christmas Carol. Running to an hour, it featured one hundred and fifty of Worsley's beautifully atmospheric paintings.

ITV was divided into regional franchises for much of its early existence and so there are multiple broadcast dates for this programme, and it appears that it was broken into episodes for broadcast in some regions. The programme does survive in full, and was at one time commercially available in the 1980s.

A Christmas Carol (1971)
Animation | TV | 25 mins
TX: 24/12/1972, BBC1
        25/12/1973, BBC2
        23/12/1974, BBC1
        22/12/1976, BBC2
        22/12/1978, BBC1

Richard Williams' beautiful, Oscar-winning animated adaptation of Dickens' tale exercises a connoisseur's taste in its selection of influences; the imagery is based directly upon 19th Century illustrations for the story, and it calls Alastair Sim back to the role of Scrooge – his performance in the 1951 film remains many people's favourite.

Michael Hordern also returns to wail Jacob Marley's accusing words at Sim's Scrooge once again.

While it hurtles through the story in a short run-time of twenty-five minutes, time is still found to touch upon moments from the original story that other adaptations omit. In a dark presaging of the imagery of Briggs' *The Snowman*, Scrooge and a Spirit fly through the dark sky to visit the bleak place 'where miners live', and witness even lonely lighthouse keepers and storm-beset mariners as they keep Christmas in their hearts. Despite its status as a 'cartoon', this is among the darker presentations of the story.

Originally aired on ABC TV in the US in 1971, this adaptation was given a theatrical release and was subsequently picked up for the first of many Christmas broadcasts by the BBC in 1972.

A Christmas Carol (1974)
Reading | Radio | 2 x 85 mins
TX: 23/12/1974 - 24/12/1974, BBC Radio London

Late night reading of Dickens' novel by David Broomfield.

Marcel Marceau presents A Christmas Carol
Drama | TV | 40 mins
TX: 21/12/1975, BBC2

Marcel Marceau plays all of the characters in this mime adaptation developed specially for television, and performed in an otherwise empty Victorian Music Hall; with narration by Michael Hordern.

A Christmas Carol (1977)
Drama | TV | 60 mins
TX: 24/12/77, BBC2
         25/12/79, BBC2

Adapted by Elaine Morgan. Starring Michael Hordern as Scrooge, with John Le Mesurier as Marley, Bernard Lee as the Ghost of Christmas Present, and Patricia Quinn as the Ghost of Christmas Past.

If you believe all of the opinions that you read on the internet, time has not been kind to this BBC adaptation; there are many complaints that it is dull or cheap. Maybe so. The whole thing is studio-bound, it's rather perfunctory at only an hour in length, and it certainly defies the contemporary understanding of the word 'lavish'.

On the other hand, this kind of production was fairly normal at the time and is just fine if you're used to it. After all, the scenery is not falling to bits, the cast are all at the very least dependable (many of them are comfortingly familiar) and there is plenty of atmosphere to be found in the confines of the studio – there is a theatrical mood to the piece that works very well if you're receptive to it.

This version is also notable in that it finally promotes Michael Hordern to the top job after he'd played Jacob Marley in two previous adaptations – not to mention providing the narration for Marcel Marceau's mime-adaptation of the story broadcast in 1975 (no, honestly). Marley is played this time round by John Le Mesurier, which would doubtless have made it confusing viewing for any children at the time who would only know these actors as the voices of Paddington Bear and Bod respectively.

A Christmas Carol (1978)

Musical | Radio | 60 mins
TX: 24/12/1978, Radio 2
        23/12/1979, Radio 2

A new production of Iwan Williams's musical adaptation (previously broadcast on the BBC in 1966), starring Roy Dotrice as Scrooge.

A Christmas Carol (1982)

Reading | TV | 4 x 15 mins
TX: 21/12/1982 - 24/12/1982, BBC2 (daily)

This four-episode reading of Dickens' tale appears to have been an offshoot of Jackanory - the director (Christine Secombe), producer (Angela Beeching), and narrator (Michael Bryant) all having worked on that show, as well as the spin-off **Spine Chillers**.

Paul Birkbeck, (a regular Jackanory artist), also provided story illustrations - presumably the subject of tracking camera shots during sections of the narration.

A Christmas Carol (1982)

Opera | Radio | 115 mins
TX: 01/01/1982, BBC Radio 3

A recording, from Covent Garden, of a new two-act opera by Thea Musgrave adapting Charles Dickens's story.

A Book at Bedtime - A Christmas Carol (1985)
Reading | Radio | 8 x 15 mins
TX: 16/12/1985 - 27/12/1985

Read by Martin Jarvis, with Denise Bryer.

Humbug!
Documentary | Radio | 30 mins / 40 mins (repeat)
TX: 22/12/1987, BBC Radio 4
        25/12/1993, BBC Radio 4

Brian Sibley looks at the history of **A Christmas Carol**. This documentary includes a rich variety of extracts from the many adaptations of the novel, as well as readings from the original text. Evidently the documentary was edited to fit a 30-minute slot on its original broadcast, as the repeat a few years later was a full ten minutes longer.

Humbug! is one of a number of radio programmes that Brian Sibley has made available on his Soundcloud account, and can be heard there for free.

Saturday Playhouse - A Christmas Carol (1990)
Drama | Radio | 90 mins
TX: 22/12/1990, Radio 4
        25/12/1992, Radio 4
        25/12/2005, BBC7
        23/12/2006, BBC7
        20/12/2009, BBC7
        26/12/2010, BBC7
        25/12/2011, Radio 4 Extra

Starring Michael Gough as Scrooge, with Freddie Jones as the narrator. Directed by Glyn Dearman.

A Christmas Carol (1993)
Ballet | TV | 90 mins
TX: 25/12/1993, BBC2

A television presentation of Christopher Gable's production for the Northern Ballet Company. Prolific TV and film composer Carl Davis provided the score, with choreography by Massimo Moricone.

Scrooge – The Musical (1995)
Musical | Radio | 150 mins
TX: 09/12/1995, BBC Radio 2
     24/12/2017, BBC Radio 4 Extra

The 1994 stage production of Leslie Bricusse's musical was performed at the Palace Theatre in Manchester. Anthony Newley starred as Scrooge, with Stratford Johns as the Ghost of Christmas Present.

A recording of this show was broadcast on Radio 2 in January 1995, and subsequently repeated the following December; it was repeated more recently on Radio 4 Extra.

A Christmas Carol (1995)
Reading | Radio | 5 x 20 mins
TX: 25/12/1995 – 29/12/1995, BBC Radio 4

Richard Wilson reads the story in daily instalments.

An Audience with Charles Dickens (1996)
Reading | TV | 4 x 30 mins, 1 x 45 mins (episode 5)
TX: 23/12/1996 - 30/12/1995, BBC Radio 4

Actor Simon Callow has written extensively about the life and work of Charles Dickens, and played the man several times on radio, film and television. These appearances have included readings of Dickens stories, including the feature-length reading of **A Christmas Carol** from 2018.

In this short 1996 series, Callow recreated the famous public readings given by Dickens. Episodes two and three, broadcast on Christmas Eve and Christmas Day, constituted a two-part reading of A Christmas Carol. The other readings comprised Bill Sikes's murder of Nancy, the trial from The Pickwick Papers, and an obscure tale called *Doctor Marigold* – none of these have a supernatural component, though you might count Sikes and Nancy among the darker tales to be told at Christmas.

A Christmas Carol (2000)
Drama | TV | 90 mins
TX: 20/12/2000, ITV

Peter Bowker's update of Dickens's tale to contemporary London could at first be construed as little more than a simple star vehicle for Ross Kemp, who was at that time working under a very lucrative and exclusive contract with ITV.

However, there is a certain amount of shrewdness in evidence here, with respect to the changes and updates made to the story and the supporting cast is excellent – for example, Michael Maloney as Bob Cratchitt, and Warren Mitchell as Scrooge's father. There is a clear effort to try and make this retelling fresh and different, most significantly with the manifestation of the third spirit, and the extrapolation of a love story from the sad fragments of Scrooge's past that we were shown in the original.

A Christmas Carol (2005)
Reading | Radio | 5 x 15 mins
TX: 25/12/2005 - 29/12/2005, BBC Radio 2

An episodic reading, broadcast at a quarter to midnight. Unfortunately, available information doesn't say who the reader was, or if this was a repeat of an earlier reading.

A Christmas Carol (2006)
Reading | Radio | 7 x 15 mins
TX: 18/12/2006 - 21/12/2006, Radio 2

Shane Ritchie takes his turn as reader. In a slightly eccentric piece of scheduling, two episodes were broadcast each night (at 10pm and then a quarter to midnight), with the exception of the penultimate evening, the 20th December, when there was only the one episode at 11.45pm.

A Book at Bedtime - A Christmas Carol (2008)
Reading | Radio | 10 x 15 mins
TX: 15/12/2008 - 26/12/2008, Radio 4

A reading of the novel broadcast on weekdays over a fortnight; David Jason was the reader this time.

Saturday Drama - A Christmas Carol (2014)
Drama | Radio | 90 mins
TX: 20/12/2014, Radio 4

Composer and dramatist Neil Brand is probably best-known to BBC audiences as the resident soundtrack expert whose clear and accessible explanations of the ways in which music interacts with and supports visual images were a frequent highlight of the long-running (sadly now deceased) Film Programme. A man with many strings to his bow, Brand has also written a number of radio dramas, some of which made effective use of long musical passages of his own composition. The descriptive power of a symphonic piece shouldn't be underestimated; the music in his 2013 adaptation of *The Wind in the Willows* expertly created landscapes of the pastoral and the emotional all at once.

Brand deployed the same combination of dialogue and music for his 2014 adaptation of **A Christmas Carol**, starring Robert Powell in the lead role, and with Ron Cook as Jacob Marley.

Sadly, Brand's adaptation has thus far gone unrepeated. Recorded in front of a live audience and with the full power of the BBC Symphony Orchestra and BBC Singers brought to bear, this lavish and absorbing treatment of the familiar story was a welcome variation on the well-played theme.

Archive on 4 – The Many Faces of Ebenezer Scrooge
Documentary | Radio | 60 mins
TX: 24/12/2016, Radio 4
       22/12/2018, Radio 4
       15/12/2020, Radio 4
       25/12/2021, Radio 4

Christopher Frayling's documentary looks at the history of A Christmas Carol, its popularity, and its many adaptations.

At the time of writing, this documentary is still available to be heard on BBC Sounds.

Friday Night is Music Night – A Christmas Carol (2016)
Musical | Radio | 120 mins
TX: 23/12/2016, Radio 2
       22/12/2017, Radio 2 (as *Sunday Night is Music Night*)

Friday Night is Music Night is a long-running Radio 2 programme that provides a full-length concert to fill an evening, ranging far and wide over the musical genres. This particular edition presented a 'concert version' of Dickens's **A Christmas Carol**, mixing a number of dramatized scenes with a variety of classic Christmas songs performed by artists including Katie Melua.

Mark Gatiss led the cast as Ebenezer Scrooge, supported by Lee Ingleby as Bob Cratchit, reuniting the pair who had previously appeared together in 2008's **Crooked House**.

A Christmas Carol (2018)
Reading | TV | 72 mins
TX: 16/12/2018, BBC4
       20/12/2020, BBC4
       11/12/2021, BBC2
       18/12/2022, BBC4

Veteran actor Simon Callow's appreciation of Charles Dickens is well-documented by this time; he has repeatedly played Dickens on stage, film and television, including a memorable turn in a Doctor Who episode featuring ghosts at Christmas. His 2011 one-man stage show in which he performed A Christmas Carol used an adaptation of the text produced by Dickens himself for his own live performances of the story, and in 2018 it was filmed for television broadcast. Callow performs the story to camera, using various atmospheric interior spaces as a backdrop.

A Christmas Carol (2019)
Drama | TV | 3 x 60 mins
TX: 22/12/2019 – 24/12/2019

Steven Knight's radical reinvention of Dickens' tale as a three-hour wallow in the miseries of the Victorian era, with added child abuse and sexual exploitation, is likely to have irked more than a few of the many who love this story, and certainly the second and third episodes were watched by a significantly smaller audience than the first. There is something of the moral snakepit about this retelling, and it is evidently not intended for a family audience.

Whether or not this exercise is a successful one, it is absolutely true to say that it boasts an excellent cast, with Guy Pearce as Scrooge and Stephen Graham as Marley. It achieves an intensity and darkness that is not necessarily out of keeping with what is, after all, a ghost story, but it's very tempting to suggest that it strays a little too far from its starting point, and in doing so loses the very spirit of Christmas that is surely the essence of the story.

A Christmas Carol (2021)
Reading | Radio | 210 mins
TX: 19/12/2021, Radio 4 Extra

An unabridged, three-and-a-half hour reading of the complete text of Dickens' story, broadcast in a single afternoon. Read by Sean Baker.

A Christmas Carol: A Ghost Story (2022)
Drama | TV | 105 mins
TX: 25/12/2022, BBC4

It's now a common event for major stage plays to be filmed in order to allow them to be broadcast in cinemas nationwide, giving a far wider audience the chance to see productions that would otherwise have been quite beyond their means or opportunity. To this end, Mark Gatiss's adaptation of *A Christmas Carol* was filmed during its Alexandra Palace run, and initially shown in cinemas in November of 2022. However, BBC4 also secured it for television broadcast on Christmas Day.

Nicholas Farrell leads the cast as Scrooge, with Mark Gatiss appearing in the role of Jacob Marley. The production is rich, and lively, with an authentic sense of dark humour and a couple of minor innovations that manage to bring some additional moments of charm to the story.

CHRISTMAS CHILLS

Documentary | Radio | 35 mins

TX: 24/12/1990, Radio 5

These days Phil Rickman is a well-known writer of supernatural and mystery novels, but in 1990 he was still working as a broadcaster on BBC Radio. **Christmas Chills** was listed in the Radio Times as being 'ghost stories for Christmas, with Phil Rickman' and while this seems to imply the reading of ghost stories, Mr Rickman has been kind enough to confirm that the programme was actually *about* seasonal ghost stories. Sadly, it seems to be lost in the abyss of old radio programmes and is unlikely to surface any time soon.

A CHRISTMAS GHOST STORY

Reading | Radio | 15 mins

TX: 23/12/1969, Radio 4

One of **A.J. Alan's ghost stories**, read by Peter Tuddenham – an actor perhaps best known to posterity as the voice of Orac in *Blake's 7*. This was the second of two stories by Alan broadcast that week, the first, **The Visitor's Book**, having been broadcast the previous day.

CHRISTMAS SPIRITS (1981)

Drama | TV | 45 mins

TX: 01/01/1981, ITV

Among the most obscure television ghost stories, **Christmas Spirits** actually boasts a fair pedigree. The cast is led by Elaine Stritch, the writing is by Willis Hall, and the whole thing is produced and directed by June Wyndham-Davis, whose name may not be well-known outside of the industry, but whose career speaks for itself. Her most notable contribution to TV legend was the suggestion that Jeremy Brett be considered for the role of Sherlock Holmes in the 1980s.

Christmas Spirits is evidently considered unremarkable in the grander scheme of things, but it is well-executed; its ideas may be familiar, but they're nonetheless creepy.

Stritch plays an American location scout who is looking for somewhere in the UK that would make a good setting for a horror movie. She thinks she's found it when she comes to Glebe Hall, but then she's allowed to stay there on her own while the residents go out for an evening. She comes to realise that she is not truly on her own, and that the ghastly events of the Hall's past still hang in the air of the building's lonelier spaces.

CHRISTMAS SPIRITS (1992)

Drama | Radio | Various

An eclectic season of ghostly dramas broadcast on Radio 4 over Christmas 1992. The season comprised the following eight plays, all of which have their own entries in this book.

- **The Haunted Man and the Ghost's Bargain** (TX: 20/12/1992)
- **A Christmas Carol (1990)** (TX: 25/12/1992)
- **After Supper Ghost Stories** (TX: 26/12/1992)
- **The Exorcism** (TX: 28/12/1992)
- **Blithe Spirit (1983)** (TX: 29/12/1992)
- **Jonas** (TX: 30/12/1992)
- **The Canterville Ghost** (TX: 31/12/1992)

- **The Turn of the Screw** (TX: 01/01/1993)

CHRISTMAS SPIRITS (2003)

Documentary | Radio | 30 mins

TX: 24/12/2003, Radio 4
      01/01/2004, Radio 4

An intriguing radio documentary about a Middlesborough spiritualist circle and the fifty-year-old audio recording of one of their séances held on Christmas Eve in 1953. The documentary includes interviews with the surviving members of the circle, and extensive extracts from the recording. There is much talk of ectoplasmic rods and so on. Ooer.

Though never made commercially available, this documentary has shown up on the internet – though, a sign of the wicked world in which we now live, hearing it today it's very tempting to assume that the whole thing is a mockumentary.

CHRISTOPHER LEE'S FIRESIDE TALES

Reading | Radio | 5 x 15 mins

TX: 26/12/2004 – 30/12/2004, Radio 2
      26/12/2011 – 30/12/2011, Radio 4 Extra
      23/12/2013 – 27/12/2013, Radio 4 Extra

After a short spell haunting Radio 2 at Christmas with **Edgar Allan Poe's Gothic Tales**, Christopher Lee returned a couple of years later to perform another short series of readings for Christmas.

There were five of these **Fireside Tales**, which were broadcast at a quarter-to-midnight daily, and they comprised:

- *The Black Cat*, by Edgar Allan Poe
- *The Man of Science*, by Jerome K. Jerome
- *John Charrington's Wedding*, by E. Nesbit
- *The Man and the Snake*, by Ambrose Bierce
- *The Monkey's Paw*, by W.W. Jacobs

CHRISTOPHER LEE'S GHOST STORIES FOR CHRISTMAS

Reading | TV | 4 x 30 mins

TX: 23/12/2000, BBC2 (The Stalls of Barchester)
26/12/2000, BBC2 (The Ash Tree)
29/12/2000, BBC2 (Number 13)
31/12/2000, BBC2 (A Warning to the Curious)
24/12/2017, BBC4 (The Stalls of Barchester,
A Warning to the Curious)

Even back in the year 2000, the idea of a television programme consisting of somebody sitting in a chair reading to the camera seemed quaint – albeit reassuringly so. That this revisiting of an old format was performed in costume and in a location imitative of the famous Christmas readings given by **M.R. James** himself only added to the comforting atmosphere offered by this invocation of the spirit of Jackanorys past.

True, the readings were enhanced by collages of imagery appropriate to the story, but these never intruded or got in the way. Nor was there any attempt to add dramatized sequences as has sometimes been the case with similar exercises before and since.

The purity of the tale-telling here made for a very welcome and enjoyable short series, and in retrospect it's rather sad that the BBC never saw fit to produce any more. Indeed, after their initial broadcast they were laid to rest and only returned as extra features on the BFI DVD releases of **A Ghost Story for Christmas** - though eventually a couple of them were disinterred to celebrate Christmas once again in 2017.

Three of the episodes are commercially available on the BFI releases, but Episode 2, The Ash Tree, remains stubbornly unavailable - though it was repeated in May 2022 to mark Lee's centenary.

This was not Christopher Lee's last word on ghost stories for Christmas at the BBC, however - he returned for two series of readings on Radio 2 in 2003 and 2004; **Edgar Allan Poe's Gothic Tales** and **Christopher Lee's Fireside Tales**.

CLASSIC GHOST STORIES (1986)

Reading/Drama | TV | 5 x 15 mins

TX: 25/12/1986 - 30/12/1986, BBC2

Billed as 'five chilling tales for dark winter nights', **Classic Ghost Stories** was broadcast late at night (sometimes well past midnight) but is nonetheless recognisable as a variation of the children's television series Jackanory - producer Angela Beeching had also produced and directed many episodes of *Jackanory* and its spin-offs *Jackanory Playhouse*, **Spine Chillers (1980)** and **A Christmas Carol (1982)**.

Classic Ghost Stories did diverge from the format a little bit, using incidental music and occasional dramatized scenes; its essence however was very much the same as the later **Christopher Lee's Ghost Stories for Christmas.** Robert Powell stepped into Monty's shoes to relate the stories, though from the solitary confines of a quiet study, rather than addressing an eager audience at a Christmas gathering as Lee later did.

The series comprised the following stories:

- *The Mezzotint*
- *The Ash Tree*
- *The Wailing Well*
- *Oh, Whistle, and I'll Come to you, my Lad*
- *The Rose Garden*

All five episodes were released on DVD by the BFI in 2013; the DVD also included the three episodes of **Spine Chillers** that featured stories by **M.R. James** (*The Mezzotint*, *A School Story* and *The Diary of Mr Poynter*, all read by Michael Bryant). This DVD was subsequently included as an extra volume in a reissue of the **Ghost Stories for Christmas** boxed set.

CLASSIC STORIES: STORIES FOR CHRISTMAS (2018)

Reading | Audio Download | various

TX: 21/12/2018, BBC Sounds

A collection of short story readings made available on BBC Sounds rather than being directly broadcast; this collection covered a variety of genres, but the following supernatural stories were included:

- *The Signalman*, by Charles Dickens; read by Christopher Harper (33 mins)
- *The Tell-Tale Heart*, by Edgar Allan Poe; read by Don Gilet (15 mins)
- *The Mezzotint*, by M R James; read by Sam Dale (29 minutes)

THE CONFESSIONS OF CHARLES LINKWORTH

Reading | Radio | 15 mins

TX: 24/12/1928, 2LO London / 5XX Daventry

The tale of a prison doctor contacted by the spirit of an executed murderer, this story from E.F. Benson's ghost story collection *The Room in the Tower*, was adapted and read for Christmas Eve by the author.

Unabridged readings of this story are easily available today, but sadly it appears that no recordings of the author reading the story exist.

COTTAGE OF MY DREAMS

Reading | Radio | 15 mins

TX: 26/12/1947, BBC Home Service Welsh

"a ghost story by S.A. Claridge"

COUNT DRACULA

Drama | TV | 150 mins / 3 x 50 mins

TX: 22/12/1977, BBC2
     19/12/1979 – 21/12/1979, BBC1

Highly regarded by many, not least for its fidelity to Bram Stoker's book, **Count Dracula** wears the eccentricities of its production well when seen today. A handful of dated video effects cannot outweigh the positives of a cast that includes Frank Finlay's Van Helsing, Jack Shepherd's Renfield, and Judi Bowker's Mina (frequently cited by critic and enthusiastic disciple of Dracula Kim Newman as his favourite version of the character).

Louis Jordan is perhaps an unexpected choice to play Dracula, especially as he does not particularly correspond with the image of the character one gets reading the book; nonetheless, he is very well-suited to the drama, particularly as it bills itself as a 'gothic romance'.

The locations are also definitive – the Whitby scenes were filmed in Whitby, and the scenes in Kingstead Cemetery were filmed in the real-life equivalent, Highgate Cemetery. It's understandable that the BBC did not send a crew behind the Iron Curtain to film Castle Dracula exteriors, but some of Highgate's more grandiose architectural features make for very persuasive stand-ins.

Originally broadcast on a single evening (bisected by a news bulletin by way of an intermission), the 1979 repeat was shown in three daily parts, once again in the run-up to Christmas. A non-Christmassy repeat in the Spring of 1993 (seemingly prompted by the release of Francis Ford Coppola's film adaptation a couple of months earlier) returned to the two-part format – and was broadcast only a few days before a repeat of the 1991 radio serial commenced on Radio 4. In those days Dracula seemed to be everywhere.

Count Dracula was given a comparatively early DVD release by the BBC in 2001, but it was only available as part of a special boxed set released by BBC Learning (alongside BBC productions of The Picture of Dorian Gray and The Hound of the Baskervilles). It was finally given a mainstream DVD release in 2007, however, and is still available.

COUNT MAGNUS

Drama | TV | 30 mins

TX: 23/12/2022, BBC2

Mark Gatiss finally completed his adaptation of **Count Magnus**, which had previously been put on hold due to the various limitations imposed by Covid restrictions, just in time for Christmas 2022. After the somewhat full-on revelation at the close of the previous year's **The Mezzotint**, **Count Magnus** actually seems a rather subtle exercise in the main, hinting much and directly showing much less.

It does, however, have a somewhat comical central performance from Jason Watkins as Mr Wraxhall, which proved a little dissonant for some of the audience. An Englishman abroad in Sweden, this Wraxhall is a font of silliness and irritation to the rather more sombre and restrained local population that he encounters.

Perhaps the intention was to echo Michael Hordern's portrayal of Parkins in **Whistle and I'll Come to You (1968)**, an eccentric and somewhat inward person who enjoys the company of his own internal monologue, never really connecting with other people. Either way, Watkins gives us a character with definite notes of innocence and haplessness, and so he remains at least a little sympathetic even as he insistently blunders into things that were best left un-blundered into.

The supporting cast is excellent, and in particular MyAnna Buring gives a highly memorable, understated performance as the enigmatic Frokken de la Gardie. Max Bremer also makes his particular corner of the story quite absorbing, as he recounts the tale of the two poachers who foolishly went into the forbidden woodland of Count Magnus.

CROOKED HOUSE

Drama | TV | 3 x 30 mins

TX: 22/12/2008 - 24/12/2008, BBC4
27/12/2008, BBC4 (feature-length omnibus)
17/12/2009 - 19/12/2009, BBC4
29/12/2010 - 31/12/2010, BBC4

Mark Gatiss's three-part serial draws inspiration not only from the ghost stories of **M.R. James** and their beloved televisual incarnations, but also from the 'portmanteau' horror anthology films that had influenced the earlier **League of Gentlemen Christmas Special**.

Each of the three episodes tells a self-contained story, but all three are linked by a common location – the haunted Geap Manor alluded to by the title - and the framing device of 'the curator' (played by Gatiss) relating past events to Ben (Lee Ingleby), a young man whose discovery of an antique door knocker in the garden of his home leads him to want to know more about the long-since-demolished manor house.

The first story, *The Wainscotting*, is set in the late 1700s and tells of a corrupt and wealthy man, Bloxham (Philip Jackson) who has recently acquired Geap Manor. He decides, with all of the recklessness of a Barchester Archdeacon, to redecorate the interior using wooden panelling of a sinister provenance. The guest cast includes Beth Goddard, Julian Rhind-Tutt and the prominent ghost story enthusiast Andy Nyman.

The Bride takes place in the 1920s, on the evening when a masked ball is held at the manor. Felix, the young heir to Geap Manor, announces his engagement at this gathering, prompting various kinds of dismay from friends and relatives. Then, a spectral figure in a wedding dress is seen, and tragic events loom out of the past to threaten the happy couple. Jean Marsh is a particularly memorable guest star in this episode, playing Lady Constance.

In the final episode, *The Knocker*, Ben fixes his antique discovery to his front door, and soon finds that Geap Manor can still cast a shadow, even long after its demolition...

Perhaps not regarded with the affection it deserves, **Crooked House** efficiently delivers three memorable tales without ever outstaying its welcome, and if it is not a heart-stopping classic that haunts the dreams of everybody who saw it, nor does it need to be. The first two tales, of haunted wooden panelling, and the hideous spectre of a wronged bride, are both atmospheric and engaging, and the third ties things up in in a way that would not, tonally speaking, have been far out of place in an Amicus film.

THE CURSE OF THE BLOCKLEIGHS

Drama | Radio | 45 mins

TX: 25/12/1948

This "Christmas Ghost Story" by John Jowett, starred Basil Radford and Naunton Wayne. This pair of character actors were best known for their on-screen partnership as Charters and Caldicott, the two gentlemen first seen asking about cricket scores in Hitchcock's film of *The Lady Vanishes*.

They went on to reprise these roles – and to play very similar characters with different names – in a succession of films and other productions. For example, in several radio comedies and comedy-thrillers by John Jowett they were 'Woolcot and Spencer'.

Therefore, while this play is billed as a Christmas ghost story, the combination of the Jowett, Wayne and Radford team suggests that this was also a comedy. It was broadcast on Christmas Day afternoon when the whole family would have been listening, after all.

To be clear, Wayne and Radford are not reprising Woolcot and Spencer here, but are instead 'Blockleigh and Blayne'. These are dual roles, in fact – they apparently double up as both contemporary characters and their ancestors, so one is inclined to speculate that the story may resemble M.R. James's *The Ash Tree*, telling of a curse incurred in the past and paid for in the present.

DAEMON

Film | TV | 65 mins

TX: 22/12/1986, Channel 4

Writer and Director Colin Finbow's Children's Film Unit was an educational project that allowed children the chance to gain experience as part of the making of a feature film. As such, the CFUs output tended to be modest in some respects, though fairly ambitious in others. They also enjoyed the patronage of industry professionals such as Susannah York, who brings gravity to the supernatural tale **Daemon** through her supporting role as a psychiatrist.

Daemon is a good example of a trend in the CFU films toward darker, more fantastical themes. Despite this, the films tended to be shown on British television during school holidays without any concession toward darker content in terms of scheduling. This was certainly true for **Daemon**, which was broadcast in the middle of the afternoon.

Ostensibly a tale of an alienated boy undergoing supernatural possession, it also functions as an exploration of themes around mental health. Young Nicholas experiences many of the signs and clichés of demonic possession, but an adult viewer might just as easily wonder if he is simply suffering from a psychiatric illness – at least until the drama makes it very clear that this is definitely a supernatural story.

The explanation for this possession turns it into something of a ghost story too, and as with another CFU feature, **Emily's Ghost**, the genre cliches that are invoked are mixed in with some fresher ideas that make it well-suited to the younger audience for whom it was intended.

THE DARKEST ROOM

Reading | Radio | 5 x 30 mins

TX: 19/12/2016 - 23/12/2016, Radio 4 Extra

A family make the mistake of moving to an old, boarded up house in a lonely location with a sinister-sounding name – Eel Point, on the Swedish island of Oland – and soon tragedy befalls them. Katrine's drowned body is found, and in the wake of this terrible loss her husband Joakim increasingly feels as if there is some supernatural force at work in and around his home.

Johan Theorin's bleak, ominous story was read in five abridged parts by Nigel Stock.

DARK MATTER

Reading | Radio | 10 x 15 mins

TX: 9/12/2019 - 20/12/2019, Radio 4

Published in time for Halloween 2010, Michelle Paver's 1930s-set novel of terror in the Arctic made it onto quite a few people's Christmas Lists that year, having been praised by reviewers as an effective psychological ghost story.

Combining a particularly eerie and lonely setting with finely-drawn characterisation, **Dark Matter** is a tale that opens up entire worlds of cold isolation.

The story is narrated by Jack, a man who initially both wallows in, and rages against, his status as an outsider; part of an expedition to the Arctic, he hopes to leave behind the failures of his ordinary life, but feels judged and excluded by his colleagues. They have pre-existing friendships and are from a different social class, and so he feels outside of the group. Jack's self-pity makes him difficult to warm to, but the tale is told so skilfully that we quickly surmise from his account of other people's behaviour toward him that he is probably his own harshest critic.

The expedition makes camp at a place called Gruhuken, and Jack quickly comes to believe that the place is haunted. Afraid of being seen as weak or unstable he does not share this opinion with anybody. Soon, disaster strikes when one man is taken ill and the group is faced with the possibility of having to abandon the expedition altogether. Jack steps up, volunteering to remain behind until the others can return, even in spite of his anxieties about the place.

His colleagues admire his nerve, as it will mean living in isolation during the onset of the relentless Arctic night; but even Jack's nerve is not enough to deal with what is to come.

Dark Matter was given an airing as Radio 4s *Book at Bedtime* in December 2019; Lee Ingleby's performance of the text was particularly evocative of the emotions in the story, making it one of the best Christmas ghost stories of recent years - though also one of the least-recognised. When the final episode was broadcast late on Friday, 20th December, it ushered the Christmas season in with a welcome shudder.

DEAD OF NIGHT: THE EXORCISM

Drama | TV | 50 mins

TX: 26/12/1973, BBC1

22/12/2007, BBC4

The supernatural anthology series **Dead of Night** (which drew its name from the celebrated British portmanteau horror film of the 1940s) began with this play by Don Taylor – though in fact it had not been produced as part of the series, but was rather an independently produced play that was added to the series roster.

It was also broadcast on bonfire night, a perverse piece of scheduling given that this story is set at, and very much *about*, Christmas – though this fact was recognised the following year when it was repeated on Boxing Day.

Like the most famous supernatural Christmas tale of all, this play explores the dissonance between privilege and poverty during a season supposedly devoted to good will and charity – but I challenge any Dickens adaptation to be one half as blunt or as harsh in its presentation of the themes as **The Exorcism**.

The story is mean and efficient, unfolding in real time. Two couples have gathered to enjoy a Christmas feast together; overflowing with bourgeois self-satisfaction, Edmund and Rachel (Edward Petherbridge and Anna Cropper) enthuse about the lovely, isolated country house they have found for themselves. Soon their peaceful evening is laid waste by the discovery that they are trapped in the house – and that the spirits of far less fortunate people who once lived and died in that place do not rest peacefully there.

It's a harsh play with a harsh, haunting ending; it was very well-received, and was subsequently adapted for the stage. Years later, this extended version of the story was adapted for BBC radio and broadcast at Christmas (see: **The Exorcism (1992)**)

Dead of Night did manage to provide a disturbing entertainment for Christmas 1972, however. In an apt inversion of the way **The Exorcism** was brought under the series umbrella, Nigel Kneale's **The Stone Tape** was produced as an episode of **Dead of Night**, but broadcast as a stand-alone play.

The three episodes of **Dead of Night** that remain in the BBC archive, including **The Exorcism**, were released on DVD in 2013. This also includes the final episode *A Woman Sobbing*, which was broadcast on the 17th December 1972, and which some may therefore feel can be counted among the ghost stories for Christmas, though I've not included it here.

THE DEAD ROOM

Drama | TV | 30 mins

TX: 24/12/2018, BBC4
     24/12/2020, BBC2
     17/12/2022, BBC4

Arriving five years after **The Tractate Middoth**, Gatiss's second **Ghost Story for Christmas** unexpectedly eschews literary adaptation, telling a completely new story. M.R. James has been said to have inspired aspects of it nonetheless, and with that in mind it's at least a little interesting to note that it's a ghost story about a teller of ghost stories.

Simon Callow plays Aubrey Judd, an actor in the later years of his career, fond of reminiscing about the good old days and cursing the state of the modern world. Ghost stories were better in the old days, too, he insists – not like this new stuff he has to read out on the radio.

Whatever influence M.R. James had on **The Dead Room**, it's tempting to suppose that Gatiss was also influenced by David Thomson's **A Child's Voice**, a short film that premiered on the BBC at Christmas in 1980, filling the gap left by the then-ended **A Ghost Story for Christmas**.

Though very different in most respects, both stories feature vainglorious central characters who read ghost stories on the radio, and who find themselves haunted by the stories that they are telling. Both plays make excellent use of the dead, dark spaces in a recording studio, and both connect to the older traditions of ghost stories on the radio.

The Dead Room met with a lukewarm reception (including from myself) but I feel that time has been kind to it, and the emotional depth of the piece gives it a strength that will likely increase with time rather than diminish.

THE DEMON CAKESTAND OF BEESTLEY CHASE

Comedy-Drama | Radio | 15 mins
TX: 22/12/1984, Radio 4
     24/12/2008, BBC7
     24/12/2009, BBC7
     24/12/2010, BBC7
     23/12/2011, Radio 4 Extra
     22/12/2016, Radio 4 Extra
     26/12/2021, Radio 4 Extra

Allegedly written by Edgar Ian Brown and **M.R. James Hendrie** (cunning pseudonyms for Ian Brown and James Hendrie), this short entertainment was described in listings and in its own credits as 'A Tale of The Mausoleum Club'. A few years later The Mausoleum Club would return to the radio in two series, *Tales of the Mausoleum Club* and *The Fall of the Mausoleum Club*, broadcast in 1987 and 1988 respectively.

Each episode was a broad yet literate parody of a Victorian fiction, with titles like *The Turn of the Knob* and *The Heart of Skegness* giving a good sense of the style of humour involved. **The Demon Cakestand...** serves as a good prelude to these series, parodying M.R. James to knockabout effect. Stephen Fry leads a cast that includes an appearance by sometime Hammer stalwart Michael Ripper.

An unrelated, but similarly literate and daft M.R. James parody, **The Teeth of Abbot Thomas**, was broadcast on Radio 4 in 1987.

THE DEMON KING

Comedy | Radio | 30 mins

TX: 26/12/1962, Home Service
14/12/2003, BBC7
01/01/2018, Radio 4 Extra
27/12/2020, Radio 4 Extra

Michael and Mollie Hardwick's adaptation of J.B. Priestley's short story tells of a Christmas pantomime doomed to shambolic failure but saved at the last moment when the inept actor cast in the role of the Demon King is reported missing, believed drunk. A mysterious understudy steps in to save the performance (and the Demon King's reputation).

Wryly amusing and good-natured throughout, this story of demonic intervention at Christmas is more entertainment than tale of terror, but one has to give the devil his due, even at Christmas. Producer Charles

Lefeaux was also behind adaptations of **A Christmas Carol** and **The Goblins Who Stole a Sexton.**

THE DEMON OF TIDWORTH

Reading | Radio | 15 mins

TX: 24/12/1929, 6BM Bournemouth

'A Wessex Ghost Story' by Mrs Richardson.

Although 'the Demon of Tidworth' seems to be a name sometimes given to one of the many ghost dogs that haunt the British Isles, in this case Mrs Richardson was writing about The Demon Drummer of Tidworth, a different example of West Country folklore that was also recounted in The Ingoldsby legends as The Dead Drummer.

Although this quarter-hour broadcast gives the impression of having been a reading, it's noticeable that in 1944 there was a radio play of the same name, and again written by Norah Richardson; that later production had a significantly longer run time, so while it's certainly not possible to know, it does appear that the different broadcasts were also different variations on the same account by Richardson.

DETECTORISTS: 2015 CHRISTMAS SPECIAL

Comedy | TV | 30 mins

TX: 23/12/2015, BBC4
       17/12/2017, BBC2

26/12/2018, BBC2
25/12/2019, BBC2

Funny and beautiful, chronicling the travails and trivial passions of very ordinary people, **Detectorists** is the distinctive work of one of Britain's currently unrecognised national treasures, the writer-actor-director-producer-author Mackenzie Crook. Crook has a particular feeling for atmosphere and mood that has made him popular among fans of the eerie, and he uses it very effectively in **Detectorists**, precisely punctuating the gentle humour.

A vertigo-inducing sense of the deeper past, of lives lived long ago, is a constant presence in all three series of **Detectorists**; ostensibly about two men, Andy and Lance (Crook and Toby Jones) who enjoy the hobby of metal-detecting, we are always reminded that their treasure hunt is as much about discovering the mysteries of the past as of finding a cache of gold coins. In one memorable scene Andy discovers a hawking whistle in the soil; hesitantly, he puts it to his lips and blows. The whistle's haunting trill echoes through the air and the two friends shiver... it's a moment that seems to deliberately recall Jonathan Miller's **Whistle and I'll Come to You**.

While the theme of the uncanny is largely sublimated throughout all three series of **Detectorists**, it takes full flight in the Christmas Special – and what better time to excavate the ghostly seams that had been underfoot for two whole series?

In the previous episode, Lance finally fulfilled his dream of discovering a genuine archaeological treasure – it now resides as an exhibit in a museum. However, he's come to believe that he has done something wrong by removing his find, that it should be returned to the earth... and that he is cursed because of what he did. Then it begins to seem as if he's being followed by the figure of 'a ghostly hooded monk'.

Although this is still very much an episode of **Detectorists** – gentle and funny – it also pastiches the M.R. James story **A Warning to the Curious**, another tale of the darker consequences of amateur archaeology and robbing the earth of its treasure.

While it never becomes truly frightening, the episode works at creating an appropriate atmosphere – conversations held by flickering firelight and the like. It's by no means the scariest thing to be broadcast in the name of Christmas, but it certainly achieves the balance of good cheer and chills that makes for a good Christmas story.

THE DEVIL'S CHRISTMAS

Reading | Radio | 4 x 15 mins

TX: 17/12/2007 – 20/12/2007, Radio 2
21/12/2008 – 24/12/2008, Radio 2

Four short daily readings of dark stories - including two popular ghost stories - for the week leading up to Christmas, performed by Christopher Eccleston (who was still being billed as 'Doctor Who star', despite having left the role a year and a half earlier).

The four stories were:

- *The Signalman*, by Charles Dickens
- *The Necklace*, by Guy de Maupassant
- *Thurlow's Christmas*, by John Kendrick Bangs
- *The She-Wolf*, by Saki

THE DICK POWELL SHOW PRESENTS: THE CLOCKS

Drama | TV | 50 mins

TX: 24/12/1962, BBC Television

A successful US anthology series, The Dick Powell Show Presents (and, after host Dick Powell's death, The Dick Powell Theater) was a comedy and drama staple for BBC television in the early 1960s.

In the UK the episodes were not generally shown in order (nor did they need to be, it was an anthology after all) but even so it's noticeable that this episode, a ghost story, was scheduled for broadcast on Christmas Eve, the last programme before the carols and midnight service.

The heroine of **The Clocks** is a widow (played by Joan Fontaine) who, just as she is contemplating marrying once again, finds herself - or believes herself to be - haunted by her late husband. His collection of clocks chime dolorously, apparently indicating his presence and displeasure.

Given the limitations of television at the time, this is quite an atmospheric play. A large part of the drama is taken up by the investigations of a professional sceptic and debunker of supernatural phenomena, Doctor Waugh (David Farrar).

This very much gives the audience the sense that everything will be explained rationally, that the haunting will be revealed as a wicked trick played upon the widow in the manner of Clouzot's *Les Diaboliques*... however, the ambiguity is well-maintained, and only at the end is the truth revealed.

DOCTOR WHO: THE CHIMES OF MIDNIGHT

Drama | Radio | 4 x 30 mins

TX: 30/11/2008 - 27/12/2008, BBC7 (weekly)

Paul McGann only played the Doctor once on television, in a mid-1990s TV movie - but during the long interregnum between televisual incarnations, *Doctor Who* found a new home in the audio medium, courtesy of independent company Big Finish. It was not long before McGann had been persuaded to return to the character, and when the television series resumed in the mid-2000s, BBC7 picked up a number of the Big Finish stories for radio broadcast, **The Chimes of Midnight** among them.

It's an intelligent, highly atmospheric story that plays with motifs of the haunted house, the murder mystery, and the Christmas ghost story. Writer Rob Shearman cited P.J. Hammond's *Sapphire & Steel* as a particular influence, and the narrative is enabled by the science-fiction device of a time paradox.

Sci-fi or not, this is a strange, spooky story about a haunted house where a murder is committed as the clock chimes strike midnight on Christmas Eve – which happens every hour...

DOCTOR WHO AND THE DAEMONS

Drama | TV | 90 mins

TX: 28/12/1971, BBC1

Though science-fiction rather than horror, **Doctor Who** has frequently engaged directly with the horror genre in one way or another, often taking familiar gothic ideas and presenting them anew with a science-fiction veneer. Sometimes entire plotlines were lifted from horror stories and refitted for a younger audience, causing great excitement among younger viewers and occasional dismay among older ones.

The 1971 story **The Daemons** is a particularly good example, drawing upon Dennis Wheatley-inflected versions of witchcraft and Satanism to create a tale of sinister covens and goat-hooved demons. Naturally, when the BBC decided to broadcast a special feature-length edit of a *Doctor Who* serial over Christmas, they chose the one with the most explicitly supernatural content.

Since it's a **Doctor Who** story, all of the supernatural elements are given a pseudo-scientific explanation, but this doesn't detract from the Mephistophelean fun. Nor does it spoil things if you happen to notice how certain elements in the story seem to have been lifted directly from **Quatermass and the Pit**, another BBC science-fiction serial concerned with alien demons that was broadcast over Christmas.

Feature-length edits of *Doctor Who* serials became a Christmas standard in the following years, with the Doctor reprising his battles with aquatic reptile-people, monstrous Welsh maggots, and giant alien spiders a day or two after Boxing Day – however, none of these were quite so bound to the horror genre as **The Daemons**, hence they are absent here.

Time and the BBC archives were not kind to **The Daemons**, and most of the original colour episodes were lost; for many years, only monochrome film telerecordings made for overseas sale remained in the hands of the BBC.

By the early 1990s, however, technology began to allow for old television to be re-colourised, and in 1992 a restored version of **The Daemons** was broadcast on Friday nights on BBC2, from late November through to mid-December.

DOCTOR WHO: THE UNQUIET DEAD

Drama | TV | 45 mins

TX: 27/12/2005, BBC3

Just as **Doctor Who** is no stranger to tales of ghastly things emerging from shadowy corners, nor has it been a stranger to the Christmas season since its revival in 2005; however, few of the Christmas and New Year special episodes have ever aspired to be particularly dark or ghostly.

Yet, when the new **Doctor Who** was launched, a story about ghosts at Christmas time appeared almost immediately. Only the third episode in the run, **The Unquiet Dead** was broadcast in April, but happily it was given a Christmas repeat a few months later.

Set in snowy, Victorian Cardiff and featuring Charles Dickens on one of his reading tours, **The Unquiet Dead** probably fits the season better than any of the actual Christmas specials that the show has had since, and in retrospect it ought to surprise nobody at all that this episode was the work of Mark Gatiss.

Simon Callow guest stars, bringing Charles Dickens to life once again. Dickens finds himself assisting the Doctor in an investigation into the sightings of gaseous spirits and walking corpses that are plaguing Cardiff; the story also finds time to allude to **A Christmas Carol** with the notion of Dickens' encounters with spirits over the course of a single night changing his outlook for the better. The Doctor goes out of his way to namecheck **The Signalman**, too.

While the story is perhaps overly straightforward, it is nonetheless fast-moving and entertaining – and, from the point of view of a family audience, just a little bit scary.

THE DOG

Drama | Radio | 30 mins

TX: 24/12/1976, Radio 4

One certainly has to credit **BBC Radio** with not being content to simply wheel out an **M.R. James** tale every year – their ghost story tradition goes to all sorts of unexpected places, and this is certainly one of them.

Ivan Turgenev's tale begins as a discussion about the natural and the supernatural, and quickly becomes the story of a strange haunting and of a man's relationship with his dog.

Timothy West stars as the narrator, a hussar who is disturbed at night by the sounds of a dog moving about in the dark of his room - but there is no dog when the room is lit. Acting on the advice of somebody wiser in matters ghostly than himself, he buys a dog and the nocturnal 'haunting' ceases. However, future events will come to make the haunting seem like some sort of prophecy or warning.

DON'T LOOK NOW

Drama | Radio | 60 mins

TX: 09/12/2001, Radio 4

15/12/2001, Radio 4

Broadcast as part of the *Classic Serial* strand, this one-off drama is based on a tale from Daphne Du Maurier's *Not After Midnight* collection – though the story is no doubt best known because of the highly-regarded film adaptation directed by Nicolas Roeg.

Laura and John (Anna Chancellor and Michael Feast), a married couple haunted by grief after the recent loss of their daughter, travel to Venice. There, they encounter a pair of elderly sisters, one of whom claims to be a psychic. She tells them that their daughter's spirit is with them – but that their daughter is trying to warn them to leave Venice, because they are in danger...

Ronald Frame's adaptation cuts to the razor's edge of the story without ever feeling like it's in an undue hurry. Roeg's film version is of such emphatic repute that a remake might seem like a challenge, but radio tends to do well with such things. Nonetheless, it's easy to suspect that the climax of this play is executed in a manner that acknowledges the film version. Even so, it's an effective retelling of this story with its particularly horrible climactic twist.

DO YOU BELIEVE IN GHOSTS?

Documentary | Radio | 30 mins

TX: 26/12/1952, BBC Home Service

A compilation of accounts of personal experiences with ghostly or supernatural phenomena, as submitted by BBC listeners.

DRACULA (1975)

Drama | Radio | 60 mins

TX: 01/01/1975, Radio 4

Sadly, Glyn Dearman died prematurely, aged only 57, after an accident in his home. In respect to his work as a producer of radio drama, Dearman's name was, for many years, a mark of quality; just as an example, his 1980s adaptations of the Gormenghast novels remain highly atmospheric and absorbing evocations of Mervyn Peake's fantasy world.

Dearman had, in fact, once been an actor and one of his earliest roles sits at the very heart of the Christmas Ghost Story: it was Dearman who played Tiny Tim in the 1951 film of **A Christmas Carol** alongside Alastair Sim as Scrooge.

Among his other ventures into the darker fantasies of English literature, Dearman produced three radio plays featuring Count Dracula, beginning with this Afternoon Theatre adaptation of the novel.

There is probably less to be said about this version of Dracula than about the producer, though: it's straightforward and effective, and tells the story in less than an hour. It is of course typical of the radio drama of the day, and contemporary audiences may find the style to be a little mannered – but enthusiasts of Old Time Radio are likely to adore it.

David March played the Count here, with Aubrey Woods as Van Helsing. On the two subsequent occasions that Dearman returned to the character of Dracula, March also returned to the role.

Firstly, Dracula was the narrator of Angela Carter's *Vampirella*, a tale of the sanguinary Count's lovelorn daughter starring Anna Massey. March then returned as an active character in **Sherlock Holmes vs Dracula (1981)**, which also saw Aubrey Woods reprise the role of Van Helsing.

DRACULA (1991)

Drama | Radio | 7 x 30 mins

TX: 19/12/1991 – 30/01/1992, Radio 4

Speaking entirely personally, this is far and away the most Christmassy Dracula adaptation of them all. Although its seven-episode duration carried the story right through Christmas and up to the end of January, the first episode was broadcast on the last day of term (at my school, anyway), after a heavy snowfall in the South of England.

Having travelled home on a bus through a snowy, darkening landscape, joining Jonathan Harker on his own journey into the Carpathians seemed to be as much in keeping with the mood of the day as the Christmas tree in the front room. In fact, that first episode was delayed by a technical fault and a few minutes of airtime had to be filled with Christmas Carols. As a result, I still think of Dracula whenever I hear 'We Three Kings'.

Nostalgia aside, Nick McCarty's adaptation uses its more than three-hour duration to remain very faithful to the book and benefits from a core set of solid central performances; I particularly like Finlay Welsh's extremely Dutch Van Helsing, and David McKail's Renfield – McKail opts to present Renfield not as the kind of side-show freak to which he is often reduced, but a civilised man who has suffered a tragic decline. His episodes of mania are convincing in their mix of obsession and pathos.

Frederick Jaeger gives a restrained performance as Dracula, even when delivering some of the lines that were already rendered into cliché by the passing of so many adaptations; and, despite the merits of Judi Bowker's performance in the 1977 television adaptation, Phyllis Logan will always be Mina Harker as far as I'm concerned.

Naturally the series has its off-moments and the format has its limitations – I'm none too fond of Lord Godalming's operatic battle-cry in the final struggle with Dracula's minions, and some of Malcolm Clarke's score may now seem a little obvious – but on the other side of things it often achieves a very effective mood and generally its high points correspond to those of the book. Jonathan Harker's discovery of Dracula in his coffin is initially presented as no more than the slamming and clattering sound of the coffin lid heaved to the floor, and Harker's horrified shriek at what he discovers within. Less is more, even if radio requires that a narrator then fills in the gaps.

This serial has been commercially available for most of the last twenty years, on cassette and then compact disc; it can now be acquired digitally.

More than fifteen years after this serial was broadcast, Finlay Welsh returned to face Dracula once again in a radio play – but this time he played not Van Helsing but the captain of the ship that brings Dracula and his crates of earth to England. This play, *The Voyage of the Demeter* by Robert Forrest, was broadcast in 2008 – but in February, rather than at Christmas time.

DRACULA (BBC World Service, 2006)

Drama | Radio | 2 x 60 mins

TX: 30/12/2007 - 06/01/2008, BBC World Service

Broadcast as part of the BBC World Drama strand, this radio serial was a brand-new production of Liz Lochhead's intelligent 1985 stage adaptation of Stoker's novel. To my mind the quality of the writing in this version meant that it significantly overshadowed the BBC television adaptation broadcast just a few weeks after this radio serial debuted, though as a radio serial it did of course enjoy considerably less prominence.

The TV version was given a prime-time slot just after Christmas where lots of people could see it, while the radio version could only be heard on FM radio if you stayed up 'til 2am (by which time Radio 4 had given way to the World Service for the rest of the night). As it turns out, though, 2am on a Winter's night is a pretty good time to listen to Dracula.

By chance, both of the BBC adaptations from 2006 also shared a lead actor – David Suchet, who played Van Helsing on television and the Count himself on the radio.

Jonathan Harker was played by a young up-and-comer named Tom Hiddleston, a fact that may have contributed to the consistent commercial availability of this adaptation in the years since.

The oft-overlooked character of Renfield is given greater significance and weight in Lochhead's interpretation, and although she is certainly not constrained by her source material, nor does she abandon it – the result is an adaptation that feels true to the original while also presenting the audience with a lucid and thorough exploration of the material.

DRACULA (BBC1, 2006)

Drama | TV | 90 mins

TX: 28/12/2006, BBC1

If the BBC has not had a consistent 'tradition' of dark and prestigious dramas at Christmas in the last couple of decades, it's at least true to say that it has been struggling with the habit. In the context of 2006, a feature-length adaptation of *Dracula* seemed a fairly natural development from the two extremely dark Sherlock Holmes dramas that had appeared in the days after Christmas in 2002 and 2004.

Stewart Harcourt's script presents quite a radical take on Dracula, bringing a lot of new ideas and eschewing a lot of the familiar and expected elements from the book. While I don't feel that the whole thing works particularly well, I think it does deserve credit for these attempts at variation and even innovation (though the look of Dracula in the early parts of the story is inevitably reminiscent of the character as presented in Francis Ford Coppola's 1993 film).

For one thing, there is an entirely new and fairly bold attempt to make the story at least partly driven by an explicit fear of venereal disease and impurity of the blood (and, by implication one supposes, the corruption of aristocracy itself). For another, if you're familiar with the story you can certainly look forward to being surprised by the unfamiliar ways in which the fates of familiar characters play out.

The cast are almost all notable, and in retrospect there is an all-star feel to proceedings, Tom Burke, Dan Stevens, Rafe Spall and Sophia Myles all having gone on to bigger things since.

By contrast, Marc Warren already had a good many credits to his name by 2006, and might not have been an obvious choice to play Dracula. In the main he succeeds with both aspects of the Count in this drama, the withered leech and the Byronic seducer.

As chance would have it, the BBC also produced a radio serial of Dracula that same year, adapting Liz Lochhead's stage play. I'd maintain that the radio version is a much more self-assured and intelligent take on the story, but these days I can appreciate the TV version for its eccentricity and occasional boldness.

DRACULA (2012)

Drama | Radio | 2 x 60 mins

TX: 27/12/2014 - 03/01/2015
     12/12/2020 - 19/12/2020

A particular characteristic of radio drama is its dependency on description to compensate for the lack of visuals, and this often leads to a dramatization of a novel leaning all the more heavily on the original text for its narrative voice.

This can certainly be a virtue, preserving much of the original work's feel and tone, and this adaptation of *Dracula* makes full use of the book's epistolary narrative. This does, at times, make the whole thing feel perhaps a little too much like a full-cast reading of the novel.

Nonetheless, those narrating voices are an economic and evocative means of driving the story, and there is a good deal of atmosphere to the proceedings. Rebecca Lenkiewicz preserves much of the original story in her adaptation, but hers is still a bold, slightly more sexually frank, version of the tale.

Nicky Henson's voice (always having had the character of a subdued growl) works well for Count Dracula, Ellie Kendrick is a memorable Mina, and Don Gilet a sympathetic Renfield.

While it is not the most prominent of the BBC adaptations of Stoker's novel, this two-part serial (originally broadcast as part of a season of Gothic programming in 2012) is still very solid, and deserves recognition for adding a modern tone to an old tale without upending it entirely and without it being to no good effect.

DRACULA (2020)

Drama | TV | 3 x 90 mins

TX: 01/01/2020 - 03/01/2020, BBC1

If any television series can be compared to a Christmas dinner, Stephen Moffatt and Mark Gatiss's take on Dracula is surely a good candidate; it's a very rich meal in three courses, and perhaps as many were left with indigestion as were left satisfied by the whole thing.

Personally, I really enjoyed it. It certainly has its problems, and the final act needed to be stronger – but I found it enjoyable throughout and nobody has yet attempted to force me at gunpoint to proclaim greater love for it than I feel – not even either of the writers, despite what people on the internet would like to claim about them.

Displaying the same eclecticism as their modernised revival of Sherlock Holmes, this take on Dracula constantly shifts so that even those as well-versed in the various iterations of the tale as the writers themselves are unlikely to anticipate exactly where the story will go next, even while the essential structure of the novel is closely observed.

An entire episode is devoted to Jonathan Harker's experiences in Castle Dracula – filmed at Orava Castle in Slovakia, the location used by F.W. Murnau for his seminal Dracula adaptation, *Nosferatu*. The second and arguably strongest episode concentrates on the voyage of the Demeter as it carries Dracula to his destination in England, and the story is populated with a number of engaging characters, all of whom seem to have been given genre-significant names (for example, Dorabella, apparently named after the vampire heroine in an episode of the 1970s anthology series *Supernatural*.)

Arguably this episode owes as much to Agatha Christie as Bram Stoker, and in terms of entertainment value this is no bad thing. It also contains one of the show's most overt self-indulgences when it alludes to the anthology series **Inside Number 9**; I certainly didn't mind this, and it raised a smile, but I suspect it is an example of the kind of ingredient that will have enthused some viewers, and pushed some others away.

Finally, Dracula reaches England in the third episode and digs his way into the bloodstream of London, covering familiar ground in a number of unfamiliar ways.

The show's most unambiguous strength is its cast; Dolly Wells is particularly engaging as a demure and driven conflation of Sister Agatha and Van Helsing, and Claes Bang makes for a Dracula who has something of Roger Moore's James Bond about him.

Bang is consistently entertaining to watch, whether he is being frightening, or funny (or both), and in among the many familiar faces there are notable up-and-comers like Morfydd Clarke as Mina, and Lydia West as Lucy – not to mention Matthew Beard, a young actor who feels very much as if he's recently graduated from the Benedict Cumberbatch Finishing School and is thus entirely at home in a Moffat/Gatiss script.

(Indeed, Beard has subsequently become most visible playing the Sherlock-esque Max Liebermann in the period-set detective drama *Vienna Blood*).

Inevitably, it's easy to think that Moffat and Gatiss have perhaps too much love and enthusiasm for their work, and that a project like this might have benefited had they been more ruthless when it came to the killing of their darlings. Nonetheless, love and enthusiasm as visible as theirs can count for a lot, and even if I found myself thinking that their take on Dracula was a bit of a mess sometimes, I don't think I ever stopped finding it *fun*.

When the final episode of Dracula was broadcast on BBC1, it was immediately followed on BBC2 by a documentary, **In Search of Dracula with Mark Gatiss.**

DRACULA'S GUEST

Reading | Radio | 20 mins

TX: 27/12/2019, Radio 4 Extra

Bram Stoker's short story began life as part of his most famous work, an extra episode in Jonathan Harker's journey to Castle Dracula. Though it was excised from the novel, Stoker did turn it into a short story which has given its name to collections of Stoker's short fiction ever since.

This reading by Bertie Carvel was originally presented as an interval feature during a concert broadcast on Radio 3 on the 20th April 2012 – the date which marked the centenary of Bram Stoker's death.

DRACULA RE-VISITED

Documentary | Radio | 60 mins

TX: 25/12/1974, BBC Radio London

Marjorie Bilbow investigates Bram Stoker's classic story, following in the footsteps of the novel's characters.

THE DRACULA TOUR

Reading | Radio | 15 mins

TX: 29/12/1984, BBC Radio 4

Brenda Blethyn reads Robert Westall's short story in which a woman visiting Bucharest meets and falls in love with Count Dracula...

THE DROVER'S PATH

Drama | Radio | 60 mins

TX: 23/12/2017, Radio 4 Extra

A family drama erupts into a Brontë-esque ghost story in this atmospheric play from January 2005, by Vanessa Rosenthal.

Set in the wilds of Yorkshire in the late 1800s, there are mysterious deaths, family feuds, voices on the night-wind, and so on. Apparently based on real family history, this story is perhaps a little straightforward but always evocative of its particularly haunting setting.

DUNWORTHY 13

Reading | Radio | 5 mins

TX: 25/12/1937, Regional Programme

A short reading of John Pudney's ghost story about a man working alone at telephone exchange on Christmas Eve. As you might expect in such a story, the man receives a telephone call - and it is from somebody who has a dark and sinister confession to make...

ECHOES

Reading(?) | Radio | 20 mins

TX: 24/12/1926, 5IT Birmingham

"A Ghost Story of Christmas Eve" by John Overton, set at a quarter-to-midnight. A girl wearing furs, a chauffeur and a gamekeeper with a shotgun... how will these figures in the snowy landscape interact? What is their fate? Where does the ghost come in?

Sadly, this is another of the ghost stories from the very earliest days of British radio where almost nothing is known beyond the limited information in the Radio Times listing. As it is now nearly a century old, this story may remain eternally mysterious – though I suppose it's not impossible that an old script might one day come to light.

ECHOES FROM THE ABBEY

Drama | Radio | 45 mins

TX: 26/12/2012, Radio 4 Extra
     11/12/2016, Radio 4 Extra
     19/12/2021, Radio 4 Extra

M.R. James (David March) goes to spend Christmas at Medborough Abbey, where he encounters a ghostly presence in this 1984 play by Sheila Hodgson.

Over several years, Hodgson wrote a series of James pastiches, based on the undeveloped ideas James had set down in his essay Stories I Have Tried to Write.

Despite their derivation from James's Christmas entertainments, only one of these plays - **Here I Am, Where Are You?** - was initially broadcast at Christmas; in recent years, however, **Echoes from the Abbey** and **Turn, Turn, Turn** have been given their proper status as Christmas ghost stories on Radio 4 Extra.

EDGAR ALLAN POE'S GOTHIC TALES

Reading | Radio | 3 x 15 mins

TX: 24/12/2003 - 26/12/2003, Radio 2

Though **Christopher Lee's Ghost Stories for Christmas** did not result in a second series, Lee nonetheless returned to the BBC at Christmas 2003 – this time on late night radio, reading three tales by Edgar Allan Poe.

The three tales were:

- *The Tell-Tale Heart*
- *The Cask of Amontillado*
- *The Pit and the Pendulum*

Evidently these stories were considered a successful exercise, as Lee returned to Radio 2 the following year with **Christopher Lee's Fireside Tales.**

EMILY'S GHOST

Drama | Radio | 60 mins

TX: 15/12/1994, Radio 4
 20/12/2020, Radio 4 Extra

Writer/Director Colin Finbow produced several notable dramas for younger audiences while working with the Children's Film Unit; among them was a drama called **Emily's Ghost.**

This film was shown on Channel 4 in April 1992, but was never repeated at Christmas – however a couple of years later Finbow adapted his screenplay for the radio, and this new version of the story was broadcast just before Christmas in 1994.

Emily is a lonely Victorian child who has recently come to live in a new home. She soon starts to have strange experiences and begins to suspect that she is being haunted. She has premonitions of her own death by drowning, and sometimes she sees or hears other children – children who are not really there, and cannot be heard or seen by other people.

Perhaps these children are from another time, and perhaps Emily's own life is connected to that of another girl living another life in the same house but in very different days...

In some key respects **Emily's Ghost** can seem derivative of notable British children's fantasies like *The Amazing Mr Blunden, Moondial,* or *Tom's Midnight Garden* – but the similarities to these earlier tales never crowd out the newer, fresher aspects of the story, and it remains a worthwhile exercise with an unexpected resolution.

THE EMPTY HOUSE

Reading | Radio | 2 x 15 mins

TX: 21/12/1953 – 22/12/1953, BBC Light Programme

A two-part reading of Algernon Blackwood's tale of a man and his aunt who, in a spirit of investigation, spend the night in a house said to be haunted after the murder of a young woman years earlier.

Broadcast at the appropriate hour of eleven in the evening, this reading was performed by the original Man in Black, Valentine Dyall.

THE EMPTY SLEEVE

Drama | Radio | 45 mins

TX: 11/12/2021, Radio 4 Extra

This tale of a violinist's obsession with a rare instrument and the haunting of two elderly brothers was the fourth and last of Algernon Blackwood's

John Silence stories to be adapted by Sheila Hodgson. Originally broadcast in October 1975, it was only repeated during the Christmas season as recently as 2021.

The other John Silence adaptations were broadcast all year round, but the second – **The Nemesis of Fire** – was broadcast at Christmas in 1974, and the third, **The Camp of the Dog**, was given a Christmas repeat in 1977.

The Empty Sleeve was also included in a series of readings called **Tales of the Uncanny and Supernatural**, broadcast at Christmas in 1971.

THE ENFIELD POLTERGEIST

Documentary | Radio | 40 mins

TX: 26/12/1978, Radio 4

Among the most famous stories of real-life hauntings, the story of the Enfield Poltergeist has inspired both TV dramas and motion pictures; however, back when the story was still ongoing, Radio 4 produced this documentary and decided that it was an ideal candidate for broadcast last thing at night on Boxing Day.

Built around interviews with the family at the centre of the case, and a number of other witnesses, this documentary recounts the events in an extremely matter-of-fact way, without any crass attempts at enhancing the atmosphere. As such it's rather sober, but heard today – and in view of the strong argument that the case was simply a hoax - it works equally well as a ghost story as it does a documentary.

ENOCH SOAMES

Drama | Radio | 50 mins

TX: 23/12/1948, Third Programme
     25/12/1954, Third Programme

Max Beerbohm's humorous variation on the legend of Faust tells of the fate of its title character, an untalented poet who is nonetheless convinced of his own unrecognised greatness. Certain that his name will live after him once his work is finally appreciated, Soames is approached by the Devil, who offers him a chance to visit the future and see for himself how he is remembered by posterity.

Douglas Cleverdon's adaptation of the tale was broadcast several times on BBC radio, in several different performances, beginning in 1939. The versions broadcast in 1948 and 1954 were new performances with new casts, though Dennis Arundel starred as Soames in all three.

THE EXORCISM

Drama | Radio | 90 mins

TX: 28/12/1992, Radio 4

Don Taylor's play for television, broadcast as the first episode of **Dead of Night**, had been a success and he subsequently expanded it for the theatre. Nearly twenty years later, a radio adaptation of this longer version of the play was produced and broadcast as part of the **Christmas Spirits** season on Radio 4.

The play is done justice by the new cast, and Susan Fleetwood's delivery of the final, harrowing monologue is certainly the equal of Anna Cropper's original; nothing is lost from this story by the change in medium.

See also: **DEAD OF NIGHT: THE EXORCISM**

FAMOUS GHOSTS

Talk | Radio | 15 mins

TX: 28/12/1925, 5PY Plymouth

Mr F. Pedrick Harvey broadcast a number of talks on 5PY Plymouth in the mid-1920s, and in December of 1925 he gave three talks, one a week, on a Christmas theme. The first was about 'The Art of Pantomime', the second about 'Christmas To-day', and the third was about 'Famous Ghosts'. Sadly, it's not known whether this talk recounted stories from folklore or from literature.

FANTASTIC TALES

Reading | Radio | 5 x 15 mins

TX: 18/12/2000 - 22/12/2000, Radio 4

A selection of classic fantasy stories from European writers; as the presence of Le Fanu and Maupassant in the line-up suggests, these stories are a darker shade of fantasy than the series title might suggest.

The five stories were:

- *The Shadow*, by Hans Christian Andersen, read by Peter Capaldi
- *Autumn Sorcery*, by Joseph von Eichendorff, read by Jamie Glover
- *The Holes in the Mask*, by Jean Lorrain, read by Simon Russell Beale
- *The Ghost and the Bonesetter*, by Sheridan Le Fanu, read by Sean Barrett
- *The Night*, by Guy de Maupassant, read by Tom Hollander

FEAR ON FOUR

Appointment with Fear was a very successful horror anthology series that ran on BBC radio in the 1940s and 50s, presented by Valentine Dyall in character as 'The Man in Black'. The series was revived in the 1980s as **Fear on Four.**

Running for several series and more than forty episodes, Fear on Four mixed brand-new tales with adaptations of classic short stories. In amongst these there were a couple of 'Christmas specials', and one other especially wintry tale.

Gobble Gobble
Drama | Radio | 30 mins
TX: 24/12/1992, Radio 4
01/01/1994, Radio 4
26/12/2010, Radio 4 Extra

Gobble, Gobble declares its seasonal theme immediately, and goes on to ponder the industry that brings that all-important turkey to your Christmas dining table. It also poses this question: if you went to buy a turkey from a depressed farmer – just how bad could your Christmas get?

This tale by Paul Burns is a good example of how **Fear on Four** would often eschew the more mannered, literary classics of the horror genre, and instead explore more squalid, naturalistic sources of fear.

I think it also deserves credit for being an essentially Christmassy tale of horror not simply because it is set on a turkey farm, but because it uses the dynamic of a privileged individual being forced to witness the desperation and distress sometimes inherent to the production of the comforts that others take for granted.

The Horn
Drama | Radio | 30 mins
TX: 13/12/1992, Radio 4
          31/12/2005, BBC7

Stephen Gallagher's highly atmospheric tale of motorists stranded in a blizzard recalls Sir Arthur Conan Doyle's *The Captain of the Pole-Star* while being rooted very much in modernity and urban folklore.

John Castle leads the cast as Nathan, a motorist forced to abandon his car and seek shelter when driving snow makes it impossible to go on. He meets a couple of other stranded motorists, and then they hear the horn of a large vehicle blasting through the snowstorm. They head toward it expecting to be rescued – but they are not heading toward a rescuer...

The Snowman Killing

Drama | Radio | 30 mins

TX: 03/01/1988, Radio 4
     20/12/1992, Radio 4

How could something as innocent as the act of making a snowman become sinister or disturbing? **J.C.W.** Brook answers that question in this tale – the very first episode of **Fear on Four** - of an uneasy mother (Imelda Staunton) whose children have become fascinated by a strange, eyeless snowman.

THE FEMALE GHOST

Drama | Radio | 4 x 30 mins

TX: 29/12/2010 – 31/12/2010, BBC7

Originally broadcast during the Summer of 1997, this series comprised four adaptations by Christopher Hawes of ghost stories by noted female authors.

Though the series has been repeated several times over the years, it was given a truncated outing between Christmas and New Year in 2010. The limited time in the schedule meant that the final episode was not included on this occasion – rather as a shame as it was *The Demon Lover*, by Elizabeth Bowen, and a very strong episode.

The first three episodes of the series are:

- *The Cold Embrace*, by Mary Braddon
- *Man-Size in Marble*, by E. Nesbit
- *Afterward*, by Edith Wharton

THE FIDDLER

Drama | Radio | 30 mins

TX: 22/12/1944, BBC Home Service

A ghost story by Richard Hearne – apparently the same Richard Hearne who later became well-known as the television character Mr Pastry. Details of the story are sparse, but the cast list indicates that three of the characters hold RAF ranks, suggesting that the story had a contemporary, military setting.

FIVE DAHLS

Reading | Radio | 5 x 15 mins

TX: 28/12/1998 – 01/01/1999, BBC Radio 4

A selection from Roald Dahl's Tales of the Unexpected, broadcast as part of the daily 'Book at Bedtime' slot.

The stories were:

- *Mrs Bixby and the Colonel's Coat*, read by Joanna Lumley.
- *The Hitchhiker*, read by Tom Hollander.
- *A Dip in the Pool*, read by Geoffrey Palmer.
- *Vengeance is Mine Inc*, read by William Hootkins.
- *The Way up to Heaven*, read by Patricia Routledge.

These readings were all made commercially available as part of the BBC Radio Collection's *More Tales of the Unexpected*

In 2010 Dahl's macabre tales returned to Radio 4 in a series of short dramas broadcast at Christmas, **Someone Like You.**

THE FLIES OF ISIS

Drama | Radio | 60 mins

TX: 21/12/1966, BBC Light Programme

Writer Ernest Dudley enjoyed popular success in the 1940s and 1950s with his character, Doctor Morelle. Morelle was a private detective whose initial appearance on BBC radio led to short stories, novels, a stage play, and even a Hammer film. Dudley also created the radio series *Armchair Detective*, which later transferred to television.

His radio play **The Flies of Isis** was billed as a 'thriller by gas light', and was in fact a further adventure for Edgar Allan Poe's detective Auguste Dupin (who had solved the mystery of *The Murders in the Rue Morgue*).

The story was originally meant to be called *The Beetles of Isis*, but when the radiophonic workshop advised that they could not provide the sound of beetles, but *could* do flies, the story and the title were changed accordingly.

Some years later, Dudley adapted the story for prose, reinstating the original insects, and the resulting story *The Beetle* had been intended for publication as part of an anthology of Auguste Dupin stories. The anthology was not ultimately published, but *The Beetle* – Dudley's last work before his death – was subsequently included in a collection of his stories entitled *The Department of Spooks*.

FORGET TOMORROW'S MONDAY

Factual | Radio | 45 mins

TX: 18/12/1977, BBC Light Programme

'A Sunday morning miscellany' from the production unit responsible for the daily Woman's Hour magazine programme; the last edition before Christmas 1977 took on something of a ghostly theme, with tales of 'ghostly happenings' from round the country, and actor Hugh Burden reading a ghost story. Sadly, it's not known which ghost story, though it's tempting to suppose that it was a repeat of his 1957 reading of the M.R. James tale **Lost Hearts**.

Perhaps not, though, since that story was chosen to be read as part of the Hallowe'en edition of the show the following October; the special guests on that edition were Peter Underwood (President of the Ghost Club), and actor Peter Cushing, who read the story. While we have to guess at the story read by Burden, we can still hear Cushing's contribution – an off-air recording of it can be found online.

FOUR ROUND A FIRE

Factual | Radio | 30 mins

TX: 30/12/1955, BBC Home Service Midland

'Conversation about the Supernatural'

FRANKENSTEIN (1984)

Drama | TV | 70 mins

TX: 27/12/1984, ITV

Almost entirely forgotten today, this adaptation of Mary Shelley's novel is itself something of misbegotten creature let loose into an uncaring world.

This minor television production began with a Broadway stage production of Frankenstein; considered promising in its early stages it nonetheless closed in January 1981 directly after its opening night. If it's remembered at all, it's remembered (fairly or unfairly) as a disaster.

In the UK, however, Yorkshire Television apparently saw something in the production that might make for a decent TV drama, and embarked upon an adaptation. The cast included Robert Powell as Frankenstein, David Warner as the creature, and Carrie Fisher as Elizabeth.

These names were all quite prestigious for the time, though it was a prestige not necessarily supported by the decision to record the drama on videotape. The end result has a very theatrical feel, and although this was not unusual for British television at the time, it inevitably lends a very unassuming tone to even the most ambitious drama. Today, **Frankenstein** languishes unnoticed on the filmographies of the various well-regarded actors involved.

On the other hand, despite its short runtime it makes a fair attempt at telling the story in Shelley's book, emphasizing the tragic aspects of the story rather than reducing it to a tale of a monster on the rampage.

With modest fanfare and a small amount of publicity, the drama was broadcast between Christmas and New Year, just after nine in the evening. Then it disappeared, aside from a brief life on **VHS** in the wake of the Kenneth Branagh film in the mid-1990s - although these days I notice that it's usually free to watch online in magnificent blurry-vision.

FRANKENSTEIN (2012)

Drama | Radio | 2 x 60 mins

TX: 19/12/2015 - 26/12/2015, BBC Radio 4 Extra
23/12/2021 - 30/12/2021, BBC Radio 4 Extra
(First broadcast in November 2012)

Shaun Dooley gives an award-winning turn in Lucy Catherine's adaptation of Mary Shelley's novel, bringing his particular humanity and gravity to the role of the creature.

Jamie Parker also brings an appropriate weariness and obsession to the character of Frankenstein in this drama, broadcast as part of *The Gothic Imagination*, a season of programming that also included the 2012 radio adaptation of **Dracula**.

Not untypically for radio drama, this adaptation sticks closely to the original novel, though perhaps inevitably it allows itself to be more specific and gruesome with some details that the novel was vague about.

FRANKENSTEIN, OR THE MODERN PROMETHEUS (1972)

Drama | Radio | 60 mins

TX: 23/12/1972, BBC Radio 4

Trevor Martin stars as 'The Daemon', alongside Hugh Dickson as Frankenstein, in Malcolm Hazell's compact adaptation of Mary Shelley's novel.

FRANKENSTEIN - THE REAL STORY

Drama | TV | 90 mins

TX: 29/12/1992, ITV

Director and Producer David Wickes created a lively trilogy of gothic dramas for television, beginning with 1988's *Jack the Ripper*; this was followed fairly quickly by an adaptation of *Doctor Jekyll and Mr Hyde* starring Michael Caine. Wickes then embarked on an adaptation of Frankenstein, which was dubbed, with striking confidence, 'The Real Story' - David Wickes's own website still refers to it enthusiastically as the definitive adaptation.

Nonetheless, it diverges from Mary Shelley's book in a number of respects, and in particular the Monster's friendship with an old, blind man seems to have come more directly from the James Whale films than from the novel. However, this TV movie does keep the same general shape as the book, and includes both the Arctic framing of the story, and quite a loyal version of the Bride subplot; Patrick Bergin makes for a brooding Frankenstein, and Randy Quad a sympathetic monster.

I personally find this TV movie disappointing overall, but it looks positively level-headed next to the lavish but overexcited version that escaped from Kenneth Branagh's laboratory a couple of years later, and it has a few interesting details that deserve acknowledgment.

For example, the 1973 television adaptation had already used the book's arctic ice as the backdrop for its finale, but arguably Wickes's film does it better. Also, perhaps most significantly, the essential thread of the story - of the empathic connection between Frankenstein and his creation - is an effective extrapolation of Shelley's purpose in her novel, even if it does culminate in what isn't much more than a poetic irony.

FRANKENSTEIN: THE TRUE STORY

Drama | TV | 180 mins

TX: 27/12/1975, BBC2
21/12/1976, BBC2
18/12/1983, BBC2
21/12/1994 – 22/12/1994, BBC1 (in two parts)
17/12/1996 – 18/12/1996, BBC1 (in two parts)

Not to be confused with the same year's Dan Curtis version of the tale starring Robert Foxworth, this sprawling and reassuringly lavish adaptation feels surprisingly American given that it is, apparently, a British production.

Anyway, the slightly puzzling subtitle seems to imply that this adaptation has returned to Shelley's book and/or that it's based on the exploits of real Paracelsians and grave robbers. Neither is particularly true, though this version certainly makes use of ingredients familiar to readers of the novel that had been largely absent from previous versions.

What was certainly not present in any version before was the idea of Frankenstein's creation actually starting out beautiful before slowly degrading into ugliness, rather as if he was in need of a good painting by Basil Hallward. With Dorian Gray in mind, there's also an obvious homo-eroticism in Frankenstein's initial fascination with his creation. There's a good bit of James Whale's *Bride of Frankenstein* in here too – not so much because of the use of the Bride subplot, but rather in the presence of the sinister Doctor Polidori (played by James Mason).

Christopher Isherwood's adaptation might be thought to have innovated in having its Bride, Prima (Jane Seymour) a model of physical loveliness without the deterioration of her predecessor – but this too is reminiscent of Hammer's then-recent *Frankenstein Created Woman*. It is Doctor Polidori who really carries the torch from the James Whale films, simply because of the similarity between the character and that of Doctor Praetorious (played by Ernest Thesiger) in the *The Bride of Frankenstein*. Like Praetorius, he mentors and encourages the hapless Frankenstein and it is his wickedness that pushes the drama into its darkest regions.

This adaptation is undeniably lavish, though I find it a little chaotic myself; there are plenty of interesting things in it nonetheless – and for some reason it seems utterly bound to Christmas in the minds of BBC schedulers – it's never been broadcast *except* at Christmas.

After three outings as a very long TV movie, it was split in two for a repeat in 1994 (one of many TV Frankensteins that showed up in the UK after the release of the Kenneth Branagh version) and then, one last time as part of a season of programmes supporting the documentary series **Nightmare: The Birth of Horror.**

FRANKENSTEIN (2004)

Reading | Radio | 10 x 15 mins

TX: 06/12/2004 – 17/12/2004, Radio 4

The classic horror novel by Mary Shelley, read in daily episodes by David Rintoul. This appears to have been the same reading that was originally released on CD as part of the collectable partwork *Talking Classics* in the early 1990s. This recording has been available in various formats over the years and is still commercially available as a download.

FROM UNQUIET REST

Reading | Radio | 15 mins

TX: 13/12/1961, BBC Home Service

Margaret Rutherford and Robert Eddison read poems on the subject of ghosts, as chosen by John Carroll.

THE FURTHER REALM

Documentary | Radio | 5 x 15 mins

TX: 12/12/2017 – 16/12/2017, Radio 3

Novelist Andrew Martin gives a series of five short talks on the subject of ghosts in fiction and folklore, including ghosts associated with particular seasons of the year.

Originally broadcast at Halloween as part of a strand entitled *The Essay*, this series of talks is still available to hear on the BBC website at the time of writing.

THE GHOST OF CHRISTMAS TURKEY PAST

Reading | Radio | 15 mins

TX: 28/12/1992, Radio 5

A humorous and cheekily grotesque reworking of Dickens's **A Christmas Carol**, in which a young man named Jack receives a supernatural visitation to re-educate him about his love of eating turkey. This is essentially a 'how would like it if it happened to you?' sort of morality tale, but amusingly told.

Read by Nigel Planer, the story is by children's author Jamie Rix, and appeared in his successful sequence of anthologies for younger readers, now collectively referred to as 'Grizzly Tales for Gruesome Kids'.

Nigel Planer continued to be associated with Rix's tales, narrating a series of television adaptations and audiobooks, which are still commercially available.

THE GHOST DOWNSTAIRS

Drama | TV | 60 mins

TX: 26/12/1982

In the 1980s at least, British children's drama regularly contributed unashamedly supernatural stories to the Christmas schedules, and in 1982 presented not one but two ghostly dramas within a few days of each other. The very contemporary ghost story **Ghost in the Water** rounded the year out, but on Boxing Day viewers were treated to an adaptation of one of Leon Garfield's dark Victorian tales.

The Ghost Downstairs revolves around a bargain made between the strange old man, Mr Fishbane (Cyril Cusack), who lives in the basement, and the restless clerk Mr Fast who lives upstairs... It's probably best not to make bargains with strange men when your name is so similar to that of Doctor 'Faust'...

Like the 1976 BBC version of *The Snow Queen*, this production made extensive use of illustrations by Errol Le Cain, using chromakey to insert live actors onto the fantastical backgrounds he had created.

A GHOST FOR CHRISTMAS

Reading | Radio | 4 x 15 mins

TX: 21/12/1992 – 24/12/1992, Radio 5
26/12/1995 – 29/12/1995, Radio 4
20/12/2007 – 21/12/2007, BBC7 (1 & 4 only)
26/12/2012 – 27/12/2012, Radio 4 Extra (1 & 4 only)

Four spooky stories for what we'd now call the Young Adult audience; these were initially broadcast as part of Radio 5s early evening schedule for younger audiences, and then repeated in the Children's Radio 4 slot.

Even so, there are plenty of ghost stories ostensibly for younger people that have no difficulty standing with the stuff for 'grown ups', and the most recent repeats of these stories made no effort to present them as being for a younger audience.

The stories were:

- *The Woodman's Enigma*, by Gary Kilworth; read by Edward de Souza
- *RSB Limited*, by Brian Jacques; read by Anna Keaveney
- *The Investigators*, by David Belbin; read by Edward de Souza
- *Across the Fields*, by Susan Price; read by Anna Keaveney

THE GHOST HUNTERS

Documentary | TV | 50 mins

TX: 04/12/1975, BBC1
     30/12/1977, BBC1
     16/12/1978, BBC2

Presented by Hugh Burnett, this documentary followed the efforts of people who had dedicated their lives to the study of ghosts and ghostly experiences; the hunters included Peter Underwood, then-president of The Ghost Club. The documentary follows the ghost hunters to a variety of haunted locations, including the famous Borley Rectory.

Originally broadcast in 1975, **The Ghost Hunters** was the last of three programmes presented by Hugh Burnett on the subject of strange phenomena that were broadcast on consecutive days between Christmas and New Year in 1977.

Though not originally broadcast as a series, these documentaries were collected together for this Christmas repeat. They were broadcast as a series once again in early December 1978, and then during the Summer of 1984. The other documentaries were *Out of This World* (about unidentified flying objects) and *The Mystery of Loch Ness*.

GHOST IN THE WATER

Drama | TV | 50 mins

TX: 31/12/1982, BBC1

An adaptation of the 1973 novel by Edward Chitham, this one-off drama haunted many a young viewer's imagination for years afterwards.

Ghost in the Water follows two children whose school history project leads them to investigate the tragic drowning (apparently suicide) of a young girl in a local canal many years earlier. Soon, this tragedy seems to be reaching out of the past to touch the life of young Tess in the present...

Directed by Renny Rye (who subsequently worked on the eternal Christmas classic *The Box of Delights*), **Ghost in the Water** maintains an effectively gloomy atmosphere and conjures a sense of the supernatural creeping into the everyday normality of the children's lives, but without ever compromising its suitability for a family audience. The theme music by Roger Limb is also memorably eerie.

After many years as the subject of considerable nostalgia and longing, **Ghost in the Water** was finally released on DVD in 2018, and is still commercially available.

A GHOST IN THE NIGHT

Drama | Radio | 30 mins

TX: 31/12/1971, Radio 4

A play by T.G. Nestor, apparently concerning somebody taking a bet to spend a night in a haunted house.

THE GHOST IN YOUR HOUSE

Reading | Radio | 15 mins

TX: 24/12/1943, Forces Programme

"An invitation to a séance", written by Gordon Boshell, the man who went on to co-create the popular newspaper strip *Garth*, and write the *Captain Cobwebb* novels for children.

THE GHOST OF JERRY BUNDLER

Drama | Radio | 30 mins

TX: 22/12/1927, 6LV Liverpool

A radio version of the play adaptation of *Jerry Bundler*, the story by W.W. Jacobs; this is another Christmas ghost story that is set not only at Christmas time, but among a circle of people telling ghost stories.

The assembled group of men are particularly perturbed by the tale of the highwayman said to have hanged himself in that very building and several of the party are uncomfortable at the thought of sleeping in the building overnight…

THE GHOST AND MRS MUIR

Drama | Radio | 90 mins

TX: 21/12/1974, BBC Radio 4
     23/12/1974, BBC Radio 4

Josephine Leslie's romantic ghost story (published under her pseudonym R.A. Dick) is best known for the film adaptation starring Rex Harrison as the gruff ghost of a long-dead Sea Captain – but (as is true of a good many old films based on novels) BBC radio thought they'd have a go too. Gemma Jones leads the cast as Mrs Muir, the widow who rents a cottage despite its reputation as a haunted house. Soon she encounters the ghost, played by Bryan Pringle, who does not appreciate her presence.

On closer acquaintance the two like each other better and become friends, collaborating on a sensational account of the late Captain's exploits. In the process, they fall in love, but it is not an affair with a short route to a happy ending…

GHOST POEMS – VOICES IN AN EMPTY ROOM

Reading | Radio | 40 mins

TX: 25/12/1996, Radio 4

A forty-minute programme of poetry reading around the subject of ghosts and hauntings – just the thing for ten in the evening on Christmas Day.

GHOSTS FROM THE ARCHIVES

Documentary | Radio | 60 mins

TX: 24/12/1994, Radio 2

A selection of supernaturally-themed clips and extracts from the BBC archive, presented by Gillian Reynolds.

GHOSTS IN THE MACHINE

Documentary | TV | 60 mins

TX: 24/12/2009, BBC4

A history of the supernatural on British television, and how ghosts have been portrayed on the small screen in a wide range of genres from Drama to Reality TV. Notable contributors include Jonathan Miller, and Mark Gatiss.

THE GHOSTS OF FRANGOCASTELLA

Talk | Radio | 15 mins

TX: 25/12/1952, Third Programme

Alexander Wallace Fielding DSO was an extremely well-travelled author and translator who served with the Special Operations Executive in Crete, amongst other locations.

In early 1952, 'Xan' Fielding returned to Crete to investigate a piece of local folklore relating to a small Greek army that was wiped out by a much larger Turkish force during the Greek War of Independence. Legend has it that the ghosts of the dead men haunt the plain where they died, rising to walk again on the morning of the battle's anniversary each year.

Bringing the Third Programme's Christmas Day schedule to a close, this talk by Fielding related his investigations into these ghosts and the night he spent on the plain, waiting to perhaps witness the ghost soldiers as they manifested on the anniversary of their deaths.

THE GHOSTS OF MOTLEY HALL

Richard Carpenter's comedy for younger viewers benefitted from a thin seam of charming melancholy, but spent most of its time detailing the many efforts of a community of ghosts to keep annoying mortals out of their peaceful home. The series was a success and ran for three series, with both the second and third series commencing with special Christmas-themed episodes.

The Christmas Spirit
Comedy | TV | 25 mins
TX: 24/12/1976, ITV

The ghosts find themselves falling prey to an elemental spirit that creates anger and unhappiness in its victims. They soon believe that this curse can be lifted by evoking the spirit of a Christmas from Motley Hall's distant past.

Phantomime
Comedy | TV | 25 mins
TX: 26/12/1977, ITV

The final series of Richard Carpenter's comedy series for younger viewers began, as the second had, with a Christmas episode – but this time the ghost community in Motley Hall are ignoring Christmas entirely, spending the season dissociating from each other.

Their planned isolation is disrupted, however, when three strangers – a girl and her two aunts – come into the Hall to shelter from a blizzard... to say nothing of the sudden appearance of a genie.

THE GHOSTS OF M.R. JAMES

Documentary | Radio | 30 mins

TX: 27/12/1977, Radio 4

Forty years after the great man's death, Michell Raper's documentary examines a selection of his stories.

GHOSTS (1926)

Talk | Radio | 15 mins

TX: 27/12/1926, 5SX Swansea

A talk on the subject of ghosts, by Mr. J. C. Griffiths-Jones.

GHOSTS (1928)

Talk | Radio | 15 mins

TX: 22/12/1928, 2LO London & 5XX Daventry

Gerald Heard was, amongst other things in his very busy career, a public lecturer, philosopher, historian and a writer of both ghost and science fiction stories. He was also, as it happens, a co-founder of Alcoholics Anonymous.

Throughout the 1930s Heard was a prolific broadcaster in the field of science, though his rational eye was sometimes drawn to the world of the occult and the unexplained; he presented the introductory episode of the 1934 radio series *Enquiry into the Unknown*, for example.

Similarly, in one of his earliest radio appearances he presented this special Christmas talk on the subject of ghosts, and the way that their significance in our culture had been diminished with the rise of Victorian rationalism, only for them to rise once again in (what were then) more recent times.

I've tried to avoid directly quoting the original radio times listings, but it seems worthwhile in this instance, by way of a summary:

"Mr. Heard will show, the Victorian rationalism and purblind science that killed Marley and the goblins has been itself killed by a greater knowledge that brings us again to the threshold of the unseen"

GHOSTS (1949)

Documentary | Radio | 30 mins

TX: 21/12/1949, Light Programme

Presented by journalist Dennis Bardens, this programme included a number of personal accounts from people claiming to have had first-hand experience of supernatural manifestations.

Dennis Bardens is not well-remembered today, but in retrospect he is an intriguing figure. The founding editor of the BBC current affairs programme *Panorama*, Bardens was a freelance journalist for many years, and had an interest in the paranormal.

A member of The Ghost Club and Ghost Club Society, Barden's output as an author included several books about ghosts, hauntings, mysterious phenomena and even psychic animals.

GHOSTS! (1950)

Documentary | Radio | 30 mins (?)

TX: 27/12/1950, BBC Home Service North

Accounts of real-life supernatural experiences, as sent in by listeners.

GHOSTS AND APPARITIONS

Talk | Radio | 15 mins

TX: 31/12/1929, 5SC Glasgow

"A talk by Mr. D. H. Low."

GHOSTLY EXPERIENCES

Documentary | Radio | 30 mins (?)

TX: 23/12/1954, BBC Home Service Welsh

Supernatural encounters recounted by A. G. Prys-Jones. Emlyn Pugh, Major Francis Jones, and Dillwyn Miles.

GHOST STORIES

Reading | Radio | 5 x 15 mins

TX: 29/12/1997 - 02/01/1998, Radio 4,
        23/12/2018 - 27/12/2018, Radio 4 Extra,

Radio 4 began *The Late Book* in 1995, a daily reading broadcast at half-past-midnight. What better time for a ghost story? In 1997 the strand celebrated Christmas with five ghost stories by M.R. James.

These readings by Benjamin Whitrow have been repeated many times on BBC7 and Radio 4 Extra over the years, but they finally returned to a Christmas slot in 2018, when they were once again broadcast daily in the week of Christmas.

In order of broadcast the stories were:

- Canon Alberic's Scrapbook
- Lost Hearts
- A School Story
- The Haunted Doll's House
- Rats

GHOST STORIES AT CHRISTMAS

Reading | Radio | 5 x 10 mins

TX: 27/12/2010 - 31/12/2010, Radio Scotland,

Thanks to the internet, the BBCs regional programming is usually available on a non-regional basis these days, and this series is a prime example of why that's a good thing.

Each of these newly-written ghost stories was the work of a contemporary Scottish author, and they were presented by the writer of the first tale, Denise Mina. Broadcast in a late morning slot, they could be heard over the airwaves in the Orkney Islands at ten to midday; a Sassenach like myself had to get them from the BBC iPlayer, and I ended up hearing them late at night on a train journey home - which was actually very conducive to the required atmosphere, ominously so in the case of A.L. Kennedy's contribution.

The five stories in the series were:

- *Which No Man Shall Put Asunder*, by Denise Mina
- *My Actual God*, by Ewan Morrison
- *Ghost Train*, by AL Kennedy
- *It's Me Who Keeps the Bird's Heart Beating*, by Luke Sutherland
- *The Mannie*, by James Robertson

GHOST STORIES FROM AMBRIDGE

Reading | Radio | 3 x 30 mins

TX: 30/12/2019 – 01/01/2020, Radio 4

It's said that the swamps of Louisiana harbour secret cults of people who worship the terrible Great Old One known as Cthulhu; in a similar way I'm led to believe that there are parts of the UK that conceal a surprisingly large number of people who actively listen to, and enjoy, *The Archers* – the BBC Radio soap opera that has run for longer than most people have been alive.

In more recent years *The Archers* has had a running conceit that its characters are usually engaged in some sort of amateur dramatic production over Christmas; Radio 4 listeners are then treated to a spin-off broadcast of that finished production.

In 2014 listeners could hear **Blithe Spirit (2014)**; in 2015 it was a production of the stage play *Calendar Girls*. In 2019, Ambridge's retired history professor Jim Lloyd (Jim Rowe) took to the airwaves, broadcasting from his attic to read a triptych of ghost stories to the local community; these were broadcast in the early evening over three nights by Radio 4.

In order, the three stories were:

- *The Room in the Tower*, by E.F. Benson
- *Lost Hearts*, by M.R. James
- *The Monkey's Paw*, by W.W. Jacobs

GHOST STORIES FROM THEATRELAND

Documentary | Radio | 30 mins

TX: 16/12/2022, Radio 4 Extra

Actor Jack Shepherd takes the listener on a tour of the theatres of Great Britain and the accumulated folklore of the many ghosts (of persons both famous and unknown) said to walk in them. This entertaining study of theatrical superstitions and spectres was originally broadcast at Halloween in 2015, but (like many other programmes first aired at Halloween) was subsequently moved to Christmas when it was finally repeated.

GHOST STORIES OF WALTER DE LA MARE

Reading | Radio | 5 x 15 mins

TX: 24/12/2010 – 28/12/2010, Radio 4 Extra
        31/12/2018 – 04/01/2019, Radio 4 Extra

Prolific in both prose and poetry, Walter de la Mare's output included – but certainly wasn't restricted to – a number of very well-regarded horror stories. Five of these were selected by Radio 4 Extra and adapted as readings for broadcast over Christmas in 2010, beginning on Christmas Eve.

The five stories were:

- *All Hallows*, read by Richard E. Grant
- *Seaton's Aunt*, read by Toby Jones
- *Crewe*, read by Kenneth Cranham
- *A Recluse*, read by Anthony Head
- *The Almond Tree*, read by Julian Wadham

A GHOST STORY: THE CREEPING HORROR ON CHRISTMAS EVE

Reading | Radio | 15 mins

TX: 27/12/1927, 6BM Bournemouth

An intriguingly-titled story by Major C. Eagle-Bott.

GHOST STORY

Reading | Radio | 5 x 15 mins

TX: 29/12/1986 – 2/1/1987, Radio 4

Five carefully-selected ghost stories (none of the selection is obvious or overfamiliar), read expertly by Joss Ackland.

The five stories were:

- *Midnight Express*, by Alfred Noyes
- *The Crowd*, by Ray Bradbury
- *A Little Place Off the Edgware Road*, by Graham Greene
- *Laura*, by Robert Aickman
- *The Tower*, by Marghanita Laski

A GHOST STORY FOR CHRISTMAS

Drama | TV | various

TX: 1972-1977, BBC1
     2005-Present, BBC2 & BBC4

Initially a series of eight plays broadcast annually on BBC television in the 1970s, **A Ghost Story for Christmas** primarily adapted the work of M.R. James for television, before moving to the work of other writers. All but the last of this initial run of plays were directed by Lawrence Gordon Clark.

The impact and influence of these plays was such that they have inspired a variety of similar exercises in the years since, and the lingering interest in them eventually flowered into a full-blown resurrection with the advent of the BBCs digital channels. BBC4 has repeated the plays with some regularity almost since the channel's inception, and it aired the first new entry in the series in 2005. Since that time, six more plays have been broadcast, with another rumoured to be in production at the time of writing.

In practice, the exact boundaries of **A Ghost Story for Christmas** are a little more arbitrary than might be expected. For example, Jonathan Miller's 1968 **Whistle and I'll Come to You** is associated closely with the

1970s plays, even though it was not shown at Christmas until more than thirty years after its initial broadcast. Yet, its influence on **A Ghost Story for Christmas** means that it is invariably included in the roster by enthusiasts; by this point it's simply thought of as being a de facto part of the series, and is invariably included in the various BFI DVD boxed sets bearing the series name.

Likewise, these plays are often reductively considered to be entirely devoted to the works of M.R. James. The Jamesian component is so dominant that other, unrelated BBC treatments of James's stories have been included as extras on the BFI commercial releases of the plays. Similarly, the first DVD collection of these dramas was an Australian boxed set that bore the name 'The Complete Ghost Stories of M.R. James', and which obviously excluded the three non-James plays of the 1970s run.

It's also worth noting that these plays were often considered just as suitable for Springtime as Christmas – several of them were repeated in May, sometimes with revised billing referring to them as 'An English Ghost Story' or something similar.

The last of the original run, **The Ice House**, was broadcast in 1978; while **A Ghost Story for Christmas** didn't entirely go away in the years that followed, with repeat broadcasts showing up here and there in the 1980s and 1990s, it wasn't until the advent of BBC4 that the tales returned with any regularity.

A season of repeats in 2004 celebrated the work of M.R. James with specially recorded introductions by the likes of Muriel Gray and Jeremy Dyson, and a new documentary, **M.R. James: The Corner of the Retina**.

These were followed by a second selection at Christmas in 2005, with another new documentary, **The Story of the Ghost Story**, and a brand-new M.R. James adaptation reviving the series.

Richard Fell's **A View from a Hill** very effectively imitated the economy and style of the Lawrence Gordon Clark films, and was followed in 2006 by **Number 13** - though this was, sadly, the last of Fell's Ghost Stories for Christmas (unless you include Mark Gatiss's **Crooked House**, which he produced).

In 2010 a fresh M.R. James adaptation of **Whistle and I'll Come to You** appeared on Christmas Eve. It alluded to the Jonathan Miller version in a number of respects (including the truncation of James's original story title), but significantly deviated from both the earlier play and the original story in a number of others.

All three of these newer plays were included in the *Ghost Stories for Christmas* DVD boxed set produced by the BFI, effectively quashing any potential argument about whether or not they can be considered part of the series.

Five more plays have subsequently appeared, beginning in 2013 with **The Tractate Middoth**. These have all been written by Mark Gatiss, and an affection for the 1970s plays is very apparent in each of them.

The Gatiss plays have yet to be consecrated by inclusion in a reissue of the BFI boxed set, and the 2022 DVD release of the first four is titled simply *Ghost Stories*, with no mention of Christmas. However, in 2021 the BBC repeated all of the 1970s plays as a lead-up to the Christmas broadcast of Gatiss's latest, **The Mezzotint**, which surely constitutes an endorsement all of its own.

There follows a list of all of the plays that are generally considered part of the run of **Ghost Stories for Christmas**. All of these have their own individual entries in this book.

Whistle and I'll Come to You (1968)
The Stalls of Barchester (1971)
A Warning to the Curious (1972)
Lost Hearts (1973)
The Treasure of Abbot Thomas (1974)
The Ash Tree (1975)
The Signalman (1976)
Stigma (1977)
The Ice House (1978)
A View from a Hill (2005)
Number 13 (2006)
Whistle and I'll Come to You (2010)
The Tractate Middoth (2013)
The Dead Room (2018)
Martin's Close (2019)
The Mezzotint (2021)
Count Magnus (2022)

THE GHOST TRAIN

The Ghost Train is a comedy-thriller rather than an actual ghost story per se, but a ghost story is an essential part of the plot, providing much of the tension in the narrative.

A group of people find themselves stranded at an old and isolated railway station; the station master is none too happy at the arrival of this group, and warns them of the phantom passenger train that sometimes runs on this line at night. The spectre of a train that was wrecked in a disaster years earlier, it is said to be certain death to witness this 'ghost train'...

The Ghost Train was the creation of Arnold Ridley, a successful playwright and actor who, in later life, became fixed in the popular imagination as the gentle Private Godfrey in *Dad's Army*.

The Ghost Train (1937)
Drama | TV | 40 mins
TX: 20/12/1937, BBC Television
    28/12/1937, BBC Television (repeat performance)

The successful 1923 stage play, adapted for television.

The Ghost Train (1969)
Drama | Radio | 75 mins
TX: 26/12/1969, BBC Radio 4

Tony Clayton's production of the classic play featuring the company of the New Theatre in Bromley, broadcast as part of the Repertory in Britain strand.

The Ghost Train (1998)
Drama | Radio | 90 mins
TX: 30/12/2012, BBC Radio 4

Shaun McKenna's adaptation of the classic play, originally broadcast as part of the Saturday Playhouse strand. An excellent cast includes Adam Godley, Tracy-Ann Oberman and Emily Joyce.

GHOST TRILOGY

Drama | Radio | 3 x 25 mins

TX: 22/12/1975 – 24/12/1975, Radio 4

The great Peter Barkworth performs three short stories – inevitably one is by M.R. James, but the other tales are less familiar. At 25 minutes these stories were given a little more space to breathe than the usual quarter-hour slot.

The stories were:

- Mr Ash's Studio, by H.R. Wakefield
- Number 13, by M.R. James
- The Tudor Chimney, by A. N. L. Munby

THE GIANT UNDER THE SNOW

Reading | Radio | 5 x 15 mins

TX: 28/12/1981 – 01/01/1982, Radio 4

Although under-appreciated in terms of his general popularity, the late John Gordon always had the recognition of his peers and critics; author of over twenty novels and scores of short stories ostensibly for younger readers, he was a writer of considerable skill who could draw menace from a silent landscape with economy and ease. Although his dark, strange fiction initially drew comparison with the work of Alan Garner, in the long run he was celebrated more for the Jamesian aspects of his writing and his 'children's books' were often cited by serious critics of horror fiction.

The Giant Under the Snow was Gordon's first novel, and it seems to remain the best-remembered. It's also a story set in the run-up to Christmas, and which makes much use of snowy landscapes – so a daily reading of it would certainly have made ideal Christmas entertainment for younger listeners.

However, I have included it here because it is also a story in which three children must traverse the drear limits of a winter woodland, only to discover that they are being pursued by scuttling, spidery figures - the mummified liches of long-dead warriors from the Dark Ages. As in *A Warning to the Curious*, the dead have crept out of the earth to pursue those who have taken ancient treasure from its resting place in the earth...

It seems rather unlikely that we'll ever hear the reading of the novel performed by Martin Jarvis on the BBC again, and no audiobook version of the book is currently available.

GIDEON COE'S A GHOST STORY FOR CHRISTMAS

Reading | Radio | Various

Gideon Coe is a DJ (and former *Why Don't You?* presenter) who has been a presenter on the BBCs Radio 6 Music station since its inception in 2002. In 2016 and 2018 Coe included special readings of 'a ghost story Christmas' as part of his late show.

Both readings also had specially composed soundtrack accompaniments.

The Hospice, by Robert Aickman (2016)
TX: 12/12/2016 – 15/12/2016, Radio 6 (4 x 15 mins)
         16/12/2016, Radio 4 Extra (30 mins)

Read by Gideon Coe; soundtrack by Vic Mars

The Girl I Left Behind Me, by Muriel Spark (2018)
TX: 19/12/2018, Radio 6 (1 x 15 mins)

Read by Bronwen Price; soundtrack by Alison Cotton

THE GIRL BEFORE

Drama | TV | 3 x 60 mins

TX: 19/12/2021 – 22/12/2021, BBC 1

The fairy tale of Bluebeard and his murdered wives is subtly evoked by this adaptation of J. P. Delaney's novel; ostensibly a psychological thriller, it has a strongly Gothic feel while also revelling in its modernity.

Jane (Gugu Mbatha-Raw) moves into a sophisticated modern home, built to the architect's exacting minimalist standards; prospective tenants are carefully selected and must agree to the architect's preconditions. Living there requires a tenant to leave their possessions behind – they can live in the house but must not make their own impression upon it. In fact, with all of the automated systems and cameras in the house, there is a sense that moving into the place is to put oneself into the power of the architect.

Jane's story is told in parallel with that of a couple, Simon and Emma (Jessica Plummer) who lived in the house before her. As the two stories progress, Jane makes the disturbing discovery that Emma died in the house. She has begun a relationship with Edward (David Oyelewo), the troubled architect and owner of the house, and begins to suspect that he may have played a part in Emma's fate – and that she may be following in her predecessor's doomed footsteps...

A very taut and engaging thriller, The Girl Before was likely intended for weekly broadcast but was instead shown over four nights as part of the Christmas schedules. Steeped in modernism, themes of isolation, misogyny, and recovery from trauma, it is also nakedly Gothic. It seamlessly unites very old and very new variations of overbearing yet attractive men and imperilled heroines; a Bluebeard for our times.

THE GOBLINS WHO STOLE A SEXTON

A precursor to A Christmas Carol, this short tale by Charles Dickens tells of Gabriel Grub, a mean-spirited gravedigger who hates Christmas is abducted by goblins, who seek to re-educate him about the Christmas spirit with a series of little games and entertainments...

The Goblins Who Stole a Sexton (1962)
Reading | Radio | 30 mins
TX: 24/12/1962, BBC Home Service
       25/12/1962, BBC Home Service
       17/12/1972, Radio 4
       24/12/2017, Radio 4 Extra
   26/12/2020, Radio 4 Extra

Charles Lefaux's adaptation of the cautionary tale in Dickens's *The Pickwick Papers*, performed by Ralph Richardson.

Although this is essentially a reading of the story, it is considerably enlivened by a musical score, and by a second performer singing the words of the vengeful goblin-king: "Gabriel Grub! Gabriel Grub!"

Obviously, Dickens would later revisit the central idea of this story in *A Christmas Carol*, so it's appropriate that the creative forces behind this radio adaptation of the tale – writer Charles Le Faux, narrator Ralph Richardson, and composer Christopher Whelan – would come together once again for the BBCs 1965 radio production of **A Christmas Carol.**

The Goblins Who Stole a Sexton (1984)
Reading | Radio | 15 mins
TX: 31/12/1984, Radio 4

Veteran comedian and broadcaster Charlie Chester reads Dickens's tale.

The Goblins Who Stole a Sexton (1997)
Reading | Radio | 15 mins
TX: 18/12/1997, Radio 4
     24/12/2010, BBC7
     23/12/2011, Radio 4 Extra
     25/12/2022, Radio 4 Extra

Clive Francis reads Dickens's tale.

THE GOTHIC IMAGINATION

Documentary | Radio | 3 x 20 mins

TX: 21/12/1992 – 23/12/1992, Radio 3

A series of three talks given by Philip Dodd on consecutive evenings, discussing the Gothic and its continuing relevance to the contemporary imagination.

Each talk dealt with a different theme, and in order they were:

- Murder
- The Haunted House
- The Monster.

THE GREEN MAN

Drama | TV | 3 x 60 mins

TX: 17/12/2005 - 19/12/2005, BBC4

Scholars and governesses are entirely absent from this ghostly drama based on the novel of the same name. Albert Finney instead plays Maurice, a middle-aged hotelier with a drink problem. In fact, he has a problem with his appetites in general, and is more than a little preoccupied by the thought of persuading his wife and mistress to engage in a threesome with him. Plenty of ghost stories seem to build on a character's isolation; this one is unusual in that it appears to grow out of a man's mid-life crisis.

That is, if it *is* a ghost story. The narrative certainly allows for the possibility that the spectral visions Maurice begins to experience are attributable to his alcoholism, and it can be argued that the story is about Maurice, not about the haunting. Ultimately that speculation may do no more than invoke a distinction without a difference, however. The ghostly visions are certainly alarming and this would not be the first time an audience had been encouraged to wonder if a haunting is taking place within the protagonist rather than their environs; the narrative's precise focus doesn't detract from its merits as a ghost story.

The first episode begins with a horrific sequence in which a woman is walking through dark woodland on a blustery night. She carries a lantern, and her clothing suggests that we are seeing events from the 18th or 19th century. Abruptly, she is seized by a supernatural monstrosity… at which point we leap ahead to the present day where we meet Maurice, making himself dapper for an evening telling ghost stories to the guests at his hotel. Soon though, Maurice has glimpsed a female figure on the stairs – seemingly the woman whose violent death we witnessed minutes earlier.

After this he encounters other spirits, and begins to believe that the restless soul of one Dr Underhill (a man locally reputed to have been a black magician and wife-murderer) is at work. At last, he finds himself confronted by Dr. Underhill's ghastly shade, and to his surprise Underhill offers to help him realise his deepest desires…

First broadcast over three weeks starting just before Halloween in 1990, the serial was repeated in 2005 as part of a little festival of old ghost dramas on BBC4. Episode one went out between repeats of **The Signalman** and **The Ash Tree**, and the second and third episodes acted as preludes to repeats of **Lost Hearts** and **A Warning to the Curious** respectively. More recently, the entire series was shown back-to-back on BBC4 for Halloween 2022.

THE GREEN MAN REVISITED

Reading | Radio | 25 mins

TX: 27/12/1972, Radio 3
31/12/1990, Radio 3

Despite the title, this programme appears to have been a reading of Kingsley Amis's short supernatural story *Who or What Was It?*, first published in 1972.

Purporting to be a true anecdote, Amis recounts the experience of finding himself at a country inn that reminds him very, very strongly of The Green Man, the inn in his supernatural novel of the same name published in 1969. Even the people in the bar seem to correspond to his characters. The author ponders the uncanny experience, before recounting a supernatural escalation that occurred that night after he and his wife had decided to stay at the place.

It seems natural that the story would be retitled **The Green Man Revisited** for broadcast, especially as the novel had been popular. First broadcast in May 1972, both of the repeat broadcasts seem to have been intended to present the ghost story in the context of the Christmas season – especially as while the 1990 repeat was surely prompted by the then-recent BBC1 serial of **The Green Man**, it would have made more sense to broadcast it soon after the series had finished airing, and not six weeks later; except that waiting a few weeks made it a Christmas Ghost Story.

As it happens, *Who or What Was It?* had already become a Christmas ghost story on television in the mid-70s when it was adapted as the first of the two **Haunted** episodes in 1974. Naturally the adaptation was more fictionalised than the original story, and the hotel's name was changed, giving the drama its title, **Haunted: The Ferryman**.

GREY CLAY DOLLS

Drama | TV | 25 mins

TX: 29/12/1991, Channel 4

An odd little chiller broadcast sometime after midnight, this short tells of a young man named Elton who is newly arrived in an unusual boarding house; the landlady shows a lot of interest in her new tenant, and the man upstairs goes out every day to collect buckets of mud from a nearby yard.

One night Elton sees a strange little grey figure outside his window. Soon after that, something rather nasty happens downstairs. Could any of this be something to do with that man upstairs, with his mud, and the dolls that he makes out of clay?

Faintly reminiscent of the *Mannikins of Horror* episode in the old Amicus film *Asylum*, **Grey Clay Dolls** is an entertaining little diversion featuring Ronald Pickup as the sinister Mr Gray; the doll effects are surprisingly effective given the time, and what one presumes to have been a very low budget.

This one-off drama was broadcast under the series heading *Chillers*, and was evidently intended as a pilot – but it was not followed by a series.

GUINEAS FOR THE GHOST

Drama | Radio | 45 mins

TX: 22/12/1937, Regional Programme Northern

This 'frivolous affair' by Maurice Horspool was described as being both Christmassy and intended to 'make the sides shake rather than the flesh creep', so it was evidently comedic in tone.

Set in Yorkshire, the story concerns a Canadian who comes to England to take up ownership of his ancestral home. He attempts to sell it but cannot, on account of the troublesome ghost residing in the mansion.

HAIL, HORRORS, HAIL

Documentary | Radio | 45 mins

TX: 01/01/1976, Radio 4

An 'anthology of the macabre' - with readings from literary treatments of 'monsters, ghosts, murderers and mummies' by Fenella Fielding, Charles Osborne, and the original Man in Black himself, Valentine Dyall.

HARRY PRICE: GHOST HUNTER (2015)

Drama | TV | 90 mins

TX: 27/12/2015, ITV

Based on Neil Spring's 2013 novel *The Ghost Hunters*, this drama starred Rafe Spall as a fictionalised version of real-life ghost-hunter and debunker of fraudulent mediums, Harry Price.

Price enjoyed some fame in his lifetime (and some infamy thereafter) and the contemporary perspective on him is mixed, some describing him as having been as much of a fraudster as those he exposed.

This side to Price is part of this TV drama; initially we encounter him as an unscrupulously fraudulent medium, but he soon becomes involved in the investigation of what he believes to be a genuine supernatural manifestation. Seemingly he hopes to find some sort of personal redemption in doing so.

The drama sometimes has the feel of a TV pilot, and naturally enough there were hopes that Price and his assistant Sarah Grey might return in further investigations. This didn't happen, and sadly it's not altogether surprising given the slightly lacklustre feel of this sole outing. This is not to undersell the efforts of the cast however – the makers were certainly wise in their choice of lead actors, in particular Rafe Spall whose record shows him to be no mean character actor and more than up to the job here.

HAUNTED: THE FERRYMAN

Drama | TV | 50 mins

TX: 23/12/1974, ITV
      11/12/1975, ITV

The first of two plays broadcast on ITV under the '**Haunted**' banner over Christmas in 1974, **The Ferryman** is markedly different to the period-set Christmas ghost stories that had become an annual event on the BBC at the time. In fact, **The Ferryman** was broadcast on the same evening as the BBCs **The Treasure of Abbot Thomas**, allowing for contrast.

Both of the **Haunted** dramas are nonetheless adaptations of literary material, despite the elements of modernity in both. **The Ferryman** has a contemporary setting, and is based on an anecdotal story by Kingsley Amis, *Who or What Was It?* in which he describes the experience of arriving at an inn that seemed to correspond quite specifically with the hotel that had featured in his novel *The Green Man.*

Julian Bond significantly expands upon this tale, further fictionalising it so that Kingsley Amis becomes the jaded author Sheridan Owen (Jeremy Brett), a writer of supernatural tales who is sick to death of publicity duties, and of people who actually believe in the supernatural.

Taking his wife away to the country to escape it all, he soon finds himself at an inn that seems eerily like a location from one of his stories. The people in it are also eerily similar to his characters – and as the evening progresses, he becomes convinced that the horrible events from his story are going to play out in real life...

A second drama, **Haunted: Poor Girl**, followed one week later.

See also: **THE GREEN MAN REVISITED**

HAUNTED: POOR GIRL

Drama | TV | 50 mins

TX: 30/12/1974, ITV

Beautifully shot by director Michael Apted, **Poor Girl** is perhaps less conventionally satisfying than its predecessor, **Haunted: The Ferryman**, but I nonetheless find it to be the more intriguing of the two **Haunted** episodes.

Based on a short story by Elizabeth Taylor, there is a good deal about the tale to remind one very strongly of James's *The Turn of the Screw*. A young, inexperienced tutor named Florence arrives at a large house to take on a new pupil, a young boy whose precocity and insistent interest in his governess almost verges on sexual harassment. Florence also finds herself the subject of attention from her employer, Mr Wilson (from which we may infer that the boy's own behaviour is imitative of his father's past conduct). His wife quietly disapproves of Florence, finding fault while also noticing the way her husband is noticing this new girl. Amidst all of this tension the young woman starts to have visions of people around the house and grounds, people who are not really there.

As with the heroine of *The Turn of the Screw* we are forced to ask how much of this is really happening, and how much of it might be in the mind of a fragile young person placed under considerable emotional pressure. Happily, the story does not simply imitate James's earlier tale, and it leads us into a subtle labyrinth of its own.

Elizabeth Taylor's story was adapted for television by Robin Chapman, who had adapted the **M.R. James** story **Lost Hear**ts for the BBC the previous year.

Lynne Miller leads the cast as Florence; perhaps best known today for her role as Cathy Marshall in long-running police drama *The Bill*, she's very good here as a somewhat ambiguous heroine; meanwhile, Angela Thorne is austere and quietly ominous as Mrs Wilson.

THE HAUNTED AIRMAN

Drama | TV | 70 mins

TX: 15/12/2007, BBC1

Another of producer Richard Fell's chamber-pieces for BBC4, **The Haunted Airman** was initially broadcast as a Halloween treat in 2006. Critical response was markedly unenthusiastic, but it should also be appreciated in the context of its time.

Fell repeatedly produced well-acted, well-executed dramas, in spite of the low budgets, and at a time when there clearly wasn't much of a will at the BBC to do these things on a more lavish scale, if at all. His **A View from a Hill** was the first real revival of **A Ghost Story for Christmas**, and that 'new blood' surely helped to revivify the presence of the old series in the repeat schedules, bolstering wider enthusiasm for them generally.

Anyway, **The Haunted Airman** is an adaptation of the Dennis Wheatley novel *The Haunting of Toby Jugg*, and while it reduces the supernatural aspects of the novel in favour of the psychological, it hangs the drama on two excellent actors – a pre-*Twilight* Robert Pattinson, and the poised and confident Rachael Stirling.

The wartime airman of the title, Toby Jugg (Pattinson) is confined to a wheelchair, recuperating after a serious injury received during a bombing raid. He has seen quite enough to haunt any man already, but increasingly he finds, as his fellow patients start to die one-by-one, that he is subject to terrors rooted in the present, not the past.

HAUNTED HOGMANAY

Animation | TV | 30 mins

TX: 31/12/2006, BBC1 Scotland
     29/12/2007, BBC1 Scotland

Peter Capaldi and Alex Norton star as a pair of amateur ghost hunters in this stop-motion animated short. Jeff and Thurston find themselves spending their New Year's Eve on a haunted street in Edinburgh's old town.

A second adventure for Jeff and Thurston, *Glendogie Bogey*, followed in May 2008.

THE HAUNTED HOTEL

Drama | Radio | 60 mins

TX: 16/12/2018, Radio 4 Extra
       31/12/2021, Radio 4 Extra

BBC Radio has always been more attentive to the works of Wilkie Collins than television has ever quite managed to be. Among the inevitable adaptations of **The Woman in White** and **The Moonstone**, a good many of his other novels and short stories have appeared as radio plays and serials.

Among the various one-off dramas based on Wilkie Collins's stories is this 2012 adaptation of **The Haunted Hotel**. In its bare bones this is a familiar tale of mystery and murder and ghostly revenge – but there is plenty of richness and atmosphere, well-defined characters and plot twists, to make any sense of familiarity irrelevant.

The cast includes Harry Lloyd, and Adjoa Andoh brings her smoothly elegant voice to bear as the wicked Countess whose machinations are the centre of the mystery.

THE HAUNTED HOUR

Reading | Radio | 45 mins

TX: 24/12/1929, 2LO London and 5XX Daventry

An early-evening Christmas treat of three ghost stories, by E.F. Benson, W.W. Jacobs and Desmond MacCarthy. Sadly, listings don't indicate which stories were performed, or who the reader was.

THE HAUNTED MAN AND THE GHOST'S BARGAIN

Drama | Radio | 45 mins

TX: 19/12/1990, Radio 4
　　　20/12/1992, Radio 4
　　　27/12/2007, BBC7
　　　27/12/2011, Radio 4 Extra
　　　24/12/2013, Radio 4 Extra
　　　22/12/2015, Radio 4 Extra
　　　21/12/2017, Radio 4 Extra

The last of Dickens's Christmas tales touches on similar themes and events to **A Christmas Carol**; a man has a supernatural experience that teaches him the importance of the Christmas spirit and the compassion for others inherent to it.

In this case the 'haunted man' is Redlaw, who wishes to be free of his memories of the losses, slights and wrongs done to him throughout his life. He is visited by a spirit who seems to be his doppelganger, and who offers him the chance to forget all of his pain.

Redlaw takes the bargain, even on condition that he will be able to pass his 'gift' to others. Soon he begins to understand what it would really be like if we were all free of our memories of pain and sorrow, and how stunted and bitter our sense of compassion for others would become...

HAUNTERS OF THE DEEP

Film | TV | 60 mins

TX: 01/01/1990, BBC1

Hammer veterans Andrew Keir and Barbara Ewing lead the adult cast in this Children's Film Foundation production, first aired as part of BBC's children's schedules in 1986. It was subsequently given a seasonal repeat on New Year's Day 1990.

Haunters of the Deep is a ghost story set among the handsome locations of the Cornish coast; a tin mine is being re-opened, and two local children become friends. One is the daughter of the manager at the mine, and the other the little brother of one of the miners. The two children witness the ghost of a young miner from long ago, and then learn of the local tales that say the ghosts always warn when a mining disaster is imminent...

A HAUNTING

Drama | Radio | 45 mins

TX: 28/12/2001, Radio 4

A tale of ghostly possession... or perhaps mid-life crisis... A landscape artist (John Sessions) has a strange experience and begins to behave in ways that seem entirely out of character. He comes to believe that his life is being influenced, and ruined, by the spirit of a long-dead Scottish engineer...

This radio play is an adaptation of author William Boyd's short story of the same name, which appeared in his collection *Fascination*, published in 2000.

A HAUNTING HARMONY

Drama | TV | 50 mins

TX: 30/12/1993, ITV

One of the last works for television of the prolific and acclaimed Canadian director Alvin Rackoff, **A Haunting Harmony** is a rather sedate - but beautifully filmed - Christmas ghost story about a young Canadian boy who finds himself isolated and lonely at an English Cathedral Choir school. He soon finds a friend, though, in the ghostly Welsh choirboy who haunts the Cathedral.

A Haunting Harmony does, perhaps, occasionally become a little too close to being *Songs of Praise: The Movie*, but it can certainly be said to benefit from handsome locations and the acoustics of Worcester Cathedral.

Christmas Carols are woven into the very fabric of the story and so if nothing else this most definitely feels like a *Christmas* ghost story, giving it a particularly seasonal charm.

This drama seems to have been intended for a family audience, so its gentle prioritisation of the emotional over the outright ghostly is understandable, and perfectly acceptable all the time one isn't hankering after a serious scare. However, somebody in ITV scheduling clearly took the word 'haunting' a bit too seriously, as this drama ended up being shown at a quarter-to-eleven in the evening, when every member of the audience for whom it was likely intended would have been fast asleep.

THE HAUNTING OF HELEN WALKER

Drama | TV | 90 mins

TX: 24/12/1997, BBC2

This US TV Movie may have devised a new name for its previously anonymous heroine, and placed it front and centre, but there is no attempt to disguise the names of the ghostly Peter Quint or the children Miles and Flora. It may bear a different name, but this is certainly Henry James's *The Turn of the Screw*.

Originally broadcast in the US in early December 1995, the first UK broadcast of this TV movie put it unambiguously in a Christmas slot – 11.20 in the evening on Christmas Eve. It's perhaps disappointing that this adaptation drops all of the original story's ambiguity, opting to make the ghosts very definitely real and supernatural – but this still makes for an effective ghost story, and despite any limitations you might expect this version to labour under, it still manages to display some admirable strengths.

Both of the child actors are credible – one of them is Florence Hoath, who subsequently appeared in the film adaptation of the at least slightly ghostly *Tom's Midnight Garden*, and then had a crucial role in the memorably scary Doctor Who story *The Empty Child* from 2005. The reassuring presences of Michael Gough and Diana Rigg are also felt.

THE HAUNTING OF M.R. JAMES [Series]

Drama | Radio | 5 x 15 mins

TX: 17/12/2018 – 21/12/2018, Radio 4

In 2018, tales of the supernatural returned to the twice-daily slot that had previously hosted **The Red Room** and **M.R. James at Christmas**; five of James's ghost stories were once again adapted into short dramas, this time by Neil Brand and narrated by Mark Gatiss as the voice of M.R. James.

This series was followed by a one-hour biographical drama of the same name, also written by Brand, and once again starring Mark Gatiss as Monty.

The five stories adapted were:

- *The Mezzotint*
- *Casting the Runes*
- *The Stalls of Barchester Cathedral*
- *A Warning to the Curious*
- *Rats*

THE HAUNTING OF M.R. JAMES [Drama]

Drama | Radio | 60 mins

TX: 22/12/2018, Radio 4
    20/12/2020, Radio 4
    18/12/2021, Radio 4 Extra

Mark Gatiss and Fenella Woolgar star in Neil Brand's considered biographical portrait of **M.R. James**, which also finds the time to pastiche James's own tales very effectively and with appropriate restraint.

While the story is primarily concerned with James and his attitude to the changing world in which he lives, the drama skilfully uses James's own methods of subtle implication to build a chilling atmosphere. Perhaps most importantly, the human aspect of the drama is never abandoned in favour of an empty frisson.

THE HAUNTING OF RADCLIFFE HOUSE

Film | TV | 95 mins

TX: 27/12/2014, Channel 5

Although intended as a feature-film for theatrical release, **The Haunting of Radcliffe House** – originally titled *Altar* – was acquired by Channel 5 and given a prominent place in its Christmas schedule, thus qualifying it for consideration as British television (though it did subsequently get a theatrical release in the US). A certain amount of the publicity at the time seemed to suggest that this was the return of the Christmas ghost story tradition on British television, and one has to wonder if the title-change was intended to likewise invoke more traditional tastes and expectations.

Sadly, the film itself is neither bad nor especially good, and nothing like as evocative of more old-fashioned stories as its new title manages to be.

It tells a generically familiar tale of a family who move to a big, old, isolated house, with the intention of renovating it. Soon they become aware of the dark history of the house, and those who lived and died there in the past begin to exert an influence over those who reside there in the present day. The solid cast (led by Olivia Williams and Mathew Modine) don't manage to spin any gold out of the material they're given, however.

HAUNTING WOMEN

Drama | Radio | 5 x 15 mins

TX: 24/12/2018 - 28/12/2018, Radio 4 Extra

A series of short dramas by Dermot Bolger, each telling a tragic story based on Irish folklore, and featuring a female ghost.

Originally broadcast at Halloween in 2005, these plays were subsequently disinterred several times by Radio 4 Extra - though they were only broadcast at Christmas in 2018.

The five stories were entitled:

- *The Linen Mill*
- *The Wedding Bouqet*
- *The Waiting Wall*

- *The Shimmering Dress*
- *The Riding Crop*

HERE AM I, WHERE ARE YOU?

Drama | Radio | 45 mins

TX: 29/12/1977, Radio 4

Another of Sheila Hodgson's sequence of **M.R. James** pastiches, and the only one to have originally been broadcast at Christmas.

David March returns as M.R. James, and encounters an ancient book with a curse on it, designed to send any who touch the book mad...

THE HEX

Drama | Radio | 55 mins

TX: 02/01/1981, Radio 4
  20/12/2014, Radio 4 Extra
  29/12/2019, Radio 4 Extra
  01/01/2022, Radio 4 Extra

Since this play is unambiguously an adaptation of **M.R. James**'s *Casting the Runes*, it seems odd that any effort was made to change the names of the story, or any of the characters. Two of the principals are jokily renamed Montague and Rhodes, so it's not as if the Jamesian origin was being kept a secret.

Then again, this play – which updates the action to the present-day – must have been in production relatively soon after the ITV Playhouse adaptation of the same story broadcast in April of 1979. Perhaps the changing of names was a simple matter of evading unnecessary comparison.

As it happens, there are a few ways in which the two adaptations do seem similar – they both update the story to a contemporary setting, and use broadcast media as the medium by which the villain receives the criticism that moves him to his sorcerous ire – but in all fairness these seem to be no more than the natural developments one would make when updating the story and therefore explainable entirely by coincidence.

On the other hand, Gregory Evans's decision to have his play build to its climax in the carriage of a railway train looks very much like an act of homage to the earlier film adaptation, *Night of the Demon*. Unlike these other adaptations however, **The Hex** actively preserves the ambiguity of its concluding fatality, which is also executed rather well for a radio production of its era – which is to say, in a way that may make you clench your teeth when you hear it.

While googling 'H.M. Slade' does bring up lots of results that relate to the television series *Porridge*, it is also possible to find Helen Mary Slade's short story collection *Wessex in My Blood*. Published in 1968, this book includes *The Looking Glass*, and can be acquired comparatively cheaply for those interested to read the story.

A HISTORY OF HORROR

Documentary | TV | 3 x 60 mins

TX: 29/12/2010 – 31/12/2010, BBC4

Originally broadcast throughout October 2010, this lovingly-made history of horror cinema was then given a concentrated repeat over three nights at Christmas.

Shown in the small hours (roughly 1am each night), the episodes were partnered with a repeat of Gatiss's horror anthology series **Crooked House**, and on the first night with a repeat of the 2006 *Timeshift* documentary on vampires in film, **Transylvania Babylon**.

The three parts of the documentary cover neatly-divided periods of horror entertainment: the early American/Universal era, the Hammer/British era, and the post-1968 modern era.

It benefits considerably from an effort having been made to record new interviews and acquire fresh material – Gatiss even visits the Universal archive and comes face-to-face with an authentic rubber bat from a Dracula movie. He also interviews Carla Laemmle, one of the last surviving cast members of the 1931 *Dracula*.

The documentary is also notable for Gatiss's digression from the obvious in the second episode when he examines the little subculture of British horror films that include *The Wicker Man*, *Witch-Finder General*, and the then-overlooked *Blood on Satan's Claw*. During the discussion of this last film with its director, Piers Haggard, the phrase 'folk horror' was ploughed up and subsequently sewn among a wider audience; the documentary certainly didn't invent this term, but it's widely thought to have helped popularise its usage.

Gatiss later followed this documentary series with the one-off special *Horror Europa*, though this was not given any kind of Christmas outing. However, it wasn't long before Gatiss returned with another documentary, this one landing directly in the middle of the Christmas Day schedules: *M.R. James - The Lost Ghost Story* (2013).

THE HORSEMAN

Reading | Radio | 15 mins

TX: 28/12/1950

"a ghost story by James Boyce"

THE HOUND OF THE BASKERVILLES

Perhaps the most famous of all the Sherlock Holmes stories, **The Hound of the Baskervilles** is also among the darkest, directly evoking themes of folklore and the supernatural. Beginning with the recounting of an old legend about an aristocratic family cursed with the ire of a hellhound, the story concerns an extraordinarily elaborate murder plot in a wonderfully bleak and atmospheric part of South West England. It is also one of the most-adapted and popular of the Holmes adventures, and has often been a favourite for the Christmas schedules.

The Hound of the Baskervilles (Granada, 1988)
Drama | TV | 90 mins
TX: 23/12/2004, BBC2
    27/12/2006, BBC2

Granada Television's Sherlock Holmes series brought Jeremy Brett to the role to which he was subsequently bound in popular memory. For many he remains the definitive Sherlock Holmes, and the dramas in which he starred have lost little with the passing of time.

Though Brett's Holmes debuted on ITV in the 1980s, those adventures were later picked up by the BBC and broadcast on Saturday afternoons. The feature-length adaptation of **The Hound of the Baskervilles** starring Brett was held back for broadcast at Christmas, however.

It is not, sad to say, among the very best examples of the Granada series; budgetary limitations mean that it often cannot be as lavish or as atmospheric as the story requires, or indeed as viewers of the series might have come to expect. In many respects it does not match up to the atmosphere created by other versions of this very atmospheric tale – but it does boast location filming on Dartmoor itself, and of course it has Jeremy Brett and Edward Hardwicke as Holmes and Watson.

The Hound of the Baskervilles (BBC Radio, 1988)
Drama | Radio | 2 x 60 mins
TX: 28/12/2009 - 29/12/2009, BBC Radio 4

At the present time, the only Holmes-and-Watson duo to have appeared together in adaptations of all sixty of Conan Doyle's original stories is that of Clive Merrison and Michael Williams. Their radio adventures ran for over ten years, culminating in **The Hound of the Baskervilles** in 1998.

Paradoxically, this run of adaptations had its origin in a previous adaptation of **Hound**, which had starred Roger Rees and Crawford Logan as Holmes and Watson. This dramatization was successful enough for the writer Bert Coules to propose an ongoing series, and the rest is history - but it was at this point that the cast was changed and Merrison and Williams took on the lead roles.

While Merrison's singularly vulpine take on Holmes is a favourite for many, this is not to suggest that there was anything wrong with the Rees and Logan double act, or with the version of **Hound** in which they starred. Originally broadcast as part of Radio 4s Classic Serial strand, it intermittently resurfaces, and was given a Christmas broadcast on BBC7 in 2009.

The Hound of the Baskervilles 2002)
Drama | TV | 90 mins
TX: 26/12/2002, BBC1
    24/12/2005, BBC4
    24/12/2009, BBC2
    21/12/2010, BBC4

This particularly dark adaptation of an already dark Sherlock Holmes story was a centrepiece of the BBC1 Christmas schedules in 2002; while it is very likely not everybody's idea of what Sherlock Holmes should feel like, it has much to recommend it.

For one thing, it is relentlessly atmospheric, and even while the locations could never be mistaken for the Dartmoor we're being asked to see them as, they nonetheless create the requisite mood. Ian Hart's Doctor Watson is a man of action with a capacity for chivalrous outrage, a little less implacably calm than the character we're used to, and Richard Roxburgh makes for a cold, ruthless Holmes. Some of the dramatic edges have been sharpened to make the mood a little more brutal, but this usually feels true to the story, and the tragic, sombre tone to the ending is actually consistent with the stakes being played for in the final act.

Evidently this adaptation was successful enough for a second adventure to be commissioned, again from writer Allan Cubitt – but in the event, the ill-received **Sherlock Holmes and The Case of the Silk Stocking (2004)** was of a radically different style and had little beyond the return of Ian Hart's Watson to provide any real sense of continuity between the two dramas. Nonetheless, it has a few features of interest.

THE HOUSE AT WORLD'S END

Drama | Radio | 45 mins

TX: 16/10/2003, Radio 4

Rules are made to be broken, and so I'm including this radio play here even though it has never been broadcast in December. However, I insist that my decision is far more justifiable than the BBCs consistent failure to give this drama a place in the Christmas schedules.

Consider: the play begins with the sound of 'The Holly and the Ivy' being sung by a choir, then we discover we are hearing the Christmas service at King's College, Cambridge. The scene having been set, we are introduced to a pair of students, and hear as they are invited to their professor's Christmas gathering in his rooms.

This is quite an invitation, as their professor is **M.R. James**, and they've been given a chance to hear the master performing one of his famous ghost stories, as per his personal Christmas tradition. What they hear that evening, however, is a lost tale from James's own youth, one he will never set down on paper.

Stephen Sheridan had previously written **The Teeth of Abbot Thomas** for BBC radio, a very funny and literate parody of the ghost stories of M.R. James. Sheridan once again demonstrates his comprehensive knowledge of James's tales in this considerably more straight-faced entertainment, in which the young James visits the home of his friend, Henry.

Henry's elderly uncle Magnus dies suddenly while they are there, and the local Doctor, De Lacey, shows an urgent, almost obsessive, desire to obtain one of Magnus's books.

Any seasoned James fan will already have recognised echoes of *The Tractate Middoth* and *Count Magnus* here, and to be sure there is a parade of Jamesian motifs throughout the play – but they never get in the way of the story, which is deftly-told and performed by a decent cast. Of particular note, Doctor De Lacey is played by veteran actor David Collings, who subsequently recorded a complete, unabridged reading of James's ghost stories, released on CD in 2007.

HUNTING GHOSTS WITH GATISS AND COLES

Documentary | Radio | 45 mins

TX: 24/12/2019, Radio 4
     25/12/2019, Radio 4

Broadcast late on Christmas Eve, and then repeated directly after the new radio adaptation of **The Signalman (2022)** the following day, this extremely companionable programme featured two notable BBC stalwarts – the reverend Richard Coles and Mark Gatiss – who share a passion for things ghostly. Ostensibly the record of a ghost hunt, it's perhaps more of a ghost-chat - but an extremely good-natured and insightful one.

HURST OF HURSTCOTE

Reading | Radio | 15 mins

TX: 14/12/2019, Radio 4 Extra

E. Nesbit's Poe-inflected tale of the macabre, in which a man is drawn back to the arcane interests of his youth when he suffers a terrible loss; read by Linus Roache.

THE ICE HOUSE (1978)

Drama | TV | 30 mins

TX: 25/12/1978, BBC1
        26/12/1982, BBC1
        20/12/2021, BBC4

The ultimate departure for **A Ghost Story for Christmas**, in several respects, **The Ice House** truly defies comparison with any of the plays that preceded it, or those that have come after.

Some argue that **Stigma** is not a ghost story, but there can be no argument at all about **The Ice House** – it's a macabre fantasy, an Aickmanesque tale of the strange and the sinister, but it's very, very difficult to see it as a ghost story.

A middle-aged man named Paul has escaped his life (prompted by the recent end of his marriage) and gone to a retreat in the countryside. The place is run by an attractive yet unsettling brother and sister partnership, Jessica and Clovis. As Paul notices more and more strangeness around him, as his perplexity increases, he begins to think that the solution to the mystery lies in the old ice house in the woods. Upon the outside of this structure there grows an attractive, double-bloomed flowering vine that exudes an alluring scent and a rich strangeness.

The last entry in the series, and directed now by Derek Lister rather than Lawrence Gordon Clark, **The Ice House** is also the least-regarded by many. I think this is at least partly a matter of deviation from expectation; the play offers none of the things that have previously been typical of the series, and John Bowen's story really doesn't offer any answers – easy or otherwise – to its audience.

I think, however, that there is much to appreciate here. The tone of the piece is lush, often dreamlike. The constant unease and our inability to know the truth about Clovis and Jessica, their motivations, their relationship with the vine, or the fate of those who enter the ice house – all of that ambiguity can make for a richly enigmatic half hour if one has the taste for it. I don't blame anybody for not having that taste, mind you.

THE IMP OF THE PERVERSE

Drama | TV | 35 mins

TX: 20/12/1975, BBC2

A tale of twisted, murderous urges and of haunting guilt, **The Imp of the Perverse** was the first of two Poe adaptations broadcast in the mid-70s under the title *Centre Play for Christmas*.

These special seasonal episodes of the *Centre Play* drama strand only ran for a couple of years, and it seems rather a shame that a longer series of Poe adaptations did not run concurrently with Lawrence Gordon Clark's ghost stories throughout the 1970s.

The Imp of the Perverse was adapted by Andrew Davies (who adapted **The Signalman** the following year), and starred Michael Kitchen and Lalla Ward. The second of these Poe adaptations, **William Wilson**, followed in 1976.

THE INEXPERIENCED GHOST

Reading | Radio | 25 mins

TX: 27/12/1976, Radio 4

Veteran film actor Kenneth More reads from H.G. Wells' comical (or at least, *initially* comical) ghost tale about an inept phantasm doing his best to haunt a gentleman's club.

THE INFINITE MONKEY CAGE: CHRISTMAS SPECIAL 2016

Factual | Radio | 45 mins

TX: 27/12/2016, Radio 4

A long-running success, the popular science programme **The Infinite Monkey Cage** has been grappling with hard science and attempting to make it accessible – and fun – for radio audiences since 2009. Presenters Brian Cox (physicist) and Robin Ince (comedian) balance the tone of the discussion perfectly, and this highly rational piece of entertainment is perhaps the last place you'd expect to find the supernatural at Christmas.

Yet, here it is – the Christmas special from 2016, devoted specifically to ghosts and ghost stories. They even have Mark Gatiss in the guest line-up.

Neil de Grasse Tyson (astrophysicist) is also a guest, as are Deborah Hyde (anthropologist) and the Bishop of Leeds (bishop). The resulting discussion addresses Christmas ghost stories and the importance of the supernatural to the human imagination, as well as allowing Mark Gatiss to show off his impersonation of Mr Potter, the villain in *It's a Wonderful Life*.

The Infinite Monkey Cage frightens as often as it fails to entertain, but nonetheless this particular episode is recommended listening because of the subject matter – and because at the time of writing, it's available for free on BBC Sounds.

THE INGOLDSBY LEGENDS

Reading | Radio | 10 x 15 mins

TX: 14/12/2009 – 25/12/2009, Radio 4

A small selection of stories from Richard Harris Barham's collection of folk tales, ghost stories and legends, first published in 1837. Barham wrote the tales under the pen-name of Thomas Ingoldsby, hence the title given to the collected edition of his stories.

There are more than fifty tales in all, but this radio series featured only six of them.

The stories selected for this reading were:

- *The Lady Rohesia*
- *The Leech of Folkstone*
- *Bloudie Jacke*
- *Jerry Jarvis' Wig*
- *The Spectre of Tapton*
- *A Singular Passage*

THE INN

Drama | Radio | 60 mins

TX: 24/12/2006, Radio 4
       30/12/2006, Radio 4

Scheduled to follow the annual Festival of Nine Lessons and Carols from King's College, Cambridge, an adaptation of a dark and spooky tale by Guy de Maupassant probably sounded like it would be just the thing for Christmas Eve. In the event, as good as it is, I think it's somewhat bleaker than might be expected of a story on a winter afternoon - though that's no impediment to its quality.

Maupassant's original tale combines the sense of being desperately alone with that of being haunted, elegantly intermingling the traditional idea of a restless spirit visiting its recriminations on the living, with the more acute sense of guilt carried by those who have survived the dead. While all of the story's events can be rationally explained, there is nonetheless a strong sense of the ghostly throughout.

Maupassant's story is a quick read, but Sue Glover's dramatization runs to an hour, and necessarily fleshes out the characters and events considerably. It also weights the story more toward the psychological, making it much easier to read certain events as being the product of a lonely imagination than a supernatural manifestation. The absence of Maupassant's equivocal narrative voice means the audience is more likely to take the rational perspective – but this somehow makes the story starker, more brutal, and all the more haunting.

The plot – the essence of which will be familiar to fans of contemporary horror – involves a young man who takes on the responsibility of being caretaker at a remote, alpine hostelry during the winter season when it will be completely cut-off by the weather.

Young Ulrich (Robin Laing) has never overwintered at the inn before, but he is not alone – he has the company of a veteran caretaker, Gaspard (Gareth Thomas). All is well at first – though Sue Glover asks us to see Ulrich as a more feckless creature, and his relationship with Gaspard less harmonious, than Maupassant does. These are not idle changes, and help to create a greater sense of unease as the story progresses.

Inevitably something goes wrong, and Ulrich finds himself completely alone. Soon, he will face the baleful consequences of his own isolation.

I genuinely think that this tale might be a shade of darkness too far for a Christmas Eve – especially, I suspect, for those spending Christmas alone. Nonetheless I do really like **The Inn**, not least because of the delicate (yet razor-sharp) closing monologue, delivered with exactness by

Vicki Liddelle, in which a young girl muses on the way in which something as beautiful as falling snow can be so utterly *evil*.

IN SEARCH OF DRACULA WITH MARK GATISS

Documentary | TV | 60 mins

TX: 03/01/2020, BBC2

After his documentaries about horror cinema and M.R. James, it seemed like an entirely natural development for him to produce a similar documentary about the history of Bram Stoker's creation, and the many adaptations that have followed it over the decades.

Moreover, this documentary was broadcast directly after the final episode of the BBCs new adaptation of **Dracula**, which Gatiss had co-written with Steven Moffat.

As with Gatiss's other documentaries, it boasts a wealth of new interview material; in particular there is a truly impressive swath of actresses who have had their own encounters with Dracula, such as Jenny Hanley, Jan Francis, Isla Blair, and Stephanie Beacham.

INSIDE NO. 9: CHRISTMAS SPECIALS

It would be reductive and unfair to summarise **Inside No. 9** as simply an anthology of macabre dramas drawing on the thriller and horror genres; it has a much broader spectrum of influences than this and the writing routinely aspires to a standard and style that betrays its major line of descent from television drama of the 1970s.

True, the tales are often very dark and whimsical, but the drama is always human and heartfelt in one way or another. One particular episode is set at Christmas (*Love's Great Adventure*) but is almost entirely in the realm of social realism. However, the first episodes of Series 3 and 8 were both broadcast several weeks ahead of the rest of their respective series, and were shown as Christmas specials. They do not disappoint in this role.

The Devil of Christmas (2016)
Drama | TV | 30 mins
TX: 27/12/2016, BBC2
      14/12/2018, BBC2
      19/12/2018, BBC2

The Devil of Christmas not only functions as a 'ghost story for Christmas' but actively alludes to both the televisual traditions of such ghost stories, and the 1970s thriller anthologies from which **Inside No. 9** itself partly derives.

It is presented to us as the unedited studio footage of an old play, apparently made for television. We are guided through this footage by a director's commentary – we hear the gentle tones of Derek Jacobi as the director, reminiscing about his lost youth and missed opportunities. If only he'd got the job on *Worzel Gummidge*...

Considerable effort was made to capture the particular look and feel of a video-taped TV drama from the late 70s, to the extent of using recording equipment authentic to the era and adopting a multi-camera setup (as opposed to the single-camera set up used for every other episode of the show); even the director, Graeme Harper, was a veteran of the televisual era being recreated here.

It would perhaps have been enough to see an entire episode constructed in this way, as a direct pastiche of old television – certainly, the episode's primary narrative is that of the play; a family are on holiday in Austria, staying in an alpine chalet over Christmas. Here they are told of the myth of the Krampus, the demonic spirit that walks abroad at Christmastime, punishing children who have been naughty...

There is more to the story than this, and as with the best examples of its kind, the sense of unease in the story lingers around the edges of things before finally coalescing in the dead centre. When it comes, the ending is among the most horrible that **Inside No. 9** can offer - a critic in The Guardian referred to it as 'depraved' - but it's also among the most pleasingly shocking.

The Bones of St. Nicholas (2022)
Drama | TV | 30 mins
TX: 22/12/2022, BBC2

Raucous and uncomfortable clashes of personality, class, worldview and temperament are a recurrent component of **Inside No. 9**, just as they were in the long tradition of British television drama from which the show derives. In the case of this Christmas episode, the tweedy academic Dr Jasper Parkway has booked an overnight stay in a reputedly haunted Church, on Christmas Eve... but he soon finds that due to a double-booking he has to share the space with an irritating couple who have a considerably less formal attitude than himself. The tension thus established, there only remains the question of exactly why Dr Parkway wants to be on his own quite so badly...

Not at all unexpectedly, this episode openly alludes to the televisual traditions from which it has sprung - the phrase 'a ghost story for Christmas' even gets spoken out loud by one character. Simon Callow is also among the guest cast, ensuring a solid performance but also adding to his personal credentials as a stalwart of the Christmas ghost story.

Furthermore, while **The Devil of Christmas** drew upon the televisual style and traditions of the 1970s, **The Bones of St. Nicholas** draws directly on elements of the ghost stories of M.R. James that formed the spine of the 1970s television ghost story. There is a touch of **The Treasure of Abbot Thomas** here, for example – though to say exactly what might spoil the story. **Inside No. 9** doesn't forget itself, though, and there is a much-needed humanity and gentleness provided by characters who initially seem rather irritating.

IS ANYBODY THERE?

Drama | Radio | 4 x 25 mins

TX: 30/12/1991 – 02/01/1992, Radio 5

Probably best-known today for a single, impactful image that appears in his only commissioned script for *Doctor Who* on television - the wall of a church crypt collapsing to reveal a demonic stone face with glowing green eyes – Eric Pringle was a prolific radio dramatist, and his extensive output included several stories of a gothic flavour.

A good example of this, **Is Anybody There?** was a four-part serial written for Radio 5 (in the early days of the channel a significant part of its schedule was intended for younger listeners). It tells the story of Christine (Moir Leslie), a girl who has moved into a new home, the old country house Angel Court.

Soon after she has arrived, Christine begins to think that Angel Court is haunted, and before long she encounters the spirit of Kirsty, a girl who lived there in the 1920s...

Originally broadcast in November 1990, the serial was repeated during the Christmas holidays in 1991. Christine returned for a second supernatural adventure in the sequel, **Yesterday - Once More**, broadcast at Christmas in 1993.

IT WAS A DARK AND STORMY NIGHT ON *BOOKSHELF*

Reading | Radio | 2 x 30 mins

TX: 13/12/1983 & 20/12/1983, Radio 4

Bookshelf was a long-running series in which authors were interviewed about their work; in 1983 the programme invited its listeners to submit their own contemporary ghost stories and the best of them were performed in these two special episodes broadcast in December.

As far as I'm aware there were no best-selling authors or latter-day masters of the ghost story discovered by this exercise, but it would still be nice to hear the end results if the BBC ever feel like repeating it...

JAMES STEWART

Reading | Radio | 30 mins

TX: 31/12/1973, Radio 4

With an accurate yet arguably misleading title, this programme was broadcast four times on BBC radio, including this initial repeat on New Year's Eve.

The programme consisted of the Hollywood actor James Stewart reading abridged versions of his favourite Edgar Allan Poe stories - not a combination you would necessarily have expected, but nor is it one you're going to pass over if you're a radio producer, I think.

Stewart's favourite Poe stories were *The Tell-Tale Heart* and *The Black Cat*. A reviewer in *The Listener* took time to rave over the original broadcast of these readings, describing it as 'pure radio'.

Tantalisingly, the stories were released by Audio Forum in the US as a 'BBC Study Tape', 'for educational purposes only' - so presumably the recordings are extant, but at present they have not been repeated by Radio 4 Extra, nor have they shown up online. We can but hope.

JONAS

Drama | Radio | 90 mins

TX: 30/12/1992, Radio 4

Anybody halfway-acquainted with the horror genre knows that if a teenager messes about with a Ouija board there will be a price to pay. I suppose you might argue that such Ouija board tales really just took the place of the less impromptu séances that were popular in older stories, and heard today, J.C.W. Brook's **Jonas** looks rather like an intermediary step between the two.

Since this story dates from 1975, the hapless group who decide to idly mess about with the Ouija board are not a bunch of irresponsible teenagers but rather a group of indolent middle-class adults. In the world of BBC Horror, the self-satisfied middle-classes often seem to cop it from the forces of darkness as Don Taylor's **The Exorcism** also demonstrated – and in fact Anna Cropper who had been so compelling in the TV version of that play also appears in **Jonas**.

Anyway, this particular gathering of people who weren't quite brave enough to go through with the wife-swapping decide to play about with a Ouija board. Unfortunately, whoops, it's a *cursed* Ouija board. In using it they release the spirit of a long-dead murderer…

Considered a classic by enthusiasts of radio drama, **Jonas** does feel a little 'of its time' now, and obviously it uses a story set-up that has very much been boiled into a cliché by this point – but it's still solidly presented with a good cast that also includes Prunella Scales and Julian Holloway.

JONATHAN CREEK

David Renwick's fondness for alluding to gothic fiction was already evident in his comedy writing by the time he came to reinvent the TV detective series with **Jonathan Creek**. Quite naturally, a drama series in which mysterious crimes and brutal murders were commonplace allowed this tendency free rein.

A clever reinvention of the Holmes/Watson dynamic (Jonathan is an expert in illusion working with Maddy, a determined journalist who chronicles their detective adventures) the series specialised in apparently impossible, frequently macabre crimes and mysteries. These often gave the proceedings a mystical or supernatural tone, even while the hero could be relied upon to resolve everything in a quiet blaze of rationality by the end. As with the most memorable of the Sherlock Holmes tales, even if the audience knows that the detective will calmly explain everything, there is still fun to be had by allowing oneself to accept the tale as supernatural while the mood lasts.

Though this flirtation with the ghostly and the horrific was a consistent presence in the show, it was somewhat ramped up in the feature-length Christmas specials:

Jonathan Creek: Black Canary (1998)
Drama | TV | 90 mins
TX: 24/12/1998, BBC1

Marella Carney is dead. Her husband saw her shoot herself in the garden, and yet the post-mortem says that she had been dead for hours by the time she was seen committing suicide. Moreover, another man was seen talking to Marella seconds before she shot herself and yet there are no footprints in the thick snow to show he had ever been there.

Marella had been a famous illusionist working under the stage name The Black Canary, but she retired years earlier after her twin sister - and stage double - Beryl, was killed in a horrific accident while rehearsing a trick.

The mysteries surrounding Marella's death leave her daughter, Charlotte, desperate and she reaches out to her friend from long-ago, Jonathan Creek, for help...

Jonathan Creek: Satan's Chimney (2001)
Drama | TV | 120 mins

TX: 26/12/2001, BBC1

The famous actress Vivian Brodie dies under mysterious circumstances, shot to death in a locked room with the windows unbroken. Jonathan Creek investigates – but how is Vivian's death connected to the strange and horrible stories about the ritual murder of blasphemers at an old castle owned by a film producer?

Jonathan Creek: The Grinning Man (2009)
Drama | TV | 120 mins
TX: 01/01/2009, BBC1

A young woman vanishes in the cursed room of an old mansion house, and her friend – energetic young paranormal investigator Joey Ross – contacts Jonathan Creek to ask him to assist her in her investigation.

Joey's friend is not the first person to have disappeared in the mysterious room, but can it really be the result of a curse? And is Jonathan Creek getting too old for this game?

Jonathan Creek: The Judas Tree (2010)
Drama | TV | 90 mins
TX: 31/12/2010, BBC1

Emily, newly employed as housekeeper at the mansion home of a famous mystery writer, witnesses a number of strange and mysterious occurrences. When the writer's wife, Harriet, is seen falling to her death from a first-floor window, Emily is arrested on suspicion of her murder. Emily insists that she is innocent, and Joey Ross recruits Jonathan Creek to investigate.

Jonathan Creek: Daemon's Roost (2016)
Drama | TV | 90 mins
TX: 28/12/2016, BBC1

Another house with a sinister past, Daemon's Roost was once the home of the infamous necromancer Jacob Surtees. One hundred and fifty years later the house is now the home of horror film producer Nathan Clore.

Clore had promised to tell his stepdaughter, Alison, the truth of the events that befell her family in the house many years earlier – but he is struck down by a stroke before he can share the secret. Unable to speak, he cannot no longer share the secret with Alison, and she turns to Jonathan Creek for help...

K9 & COMPANY

Drama | TV | 60 mins

TX: 28/12/1981, BBC1
     24/12/1982, BBC2

When Doctor Who finally attempted a spin-off series featuring the show's most gimmicky regular character, it probably made sense to somebody somewhere that it should be about a child-sacrificing Satanist cult active in a sleepy country village during the Christmas holidays.

Come to think of it, it made perfect sense to me at the time - but after all, mysterious cults and sleepy country villages with sinister secrets were very much a staple of British Children's television back then.

Intended as the pilot episode for a series that was never commissioned, a certain amount of the story is given over to explaining how plucky journalist - and former *Doctor Who* companion - Sarah Jane Smith (Elisabeth Sladen) comes to be in possession of a robot dog, not to mention how she comes to be staying at her aunt's house over Christmas, and how she is looking after Brendan, her aunt's young ward.

Unfortunately, it turns out that Sarah Jane's aunt happens to live in one of those English villages that has an active cult of Satan worshippers who practice human sacrifice. It gives Sarah Jane and K-9 something to do, though.

Needless to say, **K-9 & Company** is not the most frightening piece of television ever broadcast at Christmas (unless one acknowledges the full horror of that theme tune), but it does occasionally achieve a pleasantly eerie tone that makes it ideal entry-level macabre entertainment for children and people who like to remember being children at Christmas time.

KALEIDOSCOPE: COME BECK'NING GHOST

Documentary | Radio | 30 mins

TX: 22/12/1985, Radio 4
     30/12/1985, Radio 4

An episode of the regular arts documentary, given over to the history of the British ghost story, and the form's then-recent resurgence in the work of Susan Hill, Peter Straub et al. Presenter Peter Nicholls discusses the subject with contemporary writers, punctuated with story extracts read by Joss Ackland.

This documentary was repeated again in 1990 on the World Service under the banner of a different arts show *Meridian*. Happily, many episodes of *Meridian* can be heard on the BBC website, including this one - under the very slightly altered title *Come Beckoning Ghost*.

KISS KISS

Drama | Radio | 5 x 15 mins

TX: 16/12/2019 - 20/12/2019, Radio 4 Extra

A follow-up to 2009's **Someone Like You, Kiss Kiss** saw a further five of Roald Dahl's *Tales of the Unexpected* adapted for radio by Stephen Sheridan. Charles Dance returned as the narrator.

Though initially broadcast in April 2011, this second series was more recently given a Christmas repeat on Radio 4 Extra.

A third series of adaptations, **A Little Twist of Dahl**, followed in 2012

The stories adapted were:

- *William and Mary*
- *Parson's Pleasure*
- *Royal Jelly*
- *Mrs Bixby and the Colonel's Coat*
- *The Landlady*

LADY WITH POMEGRANATE

Drama | Radio | 15 mins

TX: 28/12/1954, BBC Home Service

"A ghost story by Victoria Bridgeman"

THE LAST VAMPYRE

Drama | TV | 100 mins

TX: 30/12/2005, BBC2
      31/12/2006, BBC2

One of the feature-length episodes from Granada Television's successful Sherlock Holmes series, **The Last Vampyre** is a very loose and sprawling adaptation of the short story *The Adventure of the Sussex Vampire*.

The original story could hardly have sustained the two hours of commercial television required for this production, so it's not surprising that the finished result bears so little resemblance to its source. There is of course no reason why such a creative adaptation might not also find a good story of its own to tell, but in the event this admittedly luxurious-looking episode is rather padded and uneven – it's not even held in any regard by fans of Jeremy Brett's much-admired Holmes.

Nonetheless, when BBC2 picked up the Jeremy Brett Holmes series that had once adorned the schedules of their commercial rival, they selected **The Last Vampyre** as being suitable to present as something of a Christmas treat. The story concerns a man whose aristocratic ancestor met his end at the hands of a torch-waving mob who thought him responsible for the murder of a young girl. Rather in the manner of the Baskerville curse, the inheritor of the family title is suspected of inheriting his ill-famed ancestor's wickedness – and indeed, it's locally believed that his family are all vampires.

Holmes and Watson get involved, of course, and needless to say Holmes comes considerably closer to encountering a supernatural evil in this story than he does in Conan Doyle's original – but if one really wants to hear Holmes at war with a vampire, Glyn Dearman's radio adaptation of **Sherlock Holmes Vs Dracula** delivers that without any ambiguity.

THE LATE ARRIVALS

Reading| Radio | 10 mins

TX: 17/12/1982, Radio 4

"An untraditional ghost story", written by Kenneth Hill and read by Brian Southwood.

LATE NIGHT STORY

Drama | TV | 4 x 15 mins

TX: 22/12/1978, 24/12/1978, 26/12/1978 – 27/12/1978, BBC2

A series of five horror stories about childhood, read to camera by Tom Baker. Despite the evident formal similarity to *Jackanory* and its various spin-offs, these stories were scheduled at the end of an evening's broadcasting, and the disturbing imagery of the opening credits made it very clear that this was not intended for a younger audience.

Although five stories were recorded, only four were broadcast. The fifth, *The End of the Party*, by Grahame Greene, scheduled for midnight on Thursday 28th December, was not broadcast due to industrial action. However, all five of these stories were included as an extra on the BBC DVD release of the *Doctor Who* story *The Armageddon Factor*.

Late Night Story shifted its focus for a second series in September 1979, with tales of the horrors of war read by John Mills.

The four episodes broadcast in 1978 were:

- *Sredni Vashtar*, by Saki
- *The Photograph*, by Nigel Kneale
- *The Emissary*, by Ray Bradbury
- *Nursery Tea*, by Mary Danby

LAYING A GHOST

Talk | Radio | 15 mins

TX: 27/12/1926, 5WA Cardiff

A talk by Miss Mary Manston

THE LEAGUE OF GENTLEMEN: CHRISTMAS SPECIAL

Comedy | TV | 60 mins

TX: 27/12/2000, BBC2
23/12/2002, BBC2

The four-man comedy troupe The League of Gentlemen (Jeremy Dyson, Steve Pemberton, Reece Shearsmith, and Mark Gatiss) never attempted to conceal their love of British horror in their television series; rather, this passion coalesced into the procession of bizarre, grotesque (sometimes loveable, sometimes terrifying) characters that inhabit the fictional town of Royston Vasey.

However, they completely and openly embraced these horror influences in their **Christmas Special**. Recalling the Amicus 'portmanteau' horror anthology films of the 1960s and 1970s, it comprised three separate stories within a framing narrative that told a story of its own.

Set on Christmas Eve, Royston Vasey's Christmas-hating vicar Bernice is forced to listen to the troubles of three different, despairing members of her flock. Each tells a different and very dark tale: a frustrated housewife takes revenge on her husband by resorting to voodoo, an exchange student finds himself menaced by the attentions of a vampire, and the world's worst veterinary surgeon relates the events that led to his family being cursed to wallow in blood.

Bernice does her best to lift the spirits of these sad souls, and by the end of the evening she has rediscovered the generosity and kindness brought to all men by the festival of Christmas... until a red-jacketed, white-bearded figure appears, and her terrible memories of a Christmas long-past come flooding back...

After the third and final television series in 2002, the League of Gentlemen returned for a film adaptation in 2005, after which no more news came out of the village of Royston Vasey for more than a decade.

However, in 2017, two decades after the League's stage show won the Perrier Award at the 1997 Edinburgh Fringe, three new episodes were commissioned to commemorate this anniversary. These were broadcast over three nights at Christmas, but did not have a Christmas theme per se – though the same cheerful mix of the grotesque, the disturbing and the silly that many find seasonally appropriate was still in evidence.

THE LEAGUE OF GENTLEMEN'S GHOST CHASE

Documentary | Radio | 30 mins

TX: 29/12/2010, Radio 4

It seems that quite a few radio and television programmes first broadcast at Halloween ended up repeated at Christmas, which I suppose implies a natural connection (if not equivalence) between the two festivals.

The League of Gentlemen's Ghost Chase is one such beast, in which the comedy writing/acting team known as The League of Gentlemen gather together to spend a night in The Ancient Ram Inn, said to be one of the most haunted houses in Britain.

The League approach the experience respectfully but sceptically and don't encounter anything more unexplained than some chilly air – but it's nonetheless a very engaging half hour in which we hear them given a tour of the house by the gentleman who is brave enough to live there.

He seems happy to share all of his findings and experiences with his visitors, and to complement his testimony the League also talk to a couple of spiritualists and psychic investigators.

LEAVING LILY

Drama | TV | 35 mins

TX: 23/12/1976, BBC2

Graham Baker's award-winning short film from 1975, billed as 'a First World War Ghost Story', is now somewhat obscure. If people saw it and loved it, they don't seem to be talking about it on the internet very much; it's not commercially available, and the most recent public showing of the film that I could identify was over ten years ago.

This seems a terrible shame. Apart from the acclaim given it at the time, it seems to have an interesting concept at its heart.

The story is about a young man named Tom – an intentionally apt name, I'm sure, since it is 1914 and he is about to enlist as a soldier. He spends his remaining time in the Norfolk village that is his home in the company of his girlfriend, Lily.

The couple's time together is soon overshadowed by the appearance of a disturbing figure coming out of the fens, a figure wearing the khaki uniform of a British soldier...

It's often remarked that the sheer weight of loss caused by the Great War directly led to an increased interest in the subject of spiritualism, and a boom in exploitative parlour games designed to comfort grieving families. Ghost stories have certainly dealt with the aftermath of war and the loss of so many young men – but it is an intriguing idea that a ghost story might reverse the typical orientation of such a tale, presenting loss as premonition rather than aftermath. Hopefully the film will one day return from whichever shadowed valley into which it has currently passed, so that we can appraise it for ourselves.

THE LEGEND OF SLEEPY HOLLOW (1980)

Drama | TV | 105 mins

TX: 24/12/1992, Thames Television

A US TV movie that tells an extrapolated version of Washington Irving's familiar tale of the schoolmaster Ichabod Crane, the bullying Brom Bones, and the terrifying spectre of a decapitated mercenary.

The story in its original form doesn't seem suitable for a feature-length narrative, and so some changes have been made – some of them the same as the ones Tim Burton chose to make. This seems both inevitable and reasonable in the name of pleasing an audience.

The cast is led by a wonderfully suitable Jeff Goldbum as Ichabod, and Meg Foster as Katerina. Not shown often in the UK it was nonetheless the centrepiece of the morning schedule on Christmas Eve in '92.

THE LEGEND OF SLEEPY HOLLOW (2005)

Reading | Radio | 3 x 30 mins

TX: 17/12/2005 – 31/12/2005, **BBC7** (weekly)
      09/12/2006 – 23/12/2006, **BBC7** (weekly)
      29/12/2009 – 31/12/2009, **BBC7**
      04/12/2010 – 18/12/2010, **BBC7** (weekly)

The tale of Ichabod Crane and his terrifying encounter with the headless ghost doesn't need much of a precis here; this particular version is an episodic reading from the early days of BBC7. At that time there were a lot of new readings being broadcast, and a number of the short stories had the hell repeated out of them over the next few years.

The Legend of Sleepy Hollow is certainly among that number, but the repeats often arrived back in December where it had first been broadcast, even, in 2005 and 2006, being billed under the series heading *Ghost Stories for Christmas*.

THE LINTEL

Drama | Radio | 60 mins

TX: 24/12/1992, Radio 4
 03/01/1994, Radio 4

'A seasonal ghost story', originally broadcast on Christmas Eve in the afternoon, acting as a prelude to the Festival of Nine Lessons and Carols at 3pm.

Though there is little information available about this play, the short plot summary in the Radio Times explains that a couple who are enjoying an idyllic Christmas in their country home suddenly find their holiday is interrupted. I may never know the cause of the interruption, but perhaps Radio 4 Extra will come to the rescue in due course.

THE LITTLE GHOST

Reading | Radio | 10 mins

TX: 27/12/1938, Regional Programme Northern

A short story by James R. Gregson, read by the author.

THE LOOKING GLASS

Reading | Radio| 10 mins (?)

TX: 17/12/1965, BBC Home Service

A ghost story by H.M. Slade, read by Constance Chapman as part of an edition of Home This Afternoon; this show is billed, perhaps ambitiously, as 'a magazine of interest to all' (though it does concede that it keeps 'older listeners specially in mind').

LITTLE HORRORS

Drama | Radio | 5 x 15 mins

TX: 26/12/1987 – 30/12/1987, Radio 4

A series of five 'short, nasty tales' by Angus Graham Campbell, black comedies featuring younger characters and ostensibly suitable for a 'family' audience - but these were nonetheless broadcast at a quarter-to-midnight.

The five dramas, broadcast daily between Christmas and New Year, were:

- *Conjuring with Spikenard*
- *The Skeleton and the Gypsy*
- *A Coward's Way Out*

- *The Foxglove Man*
- *Dares*

A LITTLE TWIST OF DAHL

Drama | Radio | 5 x 15 mins

TX: 24/12/2012 - 28/12/2012, Radio 4
29/12/2012, Radio 4 Extra (Series Omnibus)
18/12/2017 - 22/12/2017, Radio 4 Extra

Following on from Stephen Sheridan's **Someone Like You** in 2009 and April 2011's **Kiss Kiss**, this third selection of Roald Dahl's macabre short stories saw Charles Dance return once again as the measured (and not a little heartless) narrator.

The stories adapted this time were:

- *Taste*
- *The Way Up to Heaven*
- *The Hitch-hiker*
- *Edward the Conqueror*
- *Neck*

Stephen Sheridan would adapt five more of Dahl's tales for a fourth series, *Served with a Twist*, broadcast in July 2016.

LOSING CONTACT

Drama | Radio | 75 mins

31/12/1994, Radio 4

Bill Nighy and Caroline Harker star in this 'seasonal ghost story' by Nick Fisher. It begins with a man in need of an eye test who happens upon an unassuming, little opticians in a Soho back street, and decides to go in.

The hapless Richard is persuaded to buy a pair of specially-designed contact lenses. While the lenses do their job, they also give Richard the unexpected ability to see into the past; returning to the opticians to find it empty, he has an encounter with a strange presence in one of the basement rooms...

THE LOST GHOST STORY

Documentary | TV | 60 mins

See: **M.R. JAMES: GHOST WRITER**

LOST HEARTS (1957)

Reading | Radio | 20 mins

TX: 25/12/1957, The Third Programme

Scheduled as an interval feature during a programme of music by Schumann, this was a reading of the M.R. James story, performed by Hugh Burden.

LOST HEARTS (1973)

Drama | TV | 35 mins

TX: 25/12/1973, BBC1
25/12/1994, BBC2
19/12/2005, BBC4
20/12/2007, BBC4
24/12/2018, BBC4

In implication, **Lost Hearts** is perhaps the nastiest of the stories adapted in the **Ghost Story for Christmas** series, with occultism replacing archaeology as the prideful scholarship that conjures its own nemesis. Further, the victims this time are children - and as has been said, that fact can always be relied upon to give the screw an extra turn.

Simon Gipps-Kent plays Stephen, a young orphan sent to stay in the care of his amiable older cousin, Mr Abney. Stephen begins to see a pair of strange children around the grounds of Abney's house, and he later hears how two children benefitted from Abney's charity years earlier - but in both cases they disappeared suddenly, and were presumed to have run away.

As with the best of these tales, the implications steadily build and much becomes apparent without being stated directly – at least until the very end, when all is made dreadfully clear to us in a lingering and repugnant scene where Abney smacks his lips while contemplating the wisdom of his books.

The ghosts themselves are unusually present throughout the story, often directly visible rather than occasionally glimpsed. There are some scenes where we are 'alone' with them, when there are no mortal observers present on screen. They are less ambiguous as a result, and I've heard this aspect of the production criticised as undermining the power of the ghosts. That may be a valid observation, but there is still plenty about them that unsettles – not least the insistent playing of the boy's hurdy gurdy.

Lost Hearts was adapted for the screen by Robin Chapman, and though he did not contribute to **A Ghost Story for Christmas** again, he did adapt another ghost story for television the following year, **Haunted: Poor Girl**.

MACABRE

Drama/Reading | Radio | 45 mins

TX: 26/12/1938, BBC Regional Programme London/Midland/Wales/Western

A selection of three 'uncanny stories overheard at the fireside'. The stories were:

- *Mansions*, by Bertha Selous Philips
- *The Open Window*, by Saki
- *Thursday Evenings*, by E.F. Benson

It appears that the tales were presented as if told by three different storytellers sitting around a fire; the Radio Times listing indicates that the first and last stories were dramatized with a small cast, while the second was presented as a reading.

The Christmas 1938 performance of this programme had been significantly changed from the original 1935 broadcast, however – the third story in the original version had been *The Birthright*, by Hilda Hughes – 'by permission of Juliet Hagon'. One has to wonder if permission was subsequently withdrawn, or if it was just felt that the substitution of the Benson tale would be an improvement to the overall programme.

Moreover, Benson's *Thursday Evenings* had been part of *More Macabre*, a second trilogy of uncanny tales broadcast in May of 1936, so it would appear that the December 1938 version of **Macabre** conflated the two earlier productions.

MARKHEIM

The dark tale of a man who commits a murder on Christmas Eve, and is then confronted by a mysterious stranger who may or may not be of supernatural origin. The stranger seems to be very concerned with notions of good and evil, and perhaps with Markheim's very soul.

This short story by R.L. Stevenson is sometimes paired with his later *Dr. Jekyll & Mr Hyde*, because of the themes of duality common to both. There are also discernible similarities to Dickens' **A Christmas Carol** here – both tell of supernatural visitors intent on claiming the soul of a wicked protagonist on Christmas Eve. Stevenson's tale came some decades after Dickens's, so there may even be a connection.

There have been several adaptations of Markheim on British television and radio, so these are individually listed below.

Markheim (1952)
Drama | TV | 30 mins
TX: 28/12/1952, BBC Television

Starring Douglas Wilmer as Markheim, with Robin Bailey as The Man and Erik Chitty as The Dealer.

Markheim (1971)
Drama | Radio | 30 mins
TX: 25/12/2020, Radio 4 Extra

Starring Tom Watson as Markheim and Malcolm Hayes as the Stranger. First broadcast in September 1971.

Markheim (1974)
Drama | TV | 30 mins
TX: 24/12/1974, ITV

Made by Scottish Television, this adaptation starred Derek Jacobi as Markheim and Julian Glover as The Stranger.

10 x 10: Markheim (1990)
Drama | Radio | 10 mins
TX: 03/01/1990, BBC2

An episode of the long-running short film strand broadcast on BBC2 throughout the 1990s; this take on **Markheim** starred James Vaughan as both Markheim and his visitor, with Oscar Quitak as the Dealer.

MARK TWAIN STORIES: A GHOST STORY

Reading | Radio | 15 mins

TX: 31/12/2005, BBC7

A brief, satirically humorous (in the end, at least) tale about a man staying overnight in a haunted room. Broadcast as part of a run of five short stories by Mark Twain, the story was read by Kelsey Grammar.

MARTIN'S CLOSE

Drama | TV | 30 mins

TX: 24/12/2019, BBC4
24/12/2020, BBC2
17/12/2022, BBC4

One of the most successful of Mark Gatiss's ghost stories for Christmas, **Martin's Close** makes effective use of its framing as a murder trial; this allows Peter Capaldi's prosecuting attorney to act as a rather grave and compelling narrator of events.

The events in question are those leading up to, and following, the disappearance of one Ann Clark, a local girl who had been the victim of a cruel game played by the young Squire John Martin.

Martin is accused of Ann's murder, and put on trial for his life; to press his case, the prosecuting attorney calls on testimony that Ann was heard, and seen, after the time of her death...

Wilf Scolding is very good here as Martin, wringing out a few drops of sympathy for a character who is objectively despicable. No matter how much Martin deserves his later distress, Scolding portrays it with an almost redemptive edge of humanity.

The touches of eccentricity and humour customary to the modern **Ghost Stories for Christmas** are once again present, with Elliot Levey particularly good as 'Hanging' Judge Jeffreys, a cruel mix of crass jocularity and frightening coldness.

There is also an extra layer of narration, provided by Simon Williams wearing a cardigan and waving a glass of Madeira; though it's in keeping with the origin of James's ghost stories as entertainments told in good company, I suspect many can take or leave this aspect of the play. Even if one dislikes it, however, it can't be said to seriously impede the story.

THE MASQUE OF THE RED DEATH

Reading | Radio | 20 mins

TX: 31/12/1931, Regional Programme Midland

The classic Poe tale, read by Alan Griff.

MCLEVY: CHRISTMAS SPECIAL

Drama | Radio | 90 mins

TX: 25/12/2006, Radio 4
    19/12/2009, BBC7
    24/12/2010, BBC7
    18/12/2021, Radio 4 Extra

David Ashton's long-running Edinburgh-set crime drama was inspired by the writings of a real-life Victorian detective, James McLevy. Running on an occasional basis for more than fifteen years, the series starred Brian Cox in the lead role.

Throughout this time Cox had a very successful Hollywood career, but always found the time to return to the idiosyncratic role of McLevy, which he had very much made his own.

Naturally enough for a series set in Victorian Edinburgh, there is a Gothic mood hanging over proceedings throughout, and McLevy's Leith 'parish' constantly feels as if Edward Hyde might step out from a side alley covered in blood at any moment. However, this was dialled up somewhat in the feature-length Christmas special episode of 2006, in which McLevy pursues an apparently supernatural thief who is abroad in the city.

MEDIAEVAL GHOST STORIES

Talk | Radio | 20 mins

TX: 18/12/1928, 2ZY Manchester

A talk by eminent historian Professor A. Hamilton Thompson

THE MEZZOTINT

Drama | TV | 30 mins

TX: 24/12/2021, BBC2
     17/12/2022, BBC4

The Mezzotint is notable for having been produced under the shadow of Covid, and in fact *because* of Covid (plans to adapt **Count Magnus** had to be put on hold). This particular story lends itself well to small-scale adaptation - the most significant events in the story take place inside a picture-frame, after all - and so it was chosen when it became clear that circumstances were going to seriously inhibit a more expansive production.

Not that you would know any of this, watching it - ghost stories often work best under smaller-scale, more intimate circumstances in any case, and so it does not come across as atypical. If anything, the story has been expanded a little to make it more suitable for television.

A new ending has also been contrived which suits the play – the ending of **The Treasure of Abbot Thomas** likewise differs from the original story, with good reason and to good effect. I think the comparison is further instructive, however, in that **Abbot Thomas** knows when to cut away from a final image, and **The Mezzotint** doesn't.

The final moments are drawn out, and leave little to the imagination – and you might feel that this goes against the tone of James's ghost stories, but it should also be borne in mind that the **BBC** cannot reasonably be expected to fund a drama that is pitched only at fans of 1970s television. Contemporary expectations are perhaps being catered for here, and however one feels about that, it is likely a necessary compromise.

MIDNIGHT TALES

Reading | Radio | 5 x 15 mins

TX: 16/12/1996 – 20/12/1996, Radio 4

Originally broadcast as *A Book at Bedtime* for Halloween in 1990, these five short tales by Bram Stoker - found in the posthumously-published collection *Dracula's Guest and Other Stories* – were read by Dyfed

Thomas. They were subsequently dusted off in 1996 and broadcast in the half-past-midnight slot in the week before Christmas.

The stories were:

- *The Secret of the Growing Gold*
- *The Coming of Abel Behenna*
- *The Dream in the Dead House*
- *A Dream of Red Hands*
- *The Squaw*

MIKE RAVEN'S GHOST SHOW

Music | Radio | 120 mins

TX: 25/12/1969, Radio 2

"Dig the music, kids!"

Okay, those are the words of Christopher Neame having his DJ moment in *Dracula: AD 1972*, and not Mike Raven. Nonetheless, this is the same Mike Raven who appeared in a little cluster of horror films in the early 1970s, including *Lust for a Vampire*, where he played Count Karnstein.

This said, in 1969 he was more likely to be known as a former Pirate Radio DJ than as the star of *Crucible of Death*. Having 'gone straight' working for the BBC, he evidently decided to give his Christmas Night radio show (running from 10pm til midnight) a spooky flavour; the billing describes the show as comprising 'super music and supernatural stories'. Smashing. One can only hope there is an off-air recording of it out there somewhere.

THE MONK

Drama | Radio | 90 mins

TX: 23/12/1985, Radio 4

A dramatization of Mathew Lewis's novel, one of the most significant Gothic works of its era. Considered scandalous in its day, the tale of Ambrosio, an extremely naughty clergyman who gets up to the sort of stuff that probably wouldn't shake our jaded cynical assumptions about religious institutions these days.

Nonetheless, the perfect sort of thing for Christmas, apparently. Acclaimed actor Michael Pennington takes the lead role of Ambrosio.

THE MONKEY'S PAW

Drama | Radio | 30 mins

TX: 16/12/1958, Light Programme
        20/12/1958, BBC Home Service

Louis N. Parker's 1907 stage play of the cruel fable by W.W. Jacobs had been adapted for the BBC several times, with different versions broadcast on radio and television throughout the 1920s, 30s and 40s – but it was only with this version (starring Carleton Hobbs) that it finally arrived at Christmas.

Other versions of the story would return in various forms to haunt the season in later years, including the final reading in **Christopher Lee's Fireside Tales**.

MORE GHOST STORIES

Talk | Radio | 15 mins

TX: 22/12/1928, 5WA Cardiff

A selection of stories, told by Esylt Newberry. Newbery was fairly prolific as a broadcaster, giving talks on a variety of subjects, primarily life in other countries, especially in the East. One of her talks was on Chinese Folk Tales, which suggests that her ghost stories may have similarly been folkloric in origin.

THE MOONSTONE

These days Jack Whicher is best known by his own name, thanks to Kate Summerscale's novel about a famous Victorian murder case, and the television series that it spawned. However, as one of Scotland Yard's very first Police Detectives, Whicher enjoyed a degree of celebrity in his day that led to him being the inspiration for a number of fictional detectives, including Inspector Bucket in *Bleak House*, and the steadfast Sergeant Cuff of Wilkie Collins's **The Moonstone**.

Often cited as one of the earliest detective stories, **The Moonstone** is less of a procedural than this might imply and doesn't actually place the detective close to the heart of the mystery for much of the narrative. Rather, it follows the deeds and fortunes of the various parties who are present at the eighteenth birthday party of heiress Rachel Verinder. It is on this occasion that she inherits a fabulously valuable Indian diamond, the Moonstone, which had been acquired by her corrupt uncle years earlier. During the night, the diamond is stolen, and the subsequent police investigation proves unable to recover it. A complex mystery surrounding the stone then unfolds.

Wilkie Collins was a friend of (and occasional collaborator with) Charles Dickens, but while their stories occupy a certain amount of the same ground, Collins's tales are notable for their more intense gothic sensibility; there are deeper shadows in his work, a greater willingness to confront the sordid and the obsessive.

While his plots tend more toward the sensational, Collins does at times confront social inequity even more aggressively than Dickens, such in his depiction of the dependent social positions in which women were confined. Essentially a writer of thrillers, his most famous stories provide atmospheric entertainment leavened with a little bit of depth.

The Moonstone (1996)
Drama | TV | 2 x 60 mins / 1 x 120 mins
TX: 29/12/1996 - 30/12/1996, BBC2
    24/12/1998, BBC2

The 1996 BBC adaptation of **The Moonstone** boasted a starry cast, including a young actress called Keeley Hawes in the role of Rachel Verinder.

Evidently the darker regions of the Victorian world that Wilkie Collins liked to explore were considered ideal for the Christmas season, since a second Collins adaptation - **The Woman in White (1997)** - appeared the following year, in the same two-part format. **The Moonstone** itself was repeated the Christmas after that, edited into a single feature-length episode.

The Moonstone (2016)

Drama | TV | 5 x 50 mins

TX: 26/12/2016 - 30/12/2016, BBC1

Originally broadcast at Halloween, this serial was given a repeat less than two months later, beginning on Boxing Day; by coincidence, this was almost exactly twenty years after the previous BBC adaptation had first been broadcast.

As might be expected from the way it was confined to the weekday afternoon schedules on both occasions, this serial did not necessarily scale the prestigious and glossy heights of its immediate predecessor. It doesn't have quite the same atmosphere or mood – but it does have a good cast, with John Thompson making for an amiable Sergeant Cuff, and Sophie Ward an elegant Lady Verinder.

M.R. JAMES: THE CORNER OF THE RETINA

Documentary | TV | 30 mins

TX: 22/12/2004, BBC4
     25/12/2004, BBC4
     02/01/2005, BBC4
     23/12/2005, BBC4
     22/12/2006, BBC4

Short in duration, long on substance, this documentary about the work of M.R. James includes incisive contributions from a variety of commentators including Kim Newman, Ruth Rendell, Christopher Frayling and Muriel Gray.

First broadcast in 2004, this documentary opened a season of M.R. James-related programming for Christmas on BBC4, and was immediately followed by a repeat broadcast of Jonathan Miller's **Whistle and I'll Come to You (1968)**. Ironically, although Miller's play had inspired the annual **Ghost Story for Christmas** strand of the 1970s, and had been shown several times over the years, this 2004 broadcast was the first time it had been shown at Christmas.

M.R. JAMES AT CHRISTMAS

Drama | Radio | 5 x 15 mins

TX: 24/12/2007 - 28/12/2007, Radio 4

By the early 2000s there was a tendency, if not an actual tradition, to give the daily 15-minute serial over to stories of a macabre theme during the Christmas period. **The Red Room (2000)** is a particularly good example of this, but this 2007 series of James mini-adaptations also deserves recognition. You might argue that even by that time the inevitability of M.R. James as a Christmas choice was getting a little stale, especially with the same stories coming up again and again – but these are nonetheless well-executed and have names like Jamie Glover, Anton Lesser, Julian Rhind-Tutt and James D'arcy among the casts.

The stories were:

- *Oh, Whistle and I'll Come to You, My Lad!*
- *The Tractate Middoth*
- *Lost Hearts*
- *The Rose Garden*
- *Number 13*

The five plays were subsequently released on CD under the title *Spine Chillers;* as a follow-up, two further CDs were released by BBC Audio featuring ghost stories by M.R. James, read by Derek Jacobi. However, despite retaining Jacobi as narrator they did not continue the dramatized form of the first volume and these were only readings – nor were they broadcast on the radio.

M.R. JAMES: GHOST WRITER

Documentary | TV | 60 mins

TX: 25/12/2013, BBC2
24/12/2017, BBC4
24/12/2019, BBC4
24/12/2020, BBC2
06/12/2021, BBC4

In a 2021 interview on the podcast **The Evolution of Horror**, Mark Gatiss confided that his first M.R. James adaptation, **The Tractate Middoth**, had in fact come into existence as an adjunct to a documentary about M.R. James that he'd been commissioned to create.

As Gatiss himself pointed out, this is rather apt given that the BBC TV cycle of M.R. James adaptations had begun with the arts documentary strand series **Omnibus**. In the event, Gatiss's drama was given the greater prominence, with the documentary following directly after it like the B-side of an album.

M.R. James: Ghost Writer has been dusted off for a repeat much more frequently than **Tractate** though, and I suspect it's thought of with slightly more affection. As with Gatiss's other documentaries there is a measured, gentle quality to the presentation that feels suitably old-fashioned, and the presenter's love for the subject is, as ever, fully evident. Gatiss meets with various 'witnesses' and experts, who provide on-camera contributions to what he reminds us is his own, very personal take on the life and career of the great man.

The documentary is also illuminated with choice extracts from various BBC adaptations of James's stories, and Robert Lloyd-Parry (best known

MRS OSBORNE'S STORY

Reading | Radio | 20 mins

TX: 24/12/1950, The Third Programme

A tale of the supernatural, written and read by John Guest.

MURDER ROOMS

Drama | TV | 2 x 60 mins / 120 mins

TX: 04/01/2000 - 05/01/2000, BBC2
     25/12/2005, BBC4

Ian Richardson, a fine actor who'd already played Sherlock Holmes proper in a couple of US TV movies returned to Conan Doyle's world in this intriguing drama written by David Pirie.

As the drama's subtitle, **The Dark Beginnings of Sherlock Holmes** indicates, Richardson played not Holmes this time, but rather Joseph Bell, the medical doctor and lecturer whose observational powers helped to inspire the great detective. Indeed, Doctor Bell is said to have assisted the police in their investigations on several occasions.

With these facts in mind, David Pirie pushes the scenario a little further and develops the relationship between Doctor Bell and the young Conan Doyle into a recognisable variation on Holmes & Watson. It's worth noting, though, that Pirie also uses the fact that these two characters are *not* Holmes & Watson to defy the audience's more comfortable expectations on several counts.

For example, Robin Laing's Conan Doyle is a volatile, vulnerable young man who has not yet learned Watson's calm and steadfastness. The sad truth of Watson's alcoholic brother, deduced by Holmes from a pocket watch in *The Sign of Four*, is replaced here by the darker secret of the violent, psychiatric illness of Conan Doyle's father. Arthur is not amazed by Doctor Bell's deductions but rather infuriated, believing the older man to be making sport of his family shame.

Doctor Bell himself is certainly reminiscent of Holmes in a number of respects - though he is more of a mentor figure - but in one crucial regard he is very definitely *not* Sherlock Holmes. He is fallible, and cannot bring every villain to justice. As he himself observes, when a man does evil for no rationally identifiable reason at all, how can a rational mind hope to anticipate his actions?

There were further adventures for Conan-Doyle and Doctor Bell in late 2001, when a series of four feature-length episodes of **Murder Rooms** were broadcast - though Robin Laing had now been replaced by Charles Edwards as an older, more Watsonian Conan Doyle.

THE MUSIC ON THE HILL

Reading | Radio | 15 mins

TX: 20/12/2012, Radio 4 (read by Francesca Dymond)
     19/12/1986, Radio 4 (read by Hugh Dickson)

H.H. Munro's stories (published under the name 'Saki') are usually known for their wit and humour, and though there is frequently a macabre streak to be found in his tales it is usually balanced by that sense of levity.

The Music on the Hill is an unusual instance of a Saki tale where the nascent sense of cruelty found within so many of his stories runs free in all of its mercilessness, and does not provoke so much as a smile in mitigation.

The story has featured in Radio 4's Christmas schedules twice; first in 1986, when Hugh Dickson read it for the regular Morning Story slot, and then in 2012 when it was read by Francesca Dymond as part of a triptych of stories by Saki.

Likely to be of particular interest to those with a taste for Folk Horror, the story tells of Sylvia, a young bride who has persuaded her husband to move out to the country.

However, she does not easily take to the countryside; one day she finds a strange idol in the woods, and thinking little of its significance she removes the offering of fresh grapes laid there. We, the experienced audience of such tales, recognise the folly of her act and know that Sylvia will soon be faced with a comeuppance for her lack of respect...

MY CHRISTMAS GHOSTS

Talk | Radio | 15 mins

TX: 24/12/1926, 5PY Plymouth

A talk by H. C. L. Johns

MY CHRISTMAS GHOST STORY

Drama | Radio | 25 mins

TX: 24/12/1925, 6BM Bournemouth

A story by E. Cavan Dance

THE MYSTERIES OF UDOLPHO

Drama | Radio | 60 mins

TX: 31/12/2016, BBC Radio 4

Mrs Radcliffe's seminal Gothic narrative, which features mountains, castles, bandits, sinister foreigners, and a virtuous heroine called Emily, is given new life in this rather brisk one-hour dramatization.

A single hour is a limited canvas on which to explore a four-volume novel, but this adaptation was in the hands of playwright Hattie Naylor, who chose to focus quite specifically on the aspects of the story most likely to be effective and resonant with contemporary audiences.

Novels of the kind and vintage of *Udolpho* often present a challenge when it comes to persuading modern audiences to take them seriously – Jane Austen was mercilessly parodying Mrs Radcliffe's work less than twenty-five years after it was first published, and any vulnerability to mockery has not diminished in the intervening two centuries.

However, in amongst the various clichés and trappings of the Gothic novel, there is a fundamental seam of persistent anxiety within *Udolpho* – and indeed with other examples of the form, such as Le Fanu's *Uncle Silas* – and it is that of the continual sense of threat to the heroine's safety, mortally and/or sexually. Nor is this threat always ambient – sometimes it is made quite explicit by those who are most threatening to the heroine. Sadly, the fear created by the idea of being helpless in another person's power is one that has not dated, and Naylor highlights this aspect of the story with her careful reduction of the narrative.

THE MYSTERIOUS HORSEMAN

Drama | Radio | 10 mins

TX: 26/12/1954, BBC Home Service

"A true ghost story of an experience in East Bengal, told by W. Sheppard"

THE NEED FOR NIGHTMARE

Documentary | TV | 50 mins

TX: 15/12/1974, BBC1

Another contribution from the long-running arts documentary strand *Omnibus*, this drama-documentary portrays and investigates the 19th Century writers, Shelley, Poe, Stevenson and Stoker. Their personal nightmares – sleeping and waking – inspired the great characters of horror fiction.

This production is notable for featuring narration by horror veteran Michael Gough, an appearance by a young Ben Kingsley as Edgar Allan Poe, and one David Prowse as 'the shadow of the monster'. One presumes Prowse was a shoe-in for that role, since he'd already played Frankenstein's monster for Hammer films in 1970, and at the time this documentary was made he was fresh from playing Frankenstein's 'Monster from Hell' in Peter Cushing's last outing as the character.

THE NEMESIS OF FIRE

Drama | Radio | 45 mins

TX: 18/12/1974, Radio 4
     19/12/1974, Radio 4

The second of Sheila Hodgson's radio adaptations of Algernon Blackwood's Doctor John Silence mystery adventures, it is also perhaps the most disturbing. Responding to a plea for help from an old soldier, Silence finds himself investigating a patch of dark woodland.

He soon discovers that the place is haunted by a presence that is quite immaterial, but nonetheless destructive and can burn its victims to death.

A follow-up to **The Camp of the Dog**, Malcolm Hayes returns to the role of John Silence, a role he would reprise in two further radio plays, *Secret Worship* and **The Empty Sleeve**.

A NEW YEAR GHOST STORY

Reading | Radio | 15 mins

TX: 31/12/1927, 2LO London, 5XX Daventry

NIGHT OF THE WOLF

Drama | Radio | 90 mins

TX: 26/12/1978, Radio 4

American horror legend Vincent Price made a number of appearances on BBC Radio in the 1970s, including as the host of a horror anthology series bearing his name, *The Price of Fear*. In 1975 Price appeared alongside his wife, Coral Browne, in a feature-length play that feels now, and must have seemed then, as if it is channelling at least a little of the old Hammer Horror spirit. Originally broadcast in August, the play was presented as a Boxing Day entertainment a few years later.

Price plays Mathew Deacon, a father in search of a wayward son about whom he has become very concerned. His search leads him into the depths of the Cambridgeshire fenland, and into the mystery surrounding the sinister Northcott family.

Victor Pemberton's play has many things in its favour, most obviously its lead actors, and resists certain obvious temptations in its telling of a werewolf story. However, I think it's fair to say that it is somewhat let down by a werewolf that does not so much snarl as grunt like a pig. The werewolf does not have a lot in the way of dialogue, of course, so this downside does not weigh too heavily on the play, even if it stands out when it arrives.

A new production of The Night of the Wolf was produced by Fantom Films in 2010, starring Fenella Fielding in the Coral Browne role, and is still commercially available.

NIGHTMARE THE BIRTH OF HORROR

Documentary | TV | 4 x 60 mins

TX: 17/12/1996, BBC1   (1. Frankenstein)
      18/12/1996, BBC1   (2. Dracula)
      02/01/1997, BBC1   (3. Dr. Jekyll & Mr. Hyde)
      09/01/1997, BBC1   (4. The Hound of the Baskervilles)

In late 1996, the BBC unveiled their 'Nightmare' season, the central feature of which was a four-part documentary series **Nightmare: The Birth of Horror**, written and presented by Christopher Frayling.

Each episode looked at the creation of one of English literature's most influential horror stories, the works that influenced the authors of these books, and the long-term influence of each novel.

The series was oddly structured, with the first two episodes crunched together on consecutive nights a few days ahead of Christmas, and with the third and fourth episodes bringing up the rear well into January.

Nonetheless, Frayling's documentary was very good, and sadly it has not been made commercially available – though there was an attractively-illustrated tie-in book published by the BBC.

Each episode of **Nightmare: The Birth of Horror** was supported by repeat broadcasts of a number of horror films appropriate to each episode. This selection included another two-part broadcast of

Frankenstein: The True Story, Hammer's *Countess Dracula*, the 1941 *Jekyll & Hyde* starring Spencer Tracy, and the Basil Rathbone *Hound of the Baskervilles*.

NOT ONE RETURNS TO TELL (1937)

Drama | Radio | 40 mins

TX: 24/12/1937, Regional Programme Northern Ireland
    16/12/1948, BBC Home Service Northern Ireland

This 'Ghostly Adventure by Denis Johnston' is probably the most interesting of the ghost stories to be found in the early days of British broadcasting, not least for the way that it anticipated a legendary television ghost story by several decades.

Ghostwatch was broadcast on BBC television as a Halloween 'treat' in 1992; although it was unambiguously announced as part of the BBCs regular drama strand *Screen One*, it used the now-familiar conceit of pretending to be a live television documentary. Real, familiar television presenters fronted the programme, supposedly broadcasting from the nation's most haunted house, and legend has it that large numbers of viewers not only took it for live television, but believed the increasingly dark and sinister events on the television screen were really happening.

Ghostwatch subsequently attracted a lot of complaints, and it was even alleged that the programme had helped to precipitate a man's suicide. As a result, it's never been repeated, and its name is a byword for hoaxing an audience into believing in something scary.

So, it's fascinating to discover that the BBC Christmas schedules of 1937 included **Not One Returns to Tell**, a ghost story that was presented as if it were a live outside broadcast from a reputedly haunted castle.

This was broadcast months before Orson Welles's live coverage of the Martian invasion, and fifty-five years before *Ghostwatch*. There's no reason to suppose Orson Welles could have heard the broadcast (and in fact, he always cited Ronald Knox's 1926 *Broadcasting the Barricades* as his direct inspiration), but nonetheless he *was* friends with the writer, Irish dramatist Denis Johnston, whom he had known since the early 1930s.

Nor is there any indication that listeners were panicked into stampeding through the streets or writing to their MPs complaining of the beastly irresponsibility of the BBC. The Radio Times entry clearly describes the programme as being in imitation of a live outside broadcast (though it was recorded indoors at Broadcasting House in London), and throws in the disclaimer that 'if the listener is at all prone to nervousness, he or she is strongly advised not to listen'.

Very much like *Ghostwatch* years later, the broadcast made use of well-known broadcasting personalities playing themselves; the programme claimed to be coming from the derelict O'Cahan's Castle on the Ulster Coast, and from The Nine Glens Hotel, where it is said a young woman hanged herself on Christmas Eve more than a century before. 'Local superstition' has it that the girl's spectre sometimes manifests and any who accept the gifts she offers will die soon after.

In a further similarity to *Ghostwatch*, the programme begins in a jovial fashion with time given over to banter among the company and also to the recounting of ghostly events said to have taken place there in the past. A female scientist is present with scientific equipment to provide rational analysis of any strange events that occur – not that anybody present thinks that they will. Since it's a ghost story, something *does* happen of course.

There was a second broadcast of the play ten years later; it's known that the original was recorded, rather than broadcast live, so it's a reasonable assumption that the 1948 broadcast was a repeat rather than a new production.

Needless to say, there are no surviving recordings of either broadcast, and in fact the script was lost until 2014. In 2017 an Irish theatre group, the Wireless Mystery Theatre collaborated with the BBC to produce a new version of Johnston's play, recorded in front of a live audience. Sadly, while this was broadcast in three parts on **BBC Radio Ulster**, a wider audience has yet to have a chance to hear it.

NOT ONE RETURNS TO TELL (2017)

Drama | Radio | 3 x ?? mins

TX: 19/12/2017 – 21/12/2017, BBC Radio Ulster

The script to Dennis Johnston innovative radio play **Not One Returns to Tell** was lost at some point after its 1937 broadcast, but it resurfaced 77 years later, in the archives of Trinity College, Dublin.

The script was rediscovered by Reggie Chamberlain-King, and as part of The Wireless Mystery Theatre, he eventually succeeded in mounting a new production of the play, recorded in collaboration with the BBC. Like the original version it was recorded at Broadcasting House in London, though this time it had a live audience, and unlike the original it was then broadcast in three episodes as part of Radio Ulster's *The Arts Show*.

Sadly, the play has yet to be granted a wider audience, which seems a terrible shame – it would surely be a perfect addition to the Christmas Eve schedule on Radio 4 Extra, and would be of particular interest to fans of Christmas Ghost Stories.

NUMBER 13 (2006)

Drama | TV | 40 mins

TX: 22/12/2006, BBC4
      23/12/2006, BBC4
      18/12/2007, BBC4
      24/12/2008, BBC4
      31/12/2011, BBC4
      24/12/2017, BBC4

Richard Fell's second (and, all too soon, final) **M.R. James** adaptation returns to the familiar ground of an academic plagued by nocturnal disturbances in a guest house. If the predicament is reminiscent of Parkin's in **Whistle and I'll Come to You**, however, the story itself – and the climax – is not.

The Number 13 of the title is effectively a 'ghost room', adjacent to Number 12, in which the protagonist Professor Anderson is staying. Troubled in the night by the sounds he hears coming from the room next door, he is compelled to investigate.

Arguably less effective than the previous year's **A View from a Hill**, **Number 13** still manages to excite in its climactic sequences, even if it feels a little lacklustre up to that point.

The cast is excellent, including David Burke - returning after his appearance in the previous play - and also his son, Tom Burke, during the early days of his career (he could also be seen in BBC1s adaptation of Dracula that same year). Greg Wise plays Professor Anderson, and Paul Freeman rounds out the cast as a cathedral archivist.

THE OCCUPANT OF THE ROOM

Reading | Radio | 25 mins

TX: 25/12/1949, BBC Home Service
     29/12/1949, BBC Home Service

An Englishman holidaying in the alps is granted the use of a hotel room that is unexpectedly available after its previous occupant had suddenly disappeared. This story by Algernon Blackwood was read by the author himself.

OF THIS AND THAT BUT MAINLY ABOUT GHOSTS

Talk | Radio | 15 mins (?)

TX: 23/12/1952, BBC Home Service Northern Ireland

A talk by James Mageean

OH, WHISTLE AND I'LL COME TO YOU

Drama | Radio | 30 mins

TX: 24/12/1963, BBC Home Service
25/12/2015, Radio 4 Extra
31/12/2017, Radio 4 Extra
01/01/2023, Radio 4 Extra

While Jonathan Miller's **Whistle and I'll Come to You** is thought of as the 'original' Ghost Story for Christmas, and yet wasn't actually broadcast *at* Christmas for many years, an earlier BBC adaptation of the same M.R. James story, also starring Sir Michael Hordern, was broadcast on Christmas Eve in 1963.

Michael and Mollie Hardwick's more conventional take on the story goes some way to underlining the individuality of Miller's adaptation if you are inclined to compare them. Hordern's radio version of Parkins bears little comparison with the eccentric, inward, isolated version of the character that we encounter on television.

Not that it's necessary to compare them, of course. This radio play may not have the singular vision and icy chill of Miller's television adaptation, but it's nonetheless solid, and fills half an hour on Christmas Eve in exactly the manner intended.

OPEN BOOK – M.R. JAMES

Documentary | Radio | 30 mins

TX: 25/12/2005, Radio 4
29/12/2005, Radio 4 (extended repeat)

Kate Mosse (author of *The Mistletoe Bride & Other Haunting Tales*) discusses the ghost stories of **M.R. James** with biographer Richard Holmes, author Julie Myerson and poet and novelist Tobias Hill.

A PATTERN OF ROSES

Drama | Radio | 65 mins

TX: 29/12/1983, Channel 4
31/12/1984, Channel 4
30/12/1985, Channel 4

More of a tale of the past haunting the present than of ghosts per se, **A Pattern of Roses** nonetheless shares a number of key story elements with the previous year's **Ghost in the Water**; both are about young people who uncover a tragedy that played out long ago, and which threatens to repeat itself in the present day. Both dramas are also based upon children's novels, albeit the young protagonists in K.M. Peyton's **A Pattern of Roses** are a few years older than those in Edward Chitham's **Ghost in the Water**, at the very edge of adulthood. However, despite these core similarities the two stories also diverge significantly.

Raising the film's profile in the annals of the televisual ghost story category, **A Pattern of Roses** is directed by Lawrence Gordon Clark, who wrings all the eeriness out of the landscape that he can, but is perhaps unable to conjure anything truly sinister.

Nonetheless, Helena Bonham Carter (making her debut here, aged only sixteen) manages to bring a heartlessness and cruelty to her character that makes her memorably monstrous beyond any supernatural presence in the story; the themes of class and of young lives and youthful potential ended tragically and too soon do manage to deliver a resonance that makes the story worthwhile.

THE PERIWIG MAKER

Animation | TV | 15 mins

TX: 26/12/2004, BBC4

Subtle, dark and disturbing, this animated short film, made in Germany in 1999, draws inspiration from Daniel Defoe's *A Journal of the Plague Year*.

It depicts a wig maker who is confined to his home during the 1665 plague outbreak in London. Through his window he is able to observe the tragic events outside as they unfold – but he is never able to intervene.

In particular he watches, powerless, as a child is orphaned and her mother's corpse taken away. The child soon develops plague symptoms herself – her fate is sealed, and the wig-maker can only watch; but the helpless girl will not let him forget her...

THE PHANTOM OF THE OPERA (2007)

Drama| Radio | 4 x 30 mins

TX: 29/12/2007 – 01/01/2008, BBC7
     30/11/2008 – 21/12/2008, BBC7 (weekly)
     29/12/2009 – 01/01/2010, BBC7
     25/12/2012 – 28/12/2012, Radio 4 Extra

Big Finish is best-known as a company that produces Doctor Who-related audio dramas, but within its enormous catalogue it also has a range of adaptations of classic literature. Personally, I'm extremely fond of the production that launched this range – **The Phantom of the Opera**.

Writer and director Barnaby Edwards demonstrates an evident love for the Gaston Leroux novel in his adaptation, which may well be the most book-accurate dramatization of the story ever produced, right down to the selections of music on the soundtrack.

The cast is excellent; Peter Guinness is a smoothly sinister Phantom, Anna Massey an authoritative Madame Giry, and Helen Goldwyn's ability as both actress and singer make her an ideal Christine.

Alexander Siddig is also memorable as 'The Persian', a character from the book who was present in the Lon Chaney film but is almost invariably expunged from other adaptations.

The dramatization was quickly picked up by BBC7 and broadcast in an episodic format. Though it was repeated several times, it was evidently considered particularly suitable for the Christmas schedules.

The Phantom of the Opera (2007) hasn't been repeated on the BBC in some time, but it is still commercially available as a download from the Big Finish website.

THE PHANTOM OF THE OPERA: BEHIND THE MASK

Documentary | TV | 60 mins

TX: 26/12/2006, BBC2

I suppose if vengeful, rotting carcasses pursuing self-involved academics can be considered intrinsically Christmassy, it's not necessarily so unreasonable to wrap some tinsel around a stage musical centred on what is, after all, a particularly horrible instance of sexual harassment in the workplace.

Gaston Leroux's story of a physically unattractive composer obsessed with a young singer exerted an inexplicable appeal for Andrew Lloyd Webber, and as the write-up for this documentary asserts with alarming plausibility, the musical that resulted from this fascination became "arguably the most commercially successful work of art ever produced".

Why a documentary about it (boasting the cooperation of all the major players) deserved to be a prime-time feature of BBC2's Boxing Day schedule remains a mystery to me, but I didn't mind since I actually rather like *The Phantom of the Opera*, and it is considered a horror story, after all.

Mind you, Boxing Day does seem to be an unofficial Phantom of the Opera Day at the BBC, to judge by *The Phantom Phenomenon* (2011), and *Celebrating 35 Years of Phantom of the Opera* (2021), two Radio 2 documentaries covering much the same ground as **Behind the Mask.**

THE PICTURE OF DORIAN GRAY

Drama | Radio | 2 x 60 mins

TX: 18/12/1999 – 25/12/1999, BBC World Service

Dorian Gray has come to be surprisingly ubiquitous in audio but this particular interpretation of the story is automatically worth a listen on account of Ian McDiarmid's drily charismatic performance as Lord Henry. He gets the best lines, after all.

Jamie Glover's dark tones also make for an excellent Dorian, and Steven Pacey is a particularly well-chosen Basil Hallward. Of course, there can be no revelation of the painting in all of its moral decay to compare with that of the 1945 film – but given that, perhaps radio has the advantage of having to fall back on Oscar Wilde's potent original words to describe the most visual moment in the story.

PLAYING WITH DRACULA

Drama | Radio | 45 mins

TX: 21/12/1994, Radio 4

An entertaining murder mystery about an amateur drama group which specialises in horror productions.

The newest member of their company, Byron Redgrave, seems somewhat over-enthusiastic in his performance as a vampire, and predictably enough the group is soon being killed off. They are, apparently, at the mercy of a real-life vampire who has come amongst them. Who could it be? And is the answer as obvious as it seems?

Most of the characters in this drama have names openly derived from the characters in Bram Stoker's novel – for example, Lucy Western and Arthur Renfield - but despite this lack of subtlety the drama remains straight-faced, allowing the audience to appreciate the humorous tone without it directly intruding into the story.

A PLEASING TERROR - THE LIFE & GHOSTS OF M.R. JAMES

Documentary | TV | 50 mins

TX: 22/12/1995, Channel 4

Bill Wallis presents this documentary about M.R. James; the long list of contributors includes Ruth Rendell, Jonathan Miller, and his majesty Christopher Lee.

Although largely forgotten, this documentary was included as an extra on Network DVD's release of the 1979 adaptation of *Casting the Runes*.

THE PRICE OF FEAR (1978)

Drama | Radio | 5 x 30 mins

TX: 17/12/1973 - 21/12/1973, BBC Radio 2

The much-missed Vincent Price recorded a number of programmes for BBC radio throughout the 1970s; his distinctive tones certainly work well on radio, and they were put to ideal use when they made him the host of an anthology series that bore his name - **The Price of Fear**.

Although rather similar to the earlier Appointment With Fear (presented by Valentine Dyall, The Man in Black), it did have a not-so-subtle difference in that every week Price himself was an active participant in the drama; always an observer of events, but nonetheless involved.

Each story would be the tale of a friend, an acquaintance, or a chap Price met on the train during a long journey. On first acquaintance I found the device slightly irritating but I soon lost my discomfort with it. The idea of Price being so well acquainted with so many people who meet grisly fates is a charming absurdity that suits a show bearing his name – though to be clear, Price is an appropriately urbane narrator, and each tale is taken seriously.

Originally broadcast on the BBC World Service, the first series of five episodes was given its UK debut when Radio 2 broadcast them nightly, Monday-to-Friday in the week leading up to Christmas.

This is a pretty strong run of episodes, too, with stories from names like Bram Stoker and Roald Dahl. My personal favourite is *The Man Who Hated Scenes*, which guest-stars Peter Cushing as a gentle old man who shares a story of his own personal hell...

- *Remains to be Seen*, by Jack Ritchie
- *William and Mary*, by Roald Dahl
- *Cat's Cradle*, by Bram Stoker (based on the short story *The Squaw*)
- *So Cold, So Pale, So Fair*, by Charles Birkin
- *The Man Who Hated Scenes*, by Robert Arthur

QUATERMASS AND THE PIT

Drama | Radio | 6 x 35 mins

TX: 22/12/1958 – 26/01/1959, BBC Television

All of Nigel Kneale's **Quatermass** science fiction serials are heavily Gothic in tone, dealing with themes of possession and madness, bodily decay and murder, encounters with the alien and incomprehensible. However, the horror genre is most explicitly evoked by the third series, **Quatermass and the Pit** (sometimes overlooked, the titular use of 'Pit' alludes to an old name for Hell, establishing the presence of demons in this story from the outset).

Like a good many horror stories, **Pit** begins with an archaeological find – albeit an inadvertent one resulting from excavation in central London. What appear to be human remains and an unexploded bomb are quickly discovered to be ancient hominid remnants, and... an ancient metal structure that can only be of alien origin.

Moreover, the drama is very much about a haunting, especially in the earlier episodes, as the long history of phantasms and unsettling occurrences in the area around the excavation comes to light.

Even with André Morell's Professor Quatermass present to rationally untangle the various alarming phenomena that drive the story, it is a tale of hauntings, ghosts and goblins, and ancient evil. Quatermass theorises that our myths of the devil derive from alien creatures that have interfered with our development as a species – but there is a sense that in so doing he may in fact be confirming the existence of the devil rather than explaining it into non-existence.

Kneale later returned to this ambiguity in **The Stone Tape**, wherein any rational explanations of the ghostly phenomena ultimately achieve nothing more than the removal of a layer of veneer, revealing something significantly more horrible below.

I suspect few people today think of **Quatermass and the Pit** as having anything to do with Christmas – nonetheless, its first episode was broadcast just before Christmas. This seems very apt, given that the earlier episodes of the serial are the ones most concerned with hauntings and phantasms.

It's also interesting to note that when the Hammer film adaptation of **Pit** was premiered on BBC2 in 1973, it was shown late on Christmas night, clashing with **Lost Hearts** on BBC1, and in almost exactly the same slot as **The Stone Tape**, shown the previous year.

REBECCA (1976 & 1989)

Drama | Radio | 90 mins (1976), 90 mins (1989)

TX: 25/12/1976, Radio 4
27/12/1989, Radio 4
22/12/2018, Radio 4 Extra (repeat of the 1989 version)

Usually regarded as a suspense thriller, **Rebecca** is also a strongly Gothic story, with an easily recognisable debt to the fairy tale of Bluebeard. Moreover, there is also a sense in which Daphne du Maurier's most famous novel is, at its heart, the story of a haunting.

Every character in the novel lives in Rebecca's shadow in one way or another, long after her death. Her husband Max, the housekeeper Mrs Danvers, and most of all the heroine – 'the second Mrs de Winter' – who goes unnamed throughout, while the novel in which she is the lead character bears the name of the dead woman she has replaced.

Rebecca's absence – Rebecca's presence by her own absence – is what fills and drives this story, and so for both heroine and reader alike, Rebecca's presence is felt at every turn. It's psychological rather than supernatural, but it's still very much a ghost story.

Among the many radio and television adaptations of **Rebecca**, BBC Radio produced two that were given particular prominence in the Christmas schedules.

Both versions have solid casts, but Cynthia Pugh's 1976 *Saturday Night Theatre* adaptation has a trio of leads that would please any fan of 1960s British horror films: Richard Pasco as Maxim de Winter, Jane Asher as the young heroine, and the stellar presence of Flora Robson as the ominous Mrs Danvers.

The 1989 version, dramatized by Brian Miller, is also very good and stars Janet Maw as the heroine, with Christopher Cazenove, appropriately suave as Maxim.

THE RED ROOM (1977)

Reading | Radio | 15 mins

TX: 28/12/1977, Radio 4

Gabriel Woolf reads H.G. Wells's tale of a sceptical man who chooses to spend the night in a haunted room.

THE RED ROOM (2000)

Drama | Radio | 9 x 15 mins

TX: 18/12/2000 – 29/12/2000, Radio 4

The Woman's Hour Serial (and its later incarnation, *15 Minute Drama*) returned quite often to the idea of broadcasting supernatural stories at Christmas, but **The Red Room** remains the high watermark of the strand's contribution to the tradition. Over nine weekdays before and after Christmas, listeners were given adaptations of ten classic ghost stories, including an inevitable M.R. James tale.

However, the stories were presented within an intriguing framing narrative; a young woman is introduced to a mysterious man at a Christmas Party. He is a well-known teller of uncanny tales, Hugh Geoffrey Wallace (Ciaran Hinds), and she is Cicily Fairfield (Lia Williams), a journalist who recently gave Wallace's work a very scathing review.

Each is intrigued by the other, and soon they are fencing over various intellectual propositions, not least the existence of ghosts. Tales are traded, each supporting the teller's argument, and after the fifth tale, Hugh invites Cicily to visit him at his home in the country. He says that it is haunted, that she may witness a haunting for herself in one of the bedrooms there.

When Cicily arrives at Hugh's home they trade tales a little further before, finally, the ninth tale must be told and she goes with Hugh to the Red Room, to see if she can so easily dismiss the existence of ghosts when she witnesses what it is that waits there...

It's very unusual to find a 'portmanteau' of this kind where the framing device is probably the strongest of the tales being told, but writer Robin Brooks assembled and presented this collection with shrewdness. The title of the series refers to a ghost story by H.G. Wells in which a sceptic decides to spend the night in a supposedly haunted room - but in fact Cicily identifies herself as the real-life journalist Rebecca West (Cicily Fairfield was West's real name). The implication is clear, that the adversary whose haunted bedroom she is so willing to explore is a fictionalised version of H.G. Wells. Apt that Wells should be a character in his own story.

In reality Wells asked to meet West after she made some sharply critical observations about him in print, and she did indeed go to his home – and they subsequently became lovers. The fact that Wallace is not *exactly* Wells, however, adds a little something to the tale. This man is mysterious, and while Cicily might find him attractive, we might wonder if she is entirely wise to go so boldly into his territory.

The Red Room deploys these ambiguities beautifully, helping to lift the series above a good many other comparable collections of ghost stories.

The stories adapted for the nine episodes were as follows

- *Eveline's Visitant*, by Mary Braddon
- *Mr Tallent's Ghost*, by Mary Webb
- *Casting the Runes*, by M.R. James
- *The Spectre Bridegroom*, by Washington Irving
- *Count Magnus*, by M.R. James
- *The Buick Saloon*, by Ann Bridge
- *Jerry Bundler*, by W.W. Jacobs
- *The Bodysnatcher*, by Robert Louis Stevenson
- *The Tarn*, by Hugh Walpole

THE RIME OF THE ANCIENT MARINER

Reading | Radio | 30 mins

TX: 25/12/2006, Radio 4
     30/12/2006, Radio 4
     22/12/2019, Radio 4 Extra

Sir Ian McKellen reads Samuel Taylor Coleridge's gothic poem of awkward social experiences at weddings and the surprisingly dramatic consequences of random cruelty to animals, scheduled for 2.15 in the afternoon on Christmas Day. All the better to help the nation prepare themselves for the Queen's speech at 3pm.

SALEM'S LOT

Drama | Radio | 7 x 30 mins

TX: 15/12/1994 – 26/01/1995, Radio 4

Three years after BBC Radio 4 had broadcast a serialisation of *Dracula* at Christmas, the channel adapted another major vampire novel in the same format, and it was once again broadcast from mid-December, giving it the same sense of Christmas 'occasion' as **Dracula (1991)** had enjoyed.

Though cut from American cloth, King's treatment of the vampire story does contain recognisable echoes of Bram Stoker's: **Salem's Lot** also tells of a mysterious stranger come out of the Old World, and seeking to establish himself amidst the urban modernity of the West. However, where his antecedent felt that mighty London was the place to be, Kurt Barlow settles for Smalltown USA, a quieter place within which to extend his influence.

Salem's Lot necessarily makes some changes to the narrative from the book, and I dare say some of the American voices are less convincing than others – though there are several genuine US actors in the cast. Stuart Milligan plays the troubled author Ben Mears, but he's probably best known as Adam Klaus, the deeply sordid and disreputable magician from **Jonathan Creek** - nonetheless, he's a veteran actor with an extensive Cv in all media.

The role of head vampire Barlow is taken up by Doug Bradley, who certainly has an excellent voice and gives a great performance - I think it's probably arguable that his voice doesn't match the physical appearance of Barlow that we have described to us in episode 7, but this hardly matters. Bradley, best known for playing the Pinhead Cenobyte in the Hellraiser films, has a voice that can be made to sound uniquely abrasive and threatening, and all of his scenes are memorable.

SCARRA ROCK

Drama | Radio | 20 mins

TX: 26/12/1945, BBC Home Service

"a ghost story for Boxing Night" by Hilton Brown and read by John Laurie. Part of the regular *Wednesday Story* strand.

Sadly no other information is available - however, Hilton Brown did edit a number of short story anthologies for the BBC, including *Break For Fiction: Stories Broadcast by the BBC* and *Wednesday Stories Again.* It's entirely possible that **Scarra Rock** appears in one of these collections, but I'm not in a position to spend fifty quid on an old book to find out.

SCHALCKEN THE PAINTER

Drama | TV | 70 mins

TX: 23/12/1979, BBC1
      23/12/1981, BBC2
      28/12/1988, BBC2
      22/12/2022, BBC4

Leslie Megahey's beautiful, languorous adaptation of the Sheridan Le Fanu short story runs for over an hour, surely far longer than is required by the tale being told (it's literally quicker to read the original story than to watch the film); however, this is the primary indication that the drama does not merely seek to relate a narrative.

A product of the *Omnibus* arts documentary strand, the choice of a story centred on a real-life 17th century Dutch painter allows for an exploration of the world, the images, and the techniques of the artists of that time and place. Some scenes recreate images from Schalcken's own work, and Schalcken's repute as a master at reproducing the effect of candlelight in his paintings is reflected in the atmosphere and imagery of the film.

Nonetheless, while the film moves at a slow and careful pace, making limited use of dialogue, it is still a compelling piece, and the story itself is one of the more queasy and disturbing examples of its kind - at least in respect of its implications.

It tells us of the youth of Godfried Schalcken, when he was apprentice to Gottfried Dou. Dou's niece Rose becomes Schalcken's lover, but he does nothing to save Rose from being traded away in marriage to the mysterious and alarming Vanderhausen, an uncanny suitor who appears without preface or explanation, offering Dou a substantial payment in gold. Rose begs Schalcken to run away with her, but he does not, and Rose is married – and then she and her new husband disappear entirely without trace.

Later, Rose returns, begging for Schalcken's help once again, and once again he fails her; she disappears as suddenly as she had arrived. Years after that, quite unexpectedly, Schalcken sees Rose again – and this time he discovers the truth of the fate to which he has helped consign her.

The climax steps over a line that Le Fanu was clearly not prepared to go beyond, yet what it shows us feels devastatingly true to what Le Fanu did *not* show us. In his story, Schalcken faints away at the moment of revelation; Megahey does not spare the wretch – or us - in his telling of the story, and its horrible implications are laid entirely bare.

SCHALKEN THE PAINTER

Reading | Radio | 2 x 30 mins

TX: 25/12/2010, BBC7
14/12/2013 - 21/12/2013, Radio 4 Extra

In the early days of BBC7, a number of stories were adapted as unabridged readings for the channel's daily fantasy/science fiction slot *The Seventh Dimension*. It's tempting to assume that some of them were chosen because of an interest in other, then-unavailable adaptations, and at the time this was certainly true of **Schalken the Painter**. The TV adaptation seemed far away from commercial availability back then.

This two-part reading was performed by Ian McDiarmid, whose dry tones were well-suited to the tale and its very particular kind of sinister implication. Though the television adaptation of the story, **Schalcken the Painter**, is of course now commercially available – but it's still worth revisiting the original story.

SCREENSHOT: CHRISTMAS TV TRADITIONS

Documentary | Radio | 45 mins

TX: 23/12/2022, Radio 4

On the same evening that Mark Gatiss's TV adaptation of **Count Magnus** was first broadcast, Radio 4s regular programme about film and television turned its attention to two seasonal TV traditions – romcoms and ghost stories.

Presenter Ellen E. Jones led the discussion of the romance, while horror enthusiast Mark Kermode inevitably presented the section on 'ghost stories for Christmas', including a similarly inevitable interview with Mark Gatiss. Of particular note, the feature included an interview with composer Rachel Portman, in which she discussed her eerie score to the classic 1989 version of **The Woman in Black.**

THE SECOND PAN BOOK OF HORROR STORIES

Drama | Radio | 5 x 15 mins

TX: 13/12/2020 – 17/12/2020, Radio 4 Extra

The legendary Pan Book of Horror anthology series ran for thirty years, with the final volume appearing in 1989. A quarter of a century later, playwright Anita Sullivan selected five tales from the 1960 *Second Pan*

Book of Horror Stories, and adapted them as short dramas for BBC radio, broadcast in 2015.

Despite the sense of modernity that the Pan Book of Horror label tends to conjure (in terms of horror content), this selection of stories tends toward the classic. Sadly, there were no further excursions by Radio 4 into the Pan Horror back catalogue.

The stories chosen were:

- *The Vertical Ladder*, by William Sansom
- *The Speciality of the House*, by Stanley Ellin
- *The Black Cat*, by Edgar Allan Poe
- *Leiningen Versus the Ants*, by Carl Stephenson
- *The Judge's House*, by Bram Stoker

SEE HEAR! A Christmas Carol & The Monkey's Paw

Drama | TV | 50 mins & 30 mins

TX: 20/12/1987, BBC1 (A Christmas Carol)
     20/12/1988, BBC2 (A Christmas Carol)
     31/12/1989, BBC2 (The Monkey's Paw)

Still running today, **See Hear!** is the BBCs monthly magazine programme for deaf and hard-of-hearing viewers. In the late 1980s, the show experimented with a couple of short dramas performed entirely in British Sign Language.

The first of these was an adaptation of **A Christmas Carol**, and the second an adaptation of W.W. Jacobs' horror story **The Monkey's Paw**.

This second play was first broadcast in March, but was repeated as a Christmas special at the end of the year.

SHAKESPEARE, THE ANIMATED TALES: HAMLET

Drama | Radio | 30 mins

TX: 07/12/1992, BBC2
       13/12/1992, BBC2

Running to two series and twelve episodes, **Shakespeare: The Animated Tales** was the result of cooperation between Welsh television channel S4C and the Russian animation studio Soyuzmultifilm. Each episode of the series was a half-hour abridgement of a Shakespeare play, specially written by the author Leon Garfield; each script was recorded in audio by casts of experienced and acclaimed stage actors, and then the Russian animators worked to provide the visuals in a variety of different styles chosen to suit the different stories.

The resulting series of animations were highly acclaimed and proved a commercial success. While each episode has something to recommend it, the final episode of the first series, **Hamlet**, is particularly striking for the excellence of its haunting visuals. Painted on glass, the animated images are dreamlike and ghostly, elegantly expressing the mood of this tale of a haunted prince. The story may lack for cackling witches and blasted heaths, but this vision of Elsinore could easily double for Gormenghast.

Broadcast in the early evening on a Monday and then repeated as part of children's television the following Sunday morning, **Hamlet** closed the first series of **The Animated Tales** at a suitably dark time of the year.

Christmas was certainly tangible to those of us who were being encouraged to watch the show by our English teachers, and we were more than halfway through the advent calendar by the time Hamlet breathed his last...

THE SHEPHERD

Few ghost stories for Christmas can claim the seasonal turf quite so thoroughly as Frederick Forsyth's **The Shepherd**; written as a Christmas present for the author's first wife, it was also written on Christmas day, and set on Christmas Eve. Furthermore, in Canada it has literally become a Christmas tradition all of its own (more of that in a moment).

The story itself eschews the more obvious ghost story trappings and is about an RAF pilot flying home on Christmas Eve; despite the novelty of this setting, the basic mechanism of the story will be familiar to enthusiasts of the genre. Nonetheless, it's considered a classic, and it's a certainly a well-told and atmospheric story.

Two adaptations of this story have been broadcast at Christmas on British radio over the years, but it has a special place in Canada, where a reading is broadcast every year.

Back in 1979 the Christmas Eve edition of the Canadian Broadcasting Corporation's radio news programme, *As It Happens* included a reading of **The Shepherd** by veteran broadcaster Alan Maitland. The story proved so popular that it has been repeated on Christmas Eve nearly every year since. It's well worth a listen, and is easy to find online - including on the CBC website, where you can listen to it for free.

There is no such tradition in the UK, but the story has still made its presence felt:

The Shepherd (1983)
Reading | Radio | 3 x 20 mins
TX: 19/12/1983 – 21/12/1983, Radio 4

A three-part reading performed by Tony Britton.

The Shepherd (2016)
Reading | Radio | 25 mins
TX: 24/12/2016, Radio 3

Between the Ears is a regular programme on BBC Radio 3 that presents experimental features of a great breadth and variety. The episode broadcast on Christmas Eve 2016 was an impressive adaptation of Forsyth's **The Shepherd**.

Luke Thompson's reading of the story is complimented by authentic recordings of the Vampire aircraft described in the story, and by a capella music from an amateur choir, The Saint Martin Singers.

This extremely polished production went on to win awards, and is still available to hear on the BBC website at the time of writing.

SHERLOCK: THE ABOMINABLE BRIDE

Drama | TV | 90 mins

TX: 01/01/2016, BBC1

I fully expect that one day a fan somewhere will recreate the famous Sidney Paget illustration of Holmes and Watson in a train carriage, substituting Steven Moffat and Mark Gatiss in their place. This fan art would depict the moment when, on a train journey to Cardiff, the two men first conceived of a television incarnation of Sherlock Holmes that would quickly become a huge international success, making household names of Benedict Cumberbatch and Martin Freeman

Bridging the third and fourth series of **Sherlock**, this Christmas special changed the format, propelling Sherlock and John backwards, out of their contemporary setting and into the comfortingly traditional environs of the Victorian era.

While they were at it, the writers took the opportunity to make a little bit of a Ghost Story for Christmas out of this latest adventure for Holmes and Watson – after all, Sherlock Holmes stories have always leant toward the gothic, and the Victorian setting must have made the idea all the more tempting.

Why are our familiar, modern characters suddenly running around the world of Holmes Classic? I couldn't have cared less, personally; the characters are more than strong enough to survive the sudden change, and I was happy to just take it as a one-off.

Sadly, the drama feels obliged to explain the anomaly as more than a Christmas entertainment – it keeps the episode in continuity with the others, and goes to some effort to make it relevant to the ongoing narrative.

In my opinion this (as well as a flood of other ideas, good and bad) gets in the way of the actual story, and it threatens to become that rare case when an artist is killed by his darlings.

Nonetheless, there is still fun to be had here, and the phantasmal elements of the story are handled well. The antagonist of the title is a young woman, Emelia Ricoletti, who has apparently gone violently mad. She is seen to shoot herself in the head, and is buried – yet later she reappears, a ghostly figure with eyes full of fury. Has she risen from her own death to wreak vengeance on the living? Sherlock Holmes must find out the truth.

SHERLOCK HOLMES & THE CASE OF THE SILK STOCKING

Drama | TV | 100 mins

TX: 26/12/2004, BBC1
    26/12/2005, BBC4
    26/12/2008, BBC2

Ostensibly a follow-up to the BBCs 2002 adaptation of **The Hound of the Baskervilles**, this new case for the great detective had little directly in common with the previous adventure – the writer Allan Cubitt returned to script this new case, but in front of the camera only Ian Hart returned.

Richard Roxborough's ambiguous and not-at-all-comforting Holmes gave way to Rupert Everett's somewhat more louche take on the character; Danny Webb was replaced as Inspector Lestrade by a pre-*Midsomer Murders* Neil Dudgeon.

This drama remains thickly, darkly atmospheric and is quite compelling, though there is a modernity in evidence that can feel quite dissonant at times, whether one is a particular Holmes enthusiast or not. It is not so great a push to have Holmes in pursuit of a serial killer, but had I been wearing a monocle I'm quite sure it would have dropped out during the scene where Holmes and Watson's psychoanalyst fiancée discuss Krafft-

Ebing's sexual derangements. One does not expect to hear the word 'coprophilia' mentioned on Boxing Day, though I confess it's possible that I've simply led a rather dull life.

In any case, the cast is typically excellent with supporting roles for Jonathan Hyde, Perdita Weeks, Julian Wadham, and most notably Helen McCrory as Watson's unapologetically modern wife-to-be. There is also an appearance by a young Michael Fassbender, who in retrospect brings a certain prestige to the story.

SHERLOCK HOLMES VS DRACULA

Drama | Radio | 90 mins

TX: 19/12/1981, Radio 4
     21/12/1981, Radio 4

Responding to Bram Stoker's famous account, Doctor Watson sets the record straight by relating the previously-ignored contribution to the fight against a certain Transylvanian villain made by his friend Sherlock Holmes.

Loren D. Estleman's entertaining tale, adapted for radio by Glyn Dearman, is carefully assembled. It allows Holmes and Watson to investigate, and participate in, events familiar from Stoker's novel without contradicting or changing anything in the original story. I suspect that a more radical take may have been a little more fruitful – as it stands, it feels rather as if Holmes and Watson are mostly just peering into events from the sidelines – but clearly the intention was for this play to be fun, and it doesn't fail in that respect.

Additionally, this play functions as a follow-up to Dearman's 1975 radio adaptation of **Dracula**, with David March and Aubrey Woods reprising their earlier roles as the Count and Van Helsing respectively.

Holmes and Watson are played here by John Moffatt and Timothy West, with Nicholas Courtney as Inspector Lestrade.

A SHORT HISTORY OF VAMPIRES

Reading | Radio | 4 x 15 mins

TX: 15/12/2013 - 05/01/2014, Radio 4 Extra (weekly)
      21/12/2015 - 24/12/2015, Radio 4 Extra

Natalie Haynes presents a selection of vampire tales, specially read for BBC7, first broadcast in 2011.

- *Dracula's Guest*, by Bram Stoker; read by Dan Stevens
- *Hero Dust*, by Kristine Kathryn Rusch; read by David Horovitch
- *Israbel*, by Tanith Lee; read by Mark Bonnar and Claire Harry
- *Quid Pro Quo*, by Tanya Huff; read by Genevieve Adam

A SHORT SEASON OF GHOST FILMS

Film | TV | various

TX: 17/12/1994 - 02/01/1995, BBC2

For some reason, BBC2 didn't give this particular film season an actual title, and so it was just referred to as '...a short season of ghost films...'.

Although these were films intended for the cinema, their assembly as a season during the Christmas holidays was very much a TV event, hence I include it here. It's an interesting programme ranging from light dramas that could be shown in the daytime to Robert Wise's famously nerve-shredding *The Haunting*, shown last thing at night on Christmas Day.

There was also Stephen Weeks' odd, neglected *Ghost Story* from 1974, and Orson Welles' short film *Return to Glennascaul*, also known simply as *Orson Welles's Ghost Story* – though in the BBC schedules it seems to have been known by both titles.

- *Blithe Spirit* (TX: 17/11/1994)
- *The Haunting* (1963) (TX: 25/11/1994)
- *House on Haunted Hill* (TX: 27/11/1994)
- *Ghost Story* (1974) (TX: 28/11/1994)
- *Orson Welles's Ghost Story: Return to Glennascaul* (TX: 30/11/1994)
- *Portrait of Jennie* (TX: 30/11/1994)
- *The Return of Peter Grimm* (TX: 02/11/1995)
- *The Curse of the Cat People* (TX: 02/11/1995)

A SHORT HISTORY OF GOTHIC

Reading | Radio | 4 x 15 mins

TX: 12/12/2009 - 31/12/2009, BBC7 (weekly)

A series of four short tales read as part of *The Seventh Dimension* on BBC7, and subsequently Radio 4 Extra.

- *Markheim*, by R.L. Stevenson; read by Hugh Bonneville
- *Clytie*, by Eudora Welty; read by Barbara Barnes
- *The Lady of the House of Love*, by Angela Carter; read by Indira Varma
- *Those Who Seek Forgiveness*, by Laurell K Hamilton; read by Melanie Bond

SHORT SHOCKS: FOUR WEIRD TALES

Reading| Radio | 4 x 30 mins

TX: 28/12/1988 - 31/12/1988, Radio 4

Four tales, read by Anna Massey.

- *The Cat Jumps*, by Elizabeth Bowen
- *The Theft*, by Jennifer Johnston
- *Spirit of the House*, by Fay Weldon
- *The Old Man*, by Daphne Du Maurier

THE SIGNALMAN

The Staplehurst rail crash occurred on the 9th June 1865; as a result of this derailment there were fifty casualties among the passengers, ten of whom died.

Famously, Charles Dickens was a passenger on this train. He was not injured, and helped tend to those who were; in some cases, he watched them die. He was greatly traumatised by this experience – in the opinion of his son, he had not fully recovered from it at the time of his death, five years later - and in 1866, Dickens published a short story entitled **The Signalman**.

The Signalman of the title is an isolated, troubled man happened upon by an unnamed traveller. The Traveller is intrigued by the Signalman, who seems to be a much more complicated and layered personality than his work would require. He is also evidently troubled by something, and eventually he is persuaded to share those troubles with his guest.

It is not merely that the Signalman often sees a spectre at the mouth of the tunnel near to his hut - but that he has learned that every appearance of the spectre is a prelude to some tragedy or disaster. Having learned the pattern, he can now anticipate a terrible event, but he has no way of knowing what it will be, or how to warn others that it is coming...

The Signalman (1940)
Drama | Radio | 15 mins
TX: 25/12/1940, Forces Programme

Prolific stage and film actor Anthony Holles takes the title role in this adaptation of the Charles Dickens tale.

The Signalman had already been adapted for BBC radio in January 1936 (as *Mystery in the Cutting*) but this was the first time an adaptation had been broadcast at Christmas in the UK.

The Signalman (1956)
Reading | TV | 30 mins
TX: 25/12/1956, ITV

Only part of his long and eventful career, Emlyn Williams was known for his successful one-man show, first performed in 1951, in which he recreated the famous public readings of Charles Dickens.

A few years later Williams recorded a reading of **The Signalman**, performed while in character as Charles Dickens (and in full costume), for broadcast on ITV at Christmas in 1956.

The Signalman (1958)
Reading | Radio | 15 mins
TX: 25/12/1958, BBC Home Service
  20/12/2009, **BBC7**
  22/12/2013, Radio 4 Extra
  26/12/2014, Radio 4 Extra
  11/12/2016, Radio 4 Extra

Only two years after Emlyn Williams had performed **The Signalman** on television, he could be heard reading the tale on Christmas Day once again, this time on BBC radio.

Williams had recorded several readings from Dickens for Gramophone Records, and the BBC Home Service broadcast these readings as *Emlyn Williams in Readings from Dickens*, a 55-minute programme on Christmas night. This comprised *Mr Chops* (from 'Christmas Stories'), *Mr Bob Sawyer Gives a Bachelor Party* (from 'The Pickwick Papers', and to finish, **The Signalman**.

Though *Mr Chops* hasn't particularly troubled the airwaves since, Williams's reading of **The Signalman** has returned several times over the years, most recently in 2016.

Though abridged, it's a beautifully-performed reading, with a delicate and haunting quality, and is well worth seeking out. It's still commercially available, and is likely to resurface on BBC radio again in future.

The Signalman (1976)
Drama | TV | 38 mins
TX: 22/12/1976, BBC1
     25/12/1982, BBC1
     21/12/1991, BBC2
     25/12/2003, BBC4
     18/12/2005, BBC4
     20/12/2007, BBC4
     23/12/2008, BBC4
     24/12/2017, BBC4
     06/12/2021, BBC4

The sixth entry in the BBCs **A Ghost Story for Christmas** strand, **The Signalman** was the first of the plays (and so far, it is the only one) to adapt a literary source other than the tales of M.R. James.

This did not make for diminishing returns, however, and Lawrence Gordon Clark's **The Signalman** is among the best-regarded in the series. Indeed, it's proved to be perhaps the most ubiquitous ghost story in the history of British television – the dates listed above are only the Christmas broadcasts, it has been shown on at least four more occasions at other times of the year, and it will very likely be seen again in the television schedules of Christmases yet to come.

If this ubiquity is seen as a commendation of the play's merits, that seems fair enough. It's a very polished piece of work, with excellent atmosphere, a superb central performance by Denholm Eliot, and several genuinely alarming moments. The adaptation is by Andrew Davies, whose career would subsequently bristle with literary adaptations of this kind, most notably *Pride & Prejudice* and *Bleak House*.

It seems that viewers in 1976 were a little spoiled for ghost stories – those who had enjoyed **The Signalman** could watch **Leaving Lily** on BBC2 the following evening. They would make for an intriguing partnership since both are, in their different ways, about hauntings-as-harbingers.

The Signalman (2022)
Drama | Radio | 60 mins
TX: 25/12/2022, Radio 4

BBC Radio has long observed the ghostly traditions of Christmas, but this new adaptation of the Dickens classic returned the ghost story to a more central position in the radio schedules. No mere 15-minute reading slotted in somewhere as a concession, this one-hour drama was scheduled for Christmas Day afternoon, directly after the King's Speech.

The story was adapted on this occasion by Jonathan Holloway, whose deeply dark and uncomfortable 1997 adaptation of another railway ghost story, **The Affair at Grover Station**, demonstrated considerable skill in developing a brief tale into something more sustained and brooding.

This radio play – which one tentatively hopes could be the start of a new sequence of such tales on the radio – boasts Samuel West in the role of The Signalman, and James Purefoy as The Visitor.

Holloway takes time to sharpen some of the story's edges, however. It seems both reasonable and logical to identify the Visitor as Charles Dickens himself, as Holloway does, but that idea carries its own significant implications. After all, by the time he wrote the story Dickens was a man painfully familiar with disaster and tragedy on the railways. We might wonder, in fact, how much of Dickens is there in the agonised figure of The Signalman himself, haunted by past tragedies despite the certain knowledge and the kind reassurance of others that he could not have changed those terrible events.

Furthermore, these experiences are used to make the relationship between Visitor and Signalman somewhat less comforting and supportive than is usually the case. Who could expect the survivor of a railway crash to be calmly indulgent of a railway official with a safety-critical job who claims to be seeing ghosts and hearing the ringing of bells when there are no bells ringing?

Jonathan Holloway polishes a new gleam into the razor's edge of this familiar story, making this new version of the story more than worthwhile.

SIX GHOST STORIES

Reading| Radio | 6 x 15 mins

TX: 11/12/1985 - 18/12/1985, Radio 4

David McAlister reads a selection of supernatural stories by H.G. Wells.

- *The Moth*
- *The Story of the Late Mr Elvesham*
- *The Temptation of Harringay*
- *The Inexperienced Ghost*
- *The Stolen Body*

- *The Door in the Wall*

A SLIP IN TIME

Documentary | Radio | 40 mins

TX: 24/12/1972, Radio 4

A documentary programme collecting various true-life accounts of 'strange experiences', including ghosts and hauntings.

THE SMALL HAND

See: **SUSAN HILL'S GHOST STORY**

SOME GHOST STORIES

Reading | Radio | 20 mins

TX: 28/12/1926, 5PY Plymouth

Read by Miss Margaret Kennedy

SOME GHOST STORIES OF THE MIDLANDS

Reading | Radio | 15 mins

TX: 22/12/1923, 5IT Birmingham

Read by John Hingeley.

SOMETHING FROM THE DARK

Reading | Radio | 3 x 30 mins

TX: 24/12/1972 - 26/12/1972, BBC Radio London

Three macabre stories read for Christmas by Tom Vernon.

- *The Upper Berth,* by F. Marion Crawford
- *The Canterville Ghost,* by Oscar Wilde
- *The Cask of Amontillado,* by Edgar Allan Poe

SOMEONE LIKE YOU

Drama | Radio | 5 x 15 mins

TX: 21/12/2009 - 25/12/2009, Radio 4

Just as the television series *Tales of the Unexpected* took its name from a collection of short stories by Roald Dahl, when Radio 4 tackled the writer's macabre tales they opted to use the title of another of his short story collections, **Someone Like You**.

Stephen Sheridan's adroit adaptations were narrated sternly by Charles Dance (in a voice that has all the sheen found in polished mahogany, with all of its softness and sympathy), and the casts included radio stalwarts like Andrew Sachs, Kerry Shale, Lorelei King, and David Collings.

Broadcast as part of the Christmas schedules, three further series of Dahl adaptations followed, under the names **Kiss Kiss**, *Served with a Twist*, and **A Little Twist of Dahl** – though these were not all scheduled for Christmas broadcast.

The five stories featured in this series were:

- *The Man from the South*
- *Skin*
- *Lamb to the Slaughter*
- *Dip in the Pool*
- *Nunc Dimitis*

THE SPECKLED BAND

One of the best-regarded Sherlock Holmes short stories, **The Speckled Band** is something of a precursor to **The Hound of the Baskervilles** in its strongly gothic mood. It has a highly memorable villain, Dr Grimesby Roylott – whose machinations prompted Holmes to famously observe "when a doctor goes wrong, he is the first of criminals" – and builds to an exciting climax, when Holmes confronts a deadly killer lurking in the dark

Holmes's client on this occasion is a young woman named Helen Stoner, who believes her life to be in danger. Two years earlier, in very strange circumstances, Helen's sister died at home managing to utter the cryptic words 'the speckled band' in her final moments. Helen now believes that she will soon meet the same fate, and so turns to Sherlock Holmes for help.

Among the many adaptations of this story, the following were broadcast at Christmas:

The Speckled Band (1948)
Drama | Radio | 30 mins
TX: 27/12/1948, BBC Home Service

Howard Marion-Crawford and Finlay Currie star as Sherlock Holmes and Doctor Watson in this adaptation by John Dickson Carr. Grizelda Hervey appears as Helen Stoner, and Francis de Wolff as Dr Roylott.

The Speckled Band (1962)
Drama | Radio | 30 mins
TX: 27/12/1962, BBC Home Service
      23/12/1963, Light Programme

This episode of the radio series Sherlock Holmes starred Carleton Hobbs and Norman Shelley as Holmes and Watson, and was adapted by Michael Hardwick.

Carleton Hobbs has the unique distinction of having played not only Sherlock Holmes, but also Doctor Watson *and* Sir Arthur Conan Doyle – though he is certainly best-known for playing the great detective on BBC radio, appearing in more than seventy episodes throughout the 1950s and 1960s.

The Speckled Band (1984)
Drama | TV | 55 mins
TX: 13/12/2003, BBC2

ITVs classic 1980s Sherlock Holmes series starring Jeremy Brett made an unexpected return to British television in the early 2000s, this time on the BBC. The lavishly-filmed dramas were a perfect choice for broadcast on the darkening Saturday afternoons of Winter, and the initial run of repeats extended into December before breaking for Christmas. The final episode before the break was this especially memorable and atmospheric adaptation from May 1984.

Rosalyn Landor stars as Helen Stoner, and the veteran film actor Jeremy Kemp makes for a particularly wild and savage-looking Doctor Roylott. David Burke provides gallant assistance as Doctor Watson, and the final confrontation between detective and killer is chillingly staged.

SPINE CHILLERS

Reading | TV | x 15 mins

TX: 17/11/1980 - 19/12/1980, BBC1

One of several darker variations on the much-loved BBC Children's format *Jackanory*, it's debatable as to whether or not **Spine Chillers** can be considered Christmas television per se. It began its run in the middle of November and was broadcast on most weekday afternoons for a month; by the time Christmas was in view, ghost stories at teatime would hardly have seemed like a novelty of the season.

Certainly, **Spine Chillers** ensured that there was a run of ghostly tales as Christmas got ever-closer, including several by M.R. James (read by Michael Bryant, quite recovered from his brush with Abbot Thomas).

These episodes consisted entirely of the narrator delivering the story to camera, but unlike *Jackanory* the narrators were all dressed 'in character' and typically performed the stories while seated in highly atmospheric locations. For example, Michael Bryant sits dressed to the nines in a leather armchair before a fire, or at a desk with a wall of old books looming behind him; perhaps most memorably, Freddie Jones's reading of *The Stolen Bacillus* is performed from what looks like an Edwardian laboratory, with a human skull sitting ominously on a nearby table, keeping an eye on the viewers.

For the sake of interest, the complete run **of Spine Chillers** is as follows:

- *The Red Room*, by H. G. Wells; told by Freddie Jones (TX: 17/11/1980)
- *The Yellow Cat*, by Michael Joseph; told by John Woodvine (TX: 18/11/1980)
- *The Music on the Hill*, by Saki; told by Jonathan Pryce (TX: 20/11/1980)
- *The Mezzotint*, by M. R. James; told by Michael Bryant (TX: 21/11/1980)
- *The Treasure in the Forest*, by H. G. Wells; told by Freddie Jones (TX: 24/11/1980)
- *The Devil's Ape*, by Barnard Stacey; told by John Woodvine (TX: 25/11/1980)
- *Sredni Vashtar*, by Saki; told by Jonathan Pryce (TX: 27/11/1980)
- *A School Story*, by M. R. James; told by Michael Bryant (TX: 28/11/1980)
- *In the Avu Observatory*, by H. G. Wells; told by Freddie Jones (TX: 01/12/1980)

- *The Running Companion*, by Philippa Pearce; told by John Woodvine (TX: 02/12/1980)
- *The Penance*, by Saki; told by Jonathan Pryce (TX: 04/12/1980)
- *The Well*, by W. W. Jacobs; told by Michael Bryant (TX: 05/12/1980)
- *The Stolen Bacillus*, by H. G. Wells; told by Freddie Jones (TX: 08/12/1980)
- *A Sin of Omission*, by Ronald Chetwynd-Hayes; told by John Woodvine (TX: 09/12/1980)
- *Gabriel-Ernest*, by Saki; told by Jonathan Pryce (TX: 11/12/1980)
- *The Diary of Mr Poynter*, by M. R. James; told by Michael Bryant (TX: 12/12/1980)
- *The Flowering of the Strange Orchid*, by H. G. Wells; told by Freddie Jones (TX: 15/12/1980)
- *More Spinned Against*, by John Wyndham; told by John Woodvine (TX: 16/12/1980)
- *The Hounds of Fate*, by Saki; told by Jonathan Pryce (TX: 18/12/1980)
- *Jerry Bundler*, by W. W. Jacobs; told by Michael Bryant (TX: 19/12/1980)

A SPIRIT ELOPEMENT

Reading | Radio | 15 mins

TX: 22/12/1994, Radio4

"An amiable ghost story by Clotilde Graves."

THE SPIRIT OF THE HOUSE

Drama | Radio | 30 mins

TX: 24/12/2017, Radio 4 Extra
     26/12/2020, Radio 4 Extra

A slight, but well-told ghost story from May 1988, about a couple who, having lived abroad for thirty years, return to England to live out a quiet retirement in an idyllic home. However, their Christmas Eve is disturbed by unexplained sounds, disembodied voices...

Old-fashioned in tone - appropriately, perhaps - this is still a very effective ghost tale that seems to coincidentally echo one or two of Nigel Kneale's plays. For some reason this Christmas-set ghost story was initially broadcast in springtime, but Radio 4 Extra corrected this when it repeated the play nearly thirty years later.

STAG

Drama | TV | 3 x 60 mins

TX: 30/12/2016, BBC2

Vicious yet funny, Stag is a highly effective television comedy imitation of a certain subset of modern horror films with a clear line of descent from Deliverance; a group of civilised (read: feckless and/or hapless) people find themselves lost in the wilds and hunted by a heavily armed lunatic with a fetish for horrendous death traps.

Writers Jim Field Smith and George Kay take this scenario and play it for laughs as much as for horror, and while **Stag** never compromises its horror/thriller status, it's consistently very, very funny. The humour also has a rich, satirical edge that rises out of its premise and arguably comments upon the very kind of horror film that it so effectively imitates.

The protagonist is Ian, an unassuming geography teacher played by Jim Howick (now best known as Pat Butcher in the comedy series **Ghosts**), who has joined a stag party unannounced. The bride-to-be has instructed Ian - her brother - to join the party and ensure that her husband-to-be, Johnners (Stephen Campbell-Moore), comes through the weekend in one piece.

Ian quickly discovers that the group is entirely composed of obnoxious, hateful bullies who do not take well to a new face and are happy to let him know it. However, the group's deer-stalking weekend in the Highlands of Scotland quickly goes seriously awry when they discover that they are themselves being hunted by a sinister camouflage-clad figure. Ian's promise to keep Johnners in one piece has become considerably more high-stakes than he had expected.

One of **Stag**'s real successes is the way that it plausibly presents a group of horrible people, seemingly bound together by competitiveness and macho posturing, but who all (when free from the group and the pressures of conformity) are vulnerable, likeable and even loveable. Part of the horror, then, comes from the way that all of these people are trapped by the group of which they are part, yet they all of them help to build that prison in the first place.

Not that this is the main plot point, of course. The main plot point is the terrifying murderer traversing the highlands on a quad-bike, dedicated to slaughtering the entire group...

Although originally broadcast in three weekly episodes in early 2016, the whole series was repeated on a single night during the Christmas period later that year.

THE STALLS OF BARCHESTER

Drama | TV | 45 mins

TX: 24/12/1971, BBC1
     25/12/1995, BBC2
     25/12/2004, BBC4
     17/12/2007, BBC4
     31/10/2021, BBC4

Lawrence Gordon Clark's first **M.R. James** adaptation is still many people's favourite; restrained yet ominous, it quietly tells the story of an ambitious cleric who contrives the 'accidental' death of his archdeacon through the sly removal of a stair-rod.

The new archdeacon (Robert Hardy, excellent) soon learns, however, that his act has invoked a curse; the mysterious carvings in the archdeacon's stall in the cathedral have a sinister provenance, and bring their own kind of nemesis upon the wicked.

A model of restraint, Stalls very much set the standard for what was to follow under the Ghost Story for Christmas banner.

STIGMA

Drama | TV | 30 mins

TX: 28/12/1977, BBC1
     13/12/2021, BBC4

A significant departure for **A Ghost Story for Christmas, Stigma** was the first of the plays to completely eschew literary adaptation, and the first to have a contemporary setting. Overlooked for many years, perhaps because of its dissonance with the plays that preceded it, Clive Exton's story has an efficient cruelty to it. It depicts a curse, but offers little or no direct explanation for the events.

This is not to say that there is a mystery to the cause and effect. At a lonely house situated within a stone circle, workmen have been called in to pull up an ancient stone embedded in the front garden. The family that has recently moved in want it removed, and at the moment that it parts from the clutching earth, there is a violent disturbance of the air. Something has clearly been released, and it would be a poor observer who didn't understand that any wickedness that now unfolds has come from this moment.

Katherine (Kate Binchy), who had been observing the work, is dazed and wanders indoors. Later, she finds that she has started to bleed through unbroken skin – the stigmata implied by the title. There is a note of real, relatable distress in the story here, and it develops into a family catastrophe in a way that feels as personal as it does inevitable. Despite the supernatural forces driving events, there is a tangible sense of modernity that make the events seem all too real, adding considerably to the emotional weight of the piece.

It's been suggested that **Stigma** is overlooked because it is simply not a ghost story, but I think it's more a matter of tonal difference. It's as much of a ghost story as **The Ash Tree**, to which it has some similarities.

However, there is something essentially comfortable about a costume drama in which supernatural evil pops up to punish somebody who was a bit too clever for their own good. To have one's partner, or parent – or one's self – suddenly struck by an unexpected or unexplainable illness is, I suggest, all too recognisable as a feature of real life for many people for it to ever be comfortable viewing.

Stigma is positively brutal in that respect, so perhaps it's disregarded not so much because it isn't a ghost story, as because it's an unsparingly 'real' story – despite the supernatural trappings. I defy anybody to chuckle and knock back a brandy at the end of it, whatever the time of year.

A STING IN THE TALE: NO CONFERRING

Drama | Radio | 30 mins

TX: 25/12/2003, Radio 4
27/12/2020, Radio 4X

A Sting in the Tale was a series of five 'chilling' half-hour plays, the series title rather telegraphing the intent to pull off a twist at the end. Although most of the series was broadcast throughout January, the first episode was both broadcast at Christmas, and *set* at Christmas.

As the title implies, this story ties itself in to the eternal BBC institution University Challenge; in 1983 one college's team has a 'bonding week' over Christmas in an isolated cottage... because nothing ever went wrong in an isolated cottage. I'm sure you'll understand why I'm not going to go into any further detail, given the drama's clear intention of having a surprising ending...

THE STONE TAPE

Drama | TV | 90 mins

TX: 25/12/1972, BBC2

The title of this play by Nigel Kneale refers to the idea that hauntings are the result of past events having been 'recorded' in the structure of the buildings in which they occurred; that certain events are somehow retained within stones and can later be witnessed by those who are sensitive to these psychic residues. While this idea pre-dates Kneale's play, it is now widely referred to as the 'Stone Tape Theory'.

Kneale's tale is significantly more insidious than this might imply, however. In it, a group of research scientists take up residence in the basement of a very old building. The place is reputed to be haunted, and soon enough the scientists have themselves witnessed the screaming spectre of a young woman apparently falling to her death from the top of a flight of steps that have long since been removed from the basement.

Believing this to be evidence of a revolutionary new recording medium, the group bring all of their analytical capabilities to bear but in so doing they apparently 'wipe' the recording, dispelling the ghost. They do not realise, however, that by wiping the recording of the terrified girl, they have exposed an earlier recording of something less explainable and far less passive...

The play has themes of misogyny and emotional abuse of the same kind that resurface in *Buddyboy* (an episode of Kneale's later series *Beasts)*, and Kneale returned to the central idea of a haunting being a recording in his adaptation of Susan Hill's **The Woman in Black**. The question is at least raised by Kidd as to whether the screaming souls he hears drowning in the marsh are no more than recordings – though of course the other side of that coin, also raised in **The Stone Tape**, is that perhaps these recordings are *not* recordings, and instead of catching the impression of a terrible moment are in fact the terrible moment being repeated eternally, the screaming victims trapped forever. It's a thought that sits heavily upon the viewer when the end credits for **The Stone Tape** arrive.

A STORY FOR CHRISTMAS: THE VISITOR'S BOOK

Reading | TV | 15 mins

TX: 22/12/1974, BBC1

An occasional feature of BBC1's Christmas Day schedule in the early 1970s, **A Story for Christmas** featured John Slater rounding out the evening with a short story leading up to midnight. These were not always macabre in nature, but in 1974 the story was this ghostly tale by A.J. Alan, written for the radio, and originally broadcast at Christmas in 1927.

See also: **A.J. ALAN'S GHOST STORIES** and **THE VISITOR'S BOOK (1969)**

THE STORY OF THE GHOST STORY

Documentary | TV | 30 mins

TX: 18/12/2005, BBC4
    22/12/2005, BBC4
    23/12/2005, BBC4
    05/01/2006, BBC4
    22/12/2006, BBC4

A short documentary on the history of the ghost story, narrated by Michael Rosen and with contributions from names like Ramsey Campbell and Muriel Gray.

THE STRANGE CASE OF DR JEKYLL AND MR HYDE (1973)

Drama | TV | 120 mins

TX: 27/12/1973, BBC1

Produced by Dan Curtis, this adaptation of Jekyll & Hyde is one of his earliest gothic extravaganzas for television; he would later produce adaptations of Dorian Gray, Frankenstein, Dracula and The Turn of the Screw.

Through these adaptations Jack Palance earned the unusual distinction of having played both Dr. Jekyll and Count Dracula. Curtis's version of Dracula is somewhat truncated but still appreciated by many, not least for Palance's striking performance; his version of the character was seen to grieve over the loss of his bride years before Gary Oldman made it fashionable.

Palance is likewise credible as Mr Hyde in Curtis's 1968 adaptation of Stevenson's novel. It's no surprise that Palance can be menacing or frightening, but in particular he conveys a sense of seething, contained violence that makes his Hyde threatening from the first.

While the production is obviously studio-bound and on video-tape, it still manages to seem quite lavish, considering; the cast includes Denholm Elliot and Billie Whitelaw, both of whom bring their own assurances of quality to the proceedings; Duncan Lamont (the largely unsung supporting player in several Hammer films) also appears as a police sergeant.

Broadcast late at night, the BBC were kind enough to schedule this TV movie on the same day as an omnibus repeat of the Doctor Who story The Green Death, in which giant, fluorescent green maggots erupt from a Welsh coalmine to eat people's necks, so it was a pretty good day if you liked horror.

THE STRANGE CASE OF DR JEKYLL AND MR HYDE (1993)

Drama | Radio | 70 mins

TX: 27/12/1993, Radio 4

Robert Forrest's adaptation of Stevenson's novella is particularly memorable for a couple of significant changes to the story that nonetheless feel completely true to the source.

Firstly, it relocates the story to Stevenson's native Edinburgh; Stevenson's decision to set the story in London certainly makes sense, and as the 2009 documentary *Ian Rankin Investigates: Dr Jekyll & Mr Hyde* points out, Jekyll's house appears to have been modelled directly on the London home of Scottish anatomist William Hunter.

However, there are also reasons why Edinburgh seems like the natural home for the story, not least the sharp division between its old and new towns. Well brought-up young men like Stevenson might sometimes pass from the respectable limits of the New Town to engage in less respectable activities in the Old Town, crossing between two very different lives. Edinburgh is a city with two faces, and Jekyll and Hyde inhabit it with an ease and naturalness that requires no further explanation.

The play also introduces an entirely new character, a voice audible only to Jekyll and Hyde, and which accompanies him throughout his long descent. It would be a considerable spoiler to say more about this presence in the story, but it does ultimately lead to a satisfying, sickening, twist that is consistent with the story's themes as well as adding an extra dimension to them.

Originally broadcast as a Monday Play, the drama was repeated in early December the following year - but not as an early Christmas entertainment, rather as part of a season of programmes commemorating the centenary of R.L. Stevenson's death.

THE STRANGE CASE OF EDGAR ALLAN POE

Drama | Radio | 60 mins

TX: 25/12/1983, Radio 4
04/01/1989, Radio 4

Christopher Cook's 'Tale of Mystery and Imagination' is an investigation into the troubled life and mysterious death of Edgar Allan Poe, woven out of dramatic fiction and biographical fact.

Poe's own creation, the detective Auguste Dupin is presented here as a real-life friend of Poe, and he leads us into the strange tale of the man's life. The narrative includes readings from Poe's work (often juxtaposed with biographical episodes), and a judicious use of Debussy enhances the atmosphere considerably.

Kerry Shale leads the cast as Poe, and Dupin is played by John Moffat, who later became best known to radio listeners as Agatha Christie's detective Hercule Poirot.

STRANGE STORIES

Documentary | TV | 15 mins

TX: 28/12/1994, BBC1

A brief compilation of highlights from a trilogy of documentaries entitled *Strange Days*, which had been broadcast a week or so earlier, part of BBC2's 'Weird Night' on the 17th December.

Presumably scheduled as no more than space filler in a rather uninspiring evening schedule (stuck between *This Is Your Life* and *How Do They Do That?*), it nonetheless seems that fifteen minutes of interviews with people who had seen ghosts, had alien encounters, and been attacked by a leopard in the Gloucestershire countryside, was appropriate to the season. I'm rather sad I missed it.

STUDY ON 3 - THE HORROR STORY

Documentary | Radio | 4 x 60 mins

TX: 16/12/1971 - 06/01/1972, Radio 3

In this four-part documentary series, psychologist Dr Christopher Evans examined four different aspects of the horror story, each episode featuring guests and a reading of an appropriate horror story.

Of particular note, the second episode was devoted to the subject of Ghosts, and was broadcast the day before **The Stalls of Barchester** was first shown on BBC television.

Evidently doubling as a sort of warm-up act to the TV play, the episode featured guest Jonathan Miller with whom Evans discussed M.R. James and the characteristics of a successful ghost story. Complimenting this, the episode also included a reading of *Lost Hearts*, performed by Bernard Cribbins.

The episodes were as follows:

1: Gothic Tales (TX: 16/12/1971)
Christopher Lee and Alex Hamilton discuss Dracula, Frankenstein and other gothic characters.
Story: *The Gable Window*, by H.P. Lovecraft; read by Edward Bishop

2: Ghosts (TX: 23/12/1971)
Dr. Evans and Jonathan Miller discuss M.R. James, and ask what makes a successful ghost story.
Story: *Lost Hearts*, by M.R. James; read by Bernard Cribbins

3: Psychohorror (TX: 30/12/1971)
J.G. Ballard talks psychological horror and Jekyll & Hyde with Dr Evans.
Story: *The Gioconda of the Twilight Noon*, by J.G. Ballard; read by Hugh Dickson

4: Shock (TX: 6/1/1972
Alex Hamilton returns to talk Kipling, Dahl, and his own fiction...
Story: *The Attic Express*, by Alex Hamilton; read by Ronald Herdman

SUSAN HILL'S GHOST STORY
The Small Hand

Drama | TV | 115 mins

TX: 26/12/2019, Channel 5

A dealer in rare books discovers a gated garden that has been left to go wild; when he steps into the grounds, he feels a small hand pressing into his. A little while later he meets a strange woman who leads him to the abandoned house at the other end of the grounds. He buys the place, driven by some inner feeling he can't identify, and soon finds strange things beginning to occur around him...

The confident self-declaration of this adaptation as **Susan Hill's Ghost Story** rather gives the impression that it was intended to be the first of several such dramas. Susan Hill followed **The Woman in Black** with a number of other ghostly tales over the years, though none of them has come to be as celebrated as her first. Even so, a back-catalogue exists that would allow for further ghost story adaptations bearing the Hill name.

Whether that was the intention, or whether it was simply a marketing decision to play up the creative connection with **The Woman in Black**, **Susan Hill's Ghost Story** has so far proven to be just a one-off.

This is not altogether surprising as **A Small Hand** is a strikingly un-ghostly exercise in the main, building up to a phantom child seen in crisp, brightly-lit scenes with almost no atmosphere or any sense at all that we are witnessing a restless spirit.

There is a terrible absence of dread felt whenever this ghost is on screen. Even when he emerges, caked in the mud of the waters that drowned him, we are not reminded of Ann Clarke emerging from a pond anything like so much as we are the aftermath of a woodland scrap in an episode of *Grange Hill*.

All of this feels like a terrible shame as the cast is good, and boasts names like Douglas Henshall, Cal Macaninch, and even Adrian Rawlins. One has to wonder if Rawlings was cast in some sort of act of consecration, hoping that he might carry the spirit of **The Woman in Black** into this new drama... sadly neither he, nor any of the cast are able to do much beyond deliver their lines with conviction. Neve McIntosh comes close to saving things with her dark and unstable presence in the earlier parts of the drama, but she is not placed so centrally in the story that she can ever become the menacing lynchpin that it needed.

Upon its initial broadcast in 2019, this drama was immediately followed in the schedule by a broadcast of the 2012 film of *The Woman in Black*.

SWEET CHARIOT

Reading | Radio | 15 mins

TX: 28/12/1933, Regional Programme Western

"A Devonshire Ghost Story by Molly O'Fogerty Chapman"

Often the way with these older radio listings, there's little indication as to the actual plot of this story, but it did get this tantalising write-up in the Radio Times:

"If listeners like the thrill of a ghost story, they will turn out the light before they listen to this. There will be no blood-curdling screams, but they will find the effect very convincing all the same."

TAKE THE HIGH ROAD: MILLENIUM SPECIAL

Drama | TV | 2 x 50 mins

TX: 31/12/1999 - 01/01/2000, STV

Once a daily presence throughout the United Kingdom, the Scottish soap opera **Take the High Road** had been dropped from most of the ITV regions by the close of the century. It clung on until 2003, but in 1999 the show still had enough vigour left in it to make a special two-part story to celebrate the new Millenium.

Though referred to as the **Millenium Special**, this story was entitled *Mr. Broon*, and was not set within the show's normal continuity. This somewhat liberated it to tell a story of pagan celebrations and possession by a mysterious entity. You don't get that in *Eastenders*, more's the pity.

TALES OF THE SUPERNATURAL (1980)

Reading | Radio | 5 x 15 mins

TX: 15/12/1980 - 19/12/1980, Radio 4

A selection of short readings of classic supernatural stories, broadcast late at night in the 'A Book at Bedtime' slot.

The stories were:

- *The Library Window*, by Mrs Oliphant, read by Eileen MacCallum
- *The Crown Derby Plate*, by Marjorie Bowen, read by Diana Olssen

- *Thurnley Abbey*, by Perceval Landon, read by Tom Fleming
- *Man-size in Marble*, by E. Nesbit, read by John Shedden
- *Oh, Whistle, and I'll Come to You, My Lad*, by M.R. James, read by Robert Trotter

TALES OF THE SUPERNATURAL (2016)

Reading | Radio| 5 x 15 mins

TX: 18/12/2017 – 22/12/2017, Radio 4 Extra

Five supernatural tales by Charles Dickens, read by Adrian Scarborough, first broadcast in 2016.

- *Trial for Murder*
- *Chips Bargains with the Devil*
- *The Signalman*
- *A Madman's Manuscript*
- *The Queer Chair*

TALES OF THE UNCANNY AND SUPERNATURAL

Reading | Radio| 4 x 30 mins

TX: 20/12/1971 – 23/12/1971, Radio 4

Algernon Blackwood returned to BBC Radio, with this selection of his stories performed over four nights before Christmas by Howieson Culff.

- *The Tradition* and *The Occupant of the Room*
- *The Deferred Appointment* and *Accessory Before the Fact*
- *The Empty Sleeve*
- *Running Wolf*

THE TEETH OF ABBOT THOMAS

Comedy | Radio | 30 mins

TX: 25/12/1987, Radio 4
     01/01/1988, Radio 4
     25/12/2010, BBC7

While **The Teeth of Abbot Thomas** has a style of humour that gives it a knockabout tone, it is also a very specific parody of M.R. James ghost stories (as if the title had not given that away), and is even framed as a tale told at the insistence of 'Uncle Monty' despite his family's general lack of enthusiasm. Plenty of straightforward absurdity makes the story accessible for those who are not intimately acquainted with James's entertainments, but there's also a lot to allow James enthusiasts to giggle knowingly to themselves.

In retrospect this play also feels rather similar to the third section of **The League of Gentleman Christmas Special**; perhaps Mark Gatiss would like to adapt it for television. Anyway, it was written by Stephen Sheridan, a writer with a good many radio credits to his name, especially in the comedy genre - but he also wrote **The House at World's End**, a supernatural tale in the manner of M.R. James (and in fact, *featuring* M.R. James).

TELLING TALES: JEREMY DYSON

Documentary | Radio | 60 mins

TX: 24/12/2019, Radio 4 Extra
     22/12/2020, Radio 4 Extra
     24/12/2022, Radio 4 Extra

The accomplished writer and member of the League of Gentlemen talks ghosts and strange tales; the programme includes readings of two of Dyson's own stories.

THINGS THAT GO BUMP IN THE NIGHT

Reading | Radio | ?? mins

TX: 28/12/1951, BBC Light Programme

Broadcast as an item on the daily Woman's Hour programme, this was a true-life ghost story recounted by the person who experienced it - the American actor and songwriter Jimmy Dyrenforth.

This was not Dyrenforth's first ghostly broadcast on BBC radio - his **The Voice of Michael Vane**, 'almost a ghost story', had been broadcast on a few times, premiering on the BBC Home Service on the 30th December 1941.

THE THIRTEENTH TALE

Drama | TV | 90 mins

TX: 30/12/2013, BBC2

Although labelled, quite reasonably, as a psychological drama, it's nonetheless telling that this drama was subsequently repeated at Hallowe'en. Psychological or not, this is very much a story about a haunting, and its gothic trappings are quite undisguised.

Based on the bestselling novel by Diane Setterfield, **The Thirteenth Tale** is anchored by a double-act of two Oscar-winning actresses, Vanessa Redgrave and Olivia Coleman (albeit Coleman was a few years away from her own Oscar win at the time). Redgrave plays successful novelist Vida Winter who, on her deathbed, summons biographer Margaret Lea (Coleman) to hear a hitherto-untold tale from her life. As the story progresses, Lea begins to wonder (as do we) exactly how dark a destination this tale has...

Subtle and sinister, **The Thirteenth Tale** never moves into the realm of the supernatural, but nor does it ever need to. Perhaps this is in itself instructive in respect of the essential nature of ghost stories; with or without resort to the supernatural this is a story of past traumas and a childhood overshadowed by secrets and unspeakable truths that can even now be imagined to hang in the air of an abandoned house, or released by the words of a woman preparing to leave the world.

THREE JAPANESE GOTHIC TALES

Drama | Radio | 90 mins

TX: 26/12/2004, Radio 3

Three stories from the pen of Izumi Kyoka, 'the Japanese Edgar Allan Poe', performed by a distinguished cast that includes Toby Jones, Lia Williams and Geoffrey Palmer.

The featured stories are:

- *The Holy Man of Mount Koya*
- *A Tale of Three Who One Day in Spring*
- *A Tale of Three Who Were Blind*

THREE STORIES

Reading | Radio | 30 mins

TX: 25/12/1939, BBC Home Service

Algernon Blackwood reads three of his stories of the supernatural, each of them with a Christmas theme.

The stories were:

- *Transition*
- *The Laughter of Courage*
- *A Boy and his Bag*

TO BUILD A FIRE

Drama | TV | 50 mins

TX: 26/12/1970, BBC2
     28/12/1971, BBC1

It will very likely seem out of place to include an adaptation of Jack London's short story here, but I'd argue that this tale is one of isolation and mortal fear. In it, London presents the natural world as implacable and all-powerful, and it is easy to find malevolence in the elements as they bear down upon a lonely, isolated protagonist. To me this feels essentially similar to the dark forces at work in stories like Maupassant's **The Inn**, and Galsworthy's *Timber*, for example.

To Build a Fire is certainly a dark tale either way, and perhaps because it is so much about the terrifying power that unyielding cold has over us when we are caught out in the wilds, it appeared in BBC Christmas schedules three times in the 1970s (Radio 4 also broadcast a reading of the story in December 1978).

Simple enough to relate, the story is of a man who sets off on a journey through the cold forests of the Yukon territory; he has ignored advice from those with more experience of the fearsome temperatures of a Canadian winter, and travels alone apart from a single husky dog. In this place, in these conditions, his ability to successfully make fire will determine whether he lives or whether he dies.

To Build a Fire was the work of David Cobham, a film-maker with an evident love for the natural world. His talent for portraying wilderness and wild creatures on film was displayed in wildlife documentaries, and in narrative films like *Tarka the Otter*. The classic children's fantasy TV series *The Secret World of Polly Flint* benefits enormously from his ability to capture the pastoral magic of the sedate rural world that the young heroine inhabits and explores.

Sadly, David Cobham passed away in 2018, but his YouTube channel remains as a testament to his work, and you can watch **To Build a Fire** there.

THE TRACTATE MIDDOTH

Drama | TV | 30 mins

TX: 25/12/2013, BBC2
    24/12/2017, BBC4

After his successful documentaries *A History of Horror* (2010) and *Horror Europa* (2012), the implacable Mark Gatiss was commissioned to produce a one-hour documentary about M.R. James for broadcast at Christmas. Exploiting the opportunity this presented, Gatiss managed to secure an additional commission for a short adaptation of an M.R. James tale to accompany the documentary.

If Gatiss's earlier **Crooked House** had been the fulfilment of a wish to make his own contribution to British TVs ghost story tradition (and Gatiss says as much in the DVD commentary), a chance to continue the classic **Ghost Story for Christmas** plays begun in the 1970s must have been the only way up. Broadcast directly before his documentary, **M.R. James: Ghost Writer**, Gatiss's adaptation of **The Tractate Middoth** initiated the most successful revival of the strand so far.

Gatiss makes his own changes to James's story (including updating it to a 1960s setting), and a streak of humour has been added – an element almost entirely absent from the Lawrence Gordon Clark adaptations, but not inconsistent with James's own storytelling.

An excellent cast includes Louise Jameson, Una Stubbs, Eleanor Bron, Sacha Dhawan, and John Castle as the dastardly Eldred – not to mention David Ryall as Doctor Rant. Ryall had worked with Gatiss previously on several projects, including Jeremy Dyson's adaptation of the unsettling Robert Aickman tale *The Cicerones*.

Even if its particular quirks made this new entry feel different to its 1970s antecedents in a way that was not true of **A View from a Hill**, the exercise is nonetheless homage at its heart. It was a few years before another play arrived courtesy of Mr Gatiss, but in the long view **The Tractate Middoth** can be seen as the point where **A Ghost Story for Christmas** became a tradition once again.

TRANSYLVANIA BABYLON

Documentary | TV | 30 mins

TX: 28/12/2006, BBC4
       29/12/2010, BBC4

BBC4's prolific documentary series Timeshift covered a wide variety of subjects, though always with an emphasis on social and cultural history. Naturally enough, **Transylvania Babylon** focussed on vampires, and the long tradition of storytelling surrounding them.

THE TREASURE OF ABBOT THOMAS (1974)

Drama | TV | 37 mins

TX: 23/12/1974, BBC1
       26/12/1983, BBC1
       24/12/1993, BBC2
       23/12/2004, BBC4
       19/12/2007, BBC4
       22/11/2021, BBC4

Having starred in **The Stone Tape** a couple of years earlier, Michael Bryant could be said to have been on familiar turf when he was cast as the Reverend Justin Somerton in **The Treasure of Abbot Thomas** – he was once again playing a rather highly-strung rationalist whose reaction when confronted with a haunting is to try and dismantle it.

In Justin's case he is a debunker of séances, however, a calmly rational man whose pride does not allow for the possibility of his being seen as anything less than a purely intellectual creature. Though he takes part in what is essentially an archaeological treasure hunt, he insists, with a delicate edge of hysteria, that for him it is an academic pursuit, that to be a mere treasure hunter would be undignified and shameful.

He is, as the introduction to an earlier play almost put it, denying forces within himself that he does not wish to acknowledge. When he and his friend have solved the final riddle, Justin contrives to go and find the treasure alone and by dead of night. It is not a good idea.

The latter parts of this drama are, for me, especially effective. After Justin's dreadful experience finding the treasure, Bryant depicts the man's breakdown not with histrionics but with an excessive calm. We are left with a number of unanswered questions by the close of the story, and its final moments are executed with wonderful precision. The final cut to the credits is, for me, an example of perfect timing from which later dramas might have learned.

TUESDAY CALL

Factual | Radio | 37 mins

TX: 21/12/1976, Radio 4 ('How 'Normal' is the Paranormal?')

18/12/1979, Radio 4 ('Ghosts')

Produced by the same unit as *Woman's Hour*, Tuesday Call was a phone-in programme that allowed listeners to express their own views on a given subject, or to ask for advice and information provided by guest experts present in the studio.

Tuesday Call ran for a long time – from 1973 to 1987, when it transformed into 'Call Nick Ross' – and on two occasions it chose supernatural themes for discussion at Christmas.

In 1976 the theme was **How 'Normal' is the Paranormal**, a broad heading which included ghosts. The experts on that occasion were educational consultant Tony Buzan and Professor John Taylor, a physicist who had become very interested in parapsychology after witnessing Uri Geller's wrathful effect on household cutlery. By 1980 Taylor had concluded that the paranormal phenomena that he had investigated were all scientifically explicable – but at the time of his appearance on Tuesday Call he had not yet reached this sceptical position on the subject.

In 1979 the theme was **Ghosts** specifically, with guests Anita Gregory (a psychologist and member of the Society for Psychical Research who had investigated The Enfield Poltergeist, amongst others) and the prominent

THE TURN OF THE SCREW

Henry James's 1898 novella is the epitome of a strongly psychological ghost story. Its heroine is certainly haunted, but it is another question entirely as to whether she is being haunted by ghosts, or by herself.

The story has been adapted many times, perhaps most famously as Jack Clayton's film *The Innocents* (which was, itself, presented by the BBC as a ghost story to close Christmas Eve in 1985) and it is easy to find its influence in other works, such as Amenábar's *The Others*.

The story has no overt connection to Christmas, nor was it written as a Christmas entertainment – yet it has often appeared in the Christmas schedules, perhaps because it is a celebrated and 'respectable' example of the ghost story form. Benjamin Britten also adapted the story as an opera, and this has made a couple of appearances in the schedules over the years too.

Adaptations broadcast on British TV and Radio include:

Benjamin Britten's The Turn of the Screw (1959)
Opera | TV | 2 x 50 mins
TX: Act One: 25/12/1959, Associated Rediffusion
 Act Two: 28/12/1959, Associated Rediffusion

The Turn of the Screw (1977)
Reading | Radio | 5 x 15 mins
TX: 26/12/1977 - 30/12/1977, Radio 4

Read by Anna Massey

Benjamin Britten's The Turn of the Screw (1982)
Opera | TV | 120 mins
TX: 25/12/1982, Channel 4

A handsome film adaptation of Britten's opera, with music conducted by Sir Colin Davis.

The Turn of the Screw (1993)
Drama | Radio | 90 mins
TX: 01/01/1993, Radio 4

Directed by Glyn Dearman

The Turn of the Screw (1999)
Drama | TV | 90 mins
TX: 26/12/1999, ITV

Another of ITV's sporadic contributions to the Christmas Ghost story tradition, and a fairly credible effort too. While it does boast the presence of Colin Firth (at this point just a few years after *Pride & Prejudice*, and therefore a hot property when it came to costume dramas), he is only in one scene – though perhaps it's necessary that he's memorable given the apparent impact on the story's heroine.

In any case, the governess is played on this occasion by Jodhi May, an actress who had already made a name for herself (having won the Cannes Best Actress award in 1988, aged only thirteen). She'd also made memorable appearances in Michael Mann's feature film *The Last of the Mohicans*, and in Peter Kosminski's highly acclaimed BBC drama *Warriors*.

It's no surprise, then, that May gives an excellent performance in **The Turn of the Screw**; she's supported well by another excellent actress who had become a familiar face in ITV drama at the time, Pam Ferris, here playing Mrs Grose. Given the arguably conflicting demands of a popular adaptation of a story that is in its purest interpretation, more of a psychological portrait than an actual ghost story, this version does very well. ITV drama had a solid track record at the time, and while it does not reach the heights of **The Woman in Black** from a decade earlier, nor does it waste anybody's time.

The Turn of the Screw (2009)
Drama | TV | 90 mins
TX: 30/12/2009, BBC1
　　03/01/2010, BBC1
　　24/12/2019, BBC4
　　24/12/2021, BBC4

Handsomely presented and well-acted, yet intermittently resorting to cliché and even to breaking its own well-crafted ambiguity, this adaptation of Henry James's novella came a decade after the previous British television adaptation. It works somewhat harder at creating an atmosphere, in a way that may (to some tastes) sometimes feel a bit overdone, and the story has been relocated to the 1920s. A framing narrative has also been added, wherein the governess recounts her experiences at Bly to Dan Stevens's kind Doctor Fisher.

However, despite the hard work in evidence by all concerned, the drama occasionally demonstrates a desire to kick against the subtlety that makes the story as interesting as it inherently is. Nonetheless, a cast that boasts Sue Johnston, Nicola Walker and Michelle Dockery certainly keeps the story in safe hands.

The Turn of the Screw (2018)
Drama | Radio | 60 mins
TX: 25/12/2021, Radio 4 Extra

Originally broadcast as part of the *Love Henry James* season of James adaptations on Radio 4 in October 2018.

TURN, TURN, TURN

Drama | Radio | 45 mins

TX: 27/12/2012, Radio 4 Extra

M.R. James (David March) relates a tale of witches and vengeance in this 1977 play by Sheila Hodgson. Over a period of years, Hodgson wrote a sequence of these plays, based on story ideas described by M.R. James in his essay *Stories I Have Tried to Write*.

TWO AMERICAN GHOST STORIES

Reading | Radio | 2 x 25 mins

TX: 24/12/1991 & 31/12/1991, Radio 3

A pair of classic short stories by noted American authors, broadcast on Christmas Eve and New Year's Eve respectively.

Ghost Guessed, by Scott Bradfield (read by Garrick Hagon), tells of the exploits of the assertive and chaotic doppelganger of a mild-mannered man.

Where Is Here, by Joyce Carol Oates (read by Colin Stinton) is the unsettling tale of a man who revisits his childhood home – though the exact nature of his visitation is open to question...

UNCANNY

BBC Radio's successful true-life mystery series *The Battersea Poltergeist*, presented by Danny Robins, led to this follow up series in which Robins looked at a different real-life account of bizarre or mysterious events in each episode. After a successful first series, a number of special episodes appeared, including two that were broadcast at Christmas 2022:

Uncanny: Christmas Special
Documentary | Radio | 30 mins
TX: 23/12/2022, Radio 4

Ghostly events disrupt a family Christmas, and the terrifying experience leaves a young boy with memories that will follow him into adulthood.

Uncanny Live with Mark Gatiss
Documentary | Radio | 50 mins
TX: 30/12/2022, Radio 4

Aside from his versions of Count Magnus and A Christmas Carol airing on television, Mark Gatiss also made several radio appearances over Christmas in 2022. This special episode of Uncanny feels rather like a direct follow-up to Christmas Day's **Hunting Ghosts with Gatiss and Coles**, with Gatiss this time partnered with Danny Robins for another leisurely chat about ghosts and a little bit of investigation of real-life paranormal events.

UNIVERSAL HORROR

Film Season | TV | 9 x Various

TX: 24/12/2000 – 02/01/2001, BBC2

For many years old horror films were a commonplace in the weekly schedules of UK television, usually located late on a Friday or a Saturday night. Today, the UKs highest-profile purveyor of nostalgia Talking Pictures TV has even instated a Friday Night slot for horror films in imitation of this old tradition.

This being the case, the showing of horror films at Christmas time was something largely without novelty or seasonal mood. , and therefore not worthy of inclusion here. However, in those days there were also *seasons* of films in the schedules, and on several occasions the BBC decided that the Christmas holiday was an ideal time to present a selection of horror films. The last of these came in the year 2000 when BBC2 hosted a week-long festival of classics from the catalogue of Universal studios; Karloff and Lugosi were abroad once again.

The season also included the excellent 90-minute documentary *Universal Horror*, the title of which explains its content, I feel. Also, while it was not announced as part of the season, Bill Condon's melancholy film about the final days of director James Whale, *Gods and Monsters*, was shown on New Year's Eve as a prelude to the penultimate Universal Horror of the season, Whale's *The Bride of Frankenstein*.

The films shown were:

- *Frankenstein* (1931, TX: 24/12/2000
- *The Mummy* (1932), TX: 26/12/2000
- *Universal Horror* (1998), TX: 28/12/2000

- *The Old Dark House* (1932), TX: 28/12/2000
- *The Black Cat* (1934), TX: 29/12/2000
- *The Invisible Man* (1933), TX: 30/12/2000
- *Gods and Monsters* (1998), TX: 31/12/2000
- *Bride of Frankenstein* (1935), TX: 31/12/2000
- *The Wolf Man* (1941), TX: 02/01/2001

THE UNSETTLED DUST: THE STRANGE STORIES OF ROBERT AICKMAN

Documentary | Radio | 30 mins

TX: 15/12/2011, Radio 4

While Robert Aickman's strange stories are widely appreciated by connoisseurs of the macabre, mass popularity still eludes them. In this documentary, writer and ghost story enthusiast Jeremy Dyson examines Aickman's work and speaks to fellow Aickman fans, including Mark Gatiss and Ramsey Campbell.

THE VAMPYR – A SOAP OPERA

Opera | TV | 5 x 25 mins

TX: 29/12/1992 – 02/01/1993, BBC2
   09/01/1993, BBC2 'Vampyromnibus' repeat.

Though never forgotten, John Polidori's short story *The Vampyre* has diminished in stature over time. These days it's the tale that also came out of the ghost story competition that produced Frankenstein; in its day it was a sensation, and the progenitor of a vampire craze in European culture.

One adaptation of the story came itself to be adapted by Heinrich Marschner into a two-act opera, entitled *Der Vampyr*. Marschner's opera was a success, and is still performed today; in 1992 it was adapted as a television serial for the BBC, and broadcast in daily episodes between Christmas and New Year.

With lyrics by Charles Hart (best known for his work on *The Phantom of the Opera* with Andrew Lloyd Webber) and music performed by the BBC Philharmonic Orchestra, this was an appropriately lavish – perhaps garish – update of an old staple into the very modern world.

The story has been updated to contemporary London, with the vampire antihero Ripley unearthed and unleashed by building development in the city. Rejoicing rather overtly in its modernity, **The Vampyr** doesn't shy away from the sex and violence of the tale - one episode begins with a crime scene, the sordid and bloody aftermath of one of Ripley's kills. It's unapologetically gory.

Similarly, a scene in art gallery makes conspicuous use of the presence of Damien Hirst's controversial shark in formaldehyde. At once it seems both ironic - a sharp-toothed predatory relic out of its place and time – and emphatic, a symbol of an aggressively modern, capitalist era and location.

A VIEW FROM A HILL (2005)

Drama | TV | 40 mins

TX: 23/12/2005, BBC4

28/12/2005, BBC4
21/12/2006, BBC4
16/12/2007, BBC4
22/12/2008, BBC4
24/12/2017, BBC4

The first new entry in the **Ghost Story for Christmas** series in a quarter of a century, **A View from a Hill** contains much that is familiar and formulaic in the light of the past, but is nonetheless fresh and intriguing as well. Producer Richard Fell's choice of story could not be named among the 'usual suspects', even while defaulting to the work of **M.R. James** for inspiration.

It feels inevitable that **A View from a Hill** should be about an archaeologist who falls foul of a cursed artefact – but at the same time, a pair of haunted binoculars is still a rather novel device. The protagonist, Fanshawe (Mark Letheren), borrows these mysterious binoculars from Squire Richards, who has employed him to catalogue his late father's archaeological collection.

Fanshawe discovers that the binoculars have strange and mysterious properties – that by looking through them he can see features in the landscape that are long-since gone – for example, the spire of a church.

Increasingly distracted by the power of the binoculars, Fanshawe fails to consider that more might be seen through those lenses than just the architecture of past – or that through them, other things gone from the world might be invited back in.

Essentially a chamber-piece with a cast of only four speaking characters, **A View from a Hill** is tight and effective, with excellent performances – most notably from Pip Torrens as the haughty Squire Richards. It maintains an unsettling mood throughout, and its final moments are executed with an admirable precision.

VIOLENCE

Reading | Radio | 15 mins

TX: 19/12/1939, BBC Home Service

Algernon Blackwood's short story about a homicidal maniac closing in on an unsuspecting victim, read by the author.

THE VISITOR'S BOOK

Reading | Radio | 15 mins

TX: 22/12/1969, Radio 2

One of A.J. Alan's tales, read as part of the *Morning Story* strand, by Peter Tuddenham. This reading was followed by a second, **A Christmas Ghost Story**, in the same slot the following day.

THE VOICE OF MICHAEL VANE

Reading | Radio | 60 mins

TX: 30/12/1941, BBC Home Service

'Almost a ghost story' written and told by the actor and songwriter James 'Jimmy' Dyrenforth. Further information is rather scarce, sadly, though the availability of old printed scores online does confirm that this programme included songs and seems to have had a life as a stage production.

A WARNING TO THE CURIOUS (1954)

Drama | Radio | ??? mins

TX: 10/12/1954, BBC Home Service Midland

Sadly, almost no information is available about this adaptation of the M.R. James tale, except that it was adapted for radio by Philip Donnellan (who was later well-known as a documentary maker).

A WARNING TO THE CURIOUS (1972)

Drama | TV | 50 mins

TX: 24/12/1972, BBC1
      26/12/1992, BBC2
      24/12/2004, BBC4
      20/12/2005, BBC4

The original 2002 DVD release of this play had a cover that featured an extreme close up of the face of the lead character, Paxton, played by Peter Vaughan.

Paxton's expression was clearly readable as one of alert, of listening out for the footsteps of somebody following him. The selection of this picture was a shrewd choice that managed to represent the dominant mood of the drama in a single image.

The opening shots of tranquil woodland, haunted only by birdsong and stillness, soon give way to an alarming soundscape of jangling, whistling, tinnitus in this second of Lawrence Gordon Clark's adaptations. More than any of the others in the series, it evokes feelings of constant unease, of being pursued, of helplessness and restlessness.

Paxton's ambitions in the story are perhaps more relatable and human, less prideful, than is always true of the protagonists in this series. An amateur archaeologist, he believes he can find a lost Anglo-Saxon crown – not as a matter of self-satisfaction or academic point-scoring, not even as a matter of treasure-hunting, but seemingly as a matter of self-validation.

We discern that he is a man whose circumstances are poor – it is slyly pointed out to him that he is not a proper gentleman, and we're led to assume that he's out of work. If he is a treasure hunter it's surely because of need, not because he's greedy.

All of these details help us to sympathise with Paxton, and relate to him in his plight. There is little in him that appeals to our crueller instincts or helps us to think that he deserves the retribution he stirs up.

However, we know that Paxton is not the first to look for the lost crown; the drama begins by showing us the fate of an earlier treasure hunter, and the wracked, coughing form of William Ager – the last guardian of the lost crown. We are shown the trap, and then we are shown Paxton as he blindly walks into it. Among the many downfalls shown in these ghost stories, his is surely the most painful to watch.

A WARNING TO THE FURIOUS

Drama | Radio | 45 mins

TX: 28/12/2007, Radio 4

This amusing drama by Robin Brooks comments upon modern critical analysis of **M.R. James** while also spinning an effective Jamesian tale of its own, a story of academic pride provoking ghostly retribution.

The heedless digger in this case is Karen, a documentary maker who is visiting the Suffolk coast with her film crew. Karen wants to make a film about **M.R. James**, exploring his background and speculating about what it was that inspired the unassuming scholar to relate so many tales of dread.

She lights upon a sensationalist and poorly-supported idea that the life-long bachelor was a misogynist and that this permeates his writing. She has no real evidence to substantiate her thesis, but does not intend to let that get in her way. However, her ruthless investigations may disturb more than the sensibilities of her colleagues...

THE WATCH HOUSE

Drama | TV | 3 x 30 mins

TX: 07/12/1988 – 21/12/1988, BBC1
       28/12/1990 – 02/01/1991, BBC1

The work of award-winning children's writer Robert Westall has been surprisingly seldom-adapted for other media; a number of adaptations were produced by **BBC Radio** in the 1990s, but British television has so far only produced two: *The Machine Gunners* (memorably adapted in 1983), and *The Watch House* – which is, so far, the only one of Westall's supernatural stories to be adapted for a visual medium.

The story is set in the coastal town of Garmouth (Westall's fictionalised version of Tynemouth, in the North-East of England), where the Watch House of the title is an old volunteer lifeboat station.

Anne, a young girl staying with a local couple, discovers the Watch House; it's now a museum under the care of one of her guardians - and, as she discovers, it is not a little haunted.

The first time she is alone in the building, she sees a message - 'Ann Help' - written in the dust. If this were not unsettling enough, after wiping this message away she then sees, right before her eyes, the same words written afresh in another patch of dust. Shortly afterwards an old skull smashes out of the glass case in which it is displayed, and falls to the floor. Then Ann begins to faint, and to have disturbing visions of past events...

This ghost story is unusually brief for children's dramas of the era, running to three episodes rather than the more usual six. However, it doesn't suffer for its brevity, and it makes the most of its location filming in Tynemouth. Lead actress Diana Morrison works with strong support from veterans like James Garbutt, and the script is by William Corlett, a veteran of children's television who had also worked on the BBCs previous Westall adaptation, *The Machine Gunners*.

WATERSHIP DOWN (1978)

Film | TV | 90 mins

TX: 28/12/1985, BBC1
    31/12/1987, BBC2
    25/12/1990, BBC2

Though feature films per se are not included in this book, **Watership Down** is an exception not least because what was once considered an 'enchanting' adventure film is now widely seen as the apogee of child-inappropriate children's films, a nightmare and the father of nightmares for generations of young viewers. I would argue that the film's presence in BBC Christmas Television schedules has something to do with that, as well as illustrating how perspectives have changed.

A tale of the adventures of a band of wild rabbits searching for a new home, **Watership Down** had its UK television debut on BBC1, early on a Saturday evening during the Christmas period. Clearly intended for family viewing, it was broadcast without any complaint at all. Two years later, the film was broadcast on New Year's Eve, this time on BBC2, but again without causing any kind of uproar.

Then came 1990, when the film was broadcast on Christmas Day, at 9.30 in the morning, exactly when children of all ages could see it and very likely did so without adult intermediation or reassurance. Mum and Dad were busy, and the children were left in front of the telly with the tender, seasonal images of corpse-clogged warren tunnels, fields awash with blood, death by snare, and buck rabbits tearing lumps out of each other in a tale analogous to both the Biblical Exodus and to escapes from Iron Curtain dictatorships. **Watership Down,** The Great Terror of Childhoods had arrived.

The film had always contained that disturbing imagery, of course – but I suggest that prior to this time (and with the exception of children left in front of a rented video of what a parent naively assumed was a Disney-esque cartoon) the film was not widely seen as the legendary horror it has since become. The continuity announcer in 1990 referred to it as a 'beloved' adaptation of Richard Adams's novel, and it had not proved controversial when presented to an audience with duly-calibrated expectations.

Watership Down is certainly a dark film, but the fact of it being an animated film about rabbits in search of a new home surely throws that darkness into high contrast. Whimsy is in short supply here, but primarily it is an adventure story and it is often exciting, beautiful, melancholy and sad. There are moments of violence, or of the supernatural, and combined with the tone of the story these qualify it for inclusion in the ranks of dark tales told at Christmas.

Watership Down has continued to appal (an Easter afternoon broadcast on Channel 5 in 2016 provoked a flood of complaints) and to be associated with Christmas – a new, two-part television adaptation was broadcast at Christmas in 2018. Though perfectly credible in a number of respects, it lacked the dreamlike imagery that makes the original film as memorable and as unsettling as it is.

THE WAY YOU LOOK AT IT: GHOSTS (1945)

Documentary | Radio | 20 mins

TX: 17/12/1945, BBC Home Service

Radio announcer Lionel Gamlin presented this weekly series in which three speakers would muse upon a given theme, such as 'The Englishman Abroad', or – as in the case of this pre-Christmas episode, Ghosts.

THE WEIR

Drama | Radio | 90 mins

TX: 20/12/1998, Radio 3

Conor McPherson's stage play was first performed at The Royal Court in July 1997, whereupon it met with considerable acclaim and received an Olivier award. A few months later, a BBC radio adaptation of the play was broadcast in the Sunday Drama slot on Radio 3. Featuring several of the original cast (notably, Jim Norton and Brendan Coyle), it was aired in March of 1998, – but was repeated at the end of the year just before Christmas.

Christmas makes a perfect setting for **The Weir**, because while it is not set at Christmas, it *is* about a small group of friends sitting around, enjoying each other's company and telling stories.

The setting is a quiet little pub in the Irish countryside; a small group of local friends welcome a young woman from Dublin who has recently moved into the area.

Conversation moves to reminiscence, and reminiscences give way to unsettling stories, tales of fairies and of ghosts. As the evening wears on, the tales become darker and more personal…

Though there is certainly more to **The Weir** than the telling of ghost stories, it tells ghost stories very well; the intimate and evocative setting of the quiet pub, the gently conversational back-and-forth of the friends... it all makes for an excellent example of its kind – and of course, being a radio programme, it is especially suited to appreciation in a darkened room.

WELSH GHOST STORIES

Reading | Radio | 15 mins

TX: 24/12/1929, 5WA Cardiff
     24/12/1948, BBC Home Service

Two Christmas Eve broadcasts of what appears to be a collection of traditional Welsh ghost tales. Sadly, it isn't possible to tell whether these broadcasts were in any way related from the listing information; however, given the generic title, and the fact that the broadcasts were twenty years apart, a direct connection can't be assumed.

THE WEREWOLF

Documentary | Radio | 35 mins

TX: 28/12/1979, Radio 4

An examination of the werewolf in history, folklore, and in fiction. Presented by Dr. Bill Russell (President of the Folklore Society), this documentary also included contributions from Valentine Dyall and Michael McClain.

WHEN STANDING STONES COME DOWN TO DRINK

Documentary | Radio | 30 mins

TX: 27/12/2010, BBC Radio Scotland
     03/01/2011, BBC Radio Scotland
     29/12/2021, Radio 4 Extra

In the Northern Isles of Scotland, many of the customs and dark traditions of Hallowe'en are instead associated with Yule; the undead are said to rise from their barrows, the trolls come up from the depths of the earth, and even the standing stones of Orkney stir and go down to the loch for a drink.

Broadcaster Tom Morton explores the folklore underlying this season, which makes for perhaps the most haunted Christmas celebrated in the British Isles.

WHISTLE AND I'LL COME TO YOU (1968)

Drama | TV | 40 mins

TX: 07/05/1968, BBC1
     22/12/2004, BBC4
     21/12/2005, BBC4
     19/12/2007, BBC4
     01/12/2009, BBC4
     24/12/2021, BBC4

Jonathan Miller's sparse adaptation, produced as part of the arts documentary strand *Omnibus*, begins with a short commentary that contextualises what follows; it suggests that the play is to some degree a discussion of the author himself. In the original story Parkin is a younger man, but Michael Hordern's version of the character is more mature, and perhaps invites comparison with M.R. James - especially after the brief description of the author given at the outset.

(Not that I'd wish to lean too heavily on this assumption, but it's always seemed to me that the solitude and intellectual inwardness of Parkin in the play corresponds to some of the more repetitive speculations one may hear being made about James).

In many ways this story now seems archetypal - when Parkin finds the whistle and pockets it, it is by no means the last time an act of amateur archaeology will have dire consequences for an isolated man in one of these M.R. James adaptations.

It is arguably a more psychological take than the plays that followed, however, holding back from obliging the viewer to take a definite position on the presence of the supernatural within the story. Either way, Michael Hordern's central performance is still compelling in its eccentricity, and the play's famous climax remains deeply unsettling when viewed today.

WHISTLE AND I'LL COME TO YOU (2010)

Drama | TV | 60 mins

TX: 24/12/2010, BBC2
      29/12/2010, BBC1

Neil Cross's adaptation of the M.R. James tale invites comparison with Jonathan Miller's earlier version, if only because of the reuse of the truncated title and the similar take on Professor Parkin as a solitary and isolated older man. Nonetheless, there are significant alterations to the story that make this version unique - even if they are of the kind that has doubtless made some wonder at the decision to adapt a story and then change its most significant elements.

In this contemporary-set adaptation Parkin is still an ageing professor, but instead of a creature who lives a solitary life inside his own head, he is a married man - albeit to a woman now in the later stages of dementia.

There is no Templar preceptory, no sense of the archaeological, and the whistle is replaced with an inscribed ring found on the beach, shifting the title's implications more firmly onto the song to which James originally alluded.

Yet, the drama also manages to capture those things that might be thought essential to the story – the sense of isolation and of being pursued by something that has been raised by the professor's discovery and which will not be denied; the sense of knowing you are not alone at night, when you know that you should be.

John Hurt is excellent as Parkin, the atmosphere of the piece is compelling and unsettling, and personally I was quite won over by the quality of the execution even though I felt that the changes to the story were unnecessary and unsubtle in their implications.

Nonetheless, those changes do have an integrity to them; to grieve for somebody who is still alive, as Parkin does, is to be haunted. The relationship between his wife and what haunts him in the guest house is hardly a surprise – the mystery of the whistle in the original story has been replaced with the certainty of the ring in this version – but all the same, the themes of grief and loss, and of the way dementia may make living ghosts out of those who suffer from it, are strongly presented here.

WILLIAM WILSON

Drama | TV | 30 mins

TX: 19/12/1976

Edgar Allan Poe's tale of a man's long moral descent, and his persecution by a shadowy figure who bears the same name, William Wilson. Though their relationship is adversarial, both men increasingly resemble one another.

This was the second of two Poe tales adapted for a Christmas edition of the *Centre Play* drama strand - the other Poe-derived *Centre Play at Christmas* being **The Imp of the Perverse** (1975)

THE WILLOWS

Drama | Radio | 60 mins

TX: 17/12/2022, BBC Radio 4

One of Algernon Blackwood's best-regarded and most influential tales, The Willows was very highly-praised by H.P. Lovecraft, and can easily be seen as one of the precursors of his own stories of 'cosmic horror'. Blackwood is more restrained than Lovecraft usually chose to be, and provides much in the way of atmosphere and a sense of the Alien and the Other, but almost nothing in the way of explanation. Therein lies its strength.

The story tells of two men canoeing their way down the river Danube, who find themselves stranded on a little island thickly crowded with willow bushes. While there, they gradually become aware of other presences into whose space they have intruded...

Stef Penney's adaptation for BBC radio explores the implications of the story's temporal setting, with both of the lead characters contextualised as survivors of the Great War, and of the Influenza pandemic that followed it. The two men are journeying away from the carnage of civilisation and humanity, into the peace and stillness of the European wilds – but they have not accounted for the possibility that they would find not peaceful loneliness, but a dreadful otherness that waits in the empty places beyond the view of human society. It's a shrewd idea, making the protagonists themselves into alienated creatures before they encounter the truly alien forces in the wilderness.

The small cast of this radio play has a rather prestigious feel, with film stars Bill Pullman and Julian Sands in the lead roles.

THE WITHERED ARM

Reading | Radio | 3 x 15 mins

TX: 27/12/1978 – 29/12/1978

One of Thomas Hardy's Wessex Tales, Paul Rogers reads this story of love, obsession, jealousy, dreams and curses...

WITH INTENT TO STEAL

Reading | Radio | 30 mins

TX: 25/12/1947, BBC Third Programme

Algernon Blackwood's short story about a night spent in a haunted barn, read by the author.

THE WOLVES OF WILLOUGHBY CHASE (1994)

Drama | Radio | 90 mins

TX: 30/12/1994, BBC Radio 4
      26/12/2020, BBC Radio 4 Extra

Joan Aiken's celebrated gothic novel for younger readers is set in a richly-imagined parallel history of England where King James III is on the throne. In this alternative timeline a channel tunnel has allowed wolves to return to England, a fact that brings both atmosphere and a sense of imminent threat to the narrative.

Unsurprisingly given the gothic mood of the tale, it tells the story of a girl named Sylvia who is travelling through snowy, wolf-ravaged countryside to her new home at Willoughby Chase. When she finally arrives there, she is delivered into the clutches of a governess who would be quite at home stalking the pages of a Le Fanu novel.

(Indeed, the governess Miss Slighcarp is played here by Jane Lapotairre, who had previously played the wicked governess Mme De La Rougierre in *The Dark Angel*, the 1988 BBC adaptation of Le Fanu's *Uncle Silas*)

Aiken's story has proved to be a popular Christmas fixture; apart from this radio play, a feature film adaptation was broadcast on BBC2 on Christmas Eve 1991, and New Year's Eve 1995.

Moreover, the book was read on Jackanory twice – by June Barry in December 1968, and by Jane Carr in December 1982.

THE WOMAN IN BLACK

Susan Hill's classic ghost story from 1983 is notable for having been successfully adapted to a variety of different media. The long-running stage play was first performed in 1987, and a TV adaptation followed in 1989. A radio serial was broadcast in 1993, with a second radio dramatisation in 2004 and a feature film finally arriving in 2012.

Though the novel has many elements that suggest a tongue-in-cheek tone, it ultimately tells an intense story of an honest young man who dares to trespass on the territory of a singularly malevolent spirit, and the price he pays for doing so. Hill acknowledges her Victorian and Edwardian antecedents with a variety of little allusions, including the book's own title (nodding respectfully at Wilkie Collins's **The Woman in White**), and even the story's set-up – of a solicitor's clerk sent on a journey to somewhere remote in order to resolve the legal affairs of an ominous client – recalls Bram Stoker's Dracula. The book did not immediately gain the reputation it now enjoys and its arguable that it received a considerable lift from the stage and television productions based on it.

The Woman in Black (1984)
Reading | Radio | 8 x 15 mins

TX: 10/12/1984 - 19/12/1984 (weekdays)

The very first UK radio adaptation of Hill's novel was this eight-part reading performed by Alan Dudley on weekday afternoons. The scheduling of this reading in December is particularly apt as Hill frames her story as, if not an actual ghost story for Christmas, then at least one commenting upon that tradition while participating in it.

The Woman in Black (1989)
Drama | TV | 105 mins

TX: 24/12/1989, ITV
TX: 25/12/1994, Channel 4

Once a legendary shadow, recalled in hushed tones by those who saw it long ago, Herbert Wise's **The Woman in Black** has finally emerged from long years of (legal) non-availability and might now be said to be enjoying a renaissance. It turns out that this is one of those TV memories that is every bit as good as it had been built up to be.

Susan Hill's novel presents its narrative as an anti-Christmas Ghost Story, a tale told by a man to explain why he does not participate in the good-natured exchange of chilling tales among his family. Though this context was originally considered for inclusion, it was ultimately excised from the TV film. Given that it was to be broadcast on Christmas Eve, the loss of Christmas from Nigel Kneale's adaptation hardly seems to matter.

Kneale was, needless to say, a shrewd and skilful screenwriter, and while his version of Hill's tale is perfectly recognisable, he draws out subtleties from the story and introduces certain economies that serve it very well in the televisual medium, even while some of the changes seem trivial or unnecessary.

The young hero of the story is a solicitor's clerk named Arthur Kidd – Kipps in the book, a direct borrowing from a certain H.G. Wells novel, removed by Kneale - and as we see him enter his place of work, we are aware of a harsh, insistent sniffing. In the original version of the story this is simply the comical sound made by a colleague; Kneale changes it to the sound of a client Arthur has promised to help. The poor man's breathing has been affected by exposure to gas during the war, and Arthur is trying to help him get the pension appropriate to him and his condition.

In this simple change, Kneale has turned a comical sequence into a little sketch of Arthur's essential kindness and decency, while turning a figure of mockery into one of pathos and sympathy – not to mention, reminding us of how casually people may be cruel towards those whose lives they know little of.

This change may seem by-the-by, but I think it demonstrates the heart of Kneale's work on the story; there is a greater emphasis on humanity here, both good and bad. Moreover, the debilitated state of Arthur's client quietly prefigures the infirmity into which he is later plunged by his experiences.

One of Kneale's most impactful changes is the introduction of a wax cylinder machine; in other versions of the story the deceased Mrs Drablow can only be known by the documents she leaves behind. In this version Arthur finds her recorded journal; he gets to hear her voice - *we* get to hear her voice.

Apart from the practical impact this has, of breaking up what might otherwise have been a lengthy period without any human speech, these recordings also provide counterpoint to the spectral death-shrieks that Arthur hears echoing out of the sea-mists when he is outside the house.

He speculates that perhaps these sounds, these ghosts, are themselves no more than recordings. Perhaps so – but if ghosts are recordings, then perhaps recordings are also ghosts, and we at home might find the voice of Mrs Drablow all the more unsettling as a result.

All of this is before we even consider the presence of the Woman in Black herself, of course...

While Kneale's work on the drama is to be celebrated, it is of course no reason to overlook the work of the director Herbert Wise, or indeed any other aspect of this production. The cast are excellent, certainly including Pauline Moran whose baleful presence as the woman doesn't allow her any lines, but in one scene she does produce an extraordinarily memorable screech. Among the many stalwarts present in the cast, David Ryall, Clare Holman and Bernard Hepton are particularly good, and Adrian Rawlins makes for an excellent, humane protagonist.

For many years the only way to see this TV drama was as a grotty reproduction taken from a very short-lived early 1990s VHS release; Network's DVD/Blu-Ray release of the film shows it in all of its restored and eerie glory.

The Woman in Black (1993)
Drama | Radio | 4 x 30 mins

TX: 09/12/1993 – 30/12/1993, Radio 5
        22/12/1994 – 12/01/1995, BBC World Service

20/12/2010 – 23/12/2010, BBC 7
06/12/2015 – 27/12/2015, Radio 4 Extra
21/12/2020 – 24/12/2020, Radio 4 Extra

In broadcasting terms this radio adaptation of **The Woman in Black** came surprisingly quickly after the television film – though, at a time when most television was still only available to view just once unless you had personally recorded it, four years was a much longer interval than it might sound today.

Unlike the ITV adaptation, very few people will have even known that this radio serial existed – broadcast mid-evening in the mediumwave murk of Radio 5, I'm quite sure it will have been overlooked by all but a few, even though it would have made for good entertainment on a winter's evening nonetheless.

Happily, it has enjoyed a prolific afterlife and reached a much wider audience on the digital channels **BBC7** and **Radio 4 Extra**, which have, between them, repeated the serial more than ten times to date.

Heard today, the one serious issue the serial has is a synthesized theme tune that now sounds better-suited to a theme park ride or a story of magical fantasy than to a tale of dread – but as jarring as this is, it cannot take away the pluses.

The adaptation is straightforward and retains the book's Christmas framing device, with all the radio-friendly advantages of first-person narration that affords. The cast is also solid, but in particular the young Arthur is played by Robert Glenister, who was already an established character actor at the time, and a very familiar face on television today. To my mind John Woodvine sounds a little detached as the older, narrating voice of Arthur, as if he is reading an audiobook rather than performing a character – but this is a minor issue, and he does rise to the appropriate emotional pitch in the final episode's climax.

THE WOMAN IN WHITE (1997)

Drama | TV | 2 x 60 mins

TX: 28/12/1997 – 29/12/1997, BBC1
     25/12/2000, BBC2 (2-hour edit)

One of Wilkie Collins's best-known novels, **The Woman in White** is a story of mystery, of an encounter with a ghostly doppelganger, and of not one but two utterly dastardly villains. There's an irresponsible guardian, a clever heroine and a pair of young lovers for good measure. Fans of Gothic melodrama need look no further.

Following on from the 1996 adaptation of Collins's **The Moonstone**, which had been broadcast over Christmas, the BBC presented a new version of **The Woman in White** for Christmas 1997.

A particularly strong cast includes Tara Fitzgerald, bringing an appropriate strength of character to the courageous Marian Fairlie, and Justine Waddell appears in one of her first roles as the younger Fairlie sister, Laura. James Wilby and Simon Callow oppose them in their villainous alliance as Sir Perceval Glyde and the sinister Count Fosco. Ian Richardson also appears as the reprehensible, irresponsible Mr. Fairlie and a young Andrew Lincoln cuts a dash as the earnest Walter Hartright.

Sadly, this brief run of Wilkie Collins dramas at Christmas did not continue into a third drama the following year – though there was a feature-length repeat broadcast of **The Moonstone** on Christmas Eve

1998. Christmas 1999 was Wilkie Collins-free, but a feature-length repeat of **The Woman in White** adorned the Christmas Day schedules in 2000.

THE WOMAN'S GHOST STORY

Reading| Radio | 30 mins

TX: 25/12/1958, BBC Home Service

Algernon Blackwood gave a reading of his tale in which a woman recounts an episode from her career as a psychic investigator; the story has a slightly romantic inflection, and is memorable for featuring a ghost who is effectively 'haunted' by visitations of the living.

A WORLD OF SOUND: A GHOST FOR BREAKFAST

Reading | Radio | 15 mins

TX: 20/12/1965, BBC World Service

"Robert Stannage presents Supernatural Stories from the BBC Sound Archives"

THE WYVERN MYSTERY

Drama| TV | 120 mins

TX: 22/12/2005, BBC4

The Wyvern Mystery was considered significant enough on its first broadcast in March 2000 that it was given a Radio Times cover upon which the declarative word 'Haunted' competed for space with the glamour of the young actress who had been cast as the heroine of this 'Sunday night chiller'.

One of those instances of television briefly having the benefit of an actor during their rapid ascent to stardom, this Sheridan Le Fanu adaptation boasted Naomi Watts as its heroine, Alice. She's in good company, too, with Derek Jacobi, Iain Glenn and Jack Davenport as the men of the Fairfield clan into whose care she is taken after her father's death.

Although the drama is based on a novel that never puts the supernatural into play, it is nonetheless steeped entirely in shadows. The first appearance of the woman Vrau, coming at the end of the first episode, would not disgrace any horror film; Aisling O'Sullivan's performance as the blind assassin is both unsettling and uncanny.

Arguably the story itself is unlikely to surprise anybody who has a reasonable familiarity with Gothic novels, but it's effective nonetheless. Even so, the series didn't seem to make much of an impact on its first broadcast.

In 2005 it was dusted off for a feature-length repeat as part of BBC4s season of ghostly tales for Christmas, alongside a number of Lawrence Gordon Clark's ghost stories from the 1970s. This broadcast of **The Wyvern Mystery** came after a repeat of **The Story of the Ghost Story**, and was followed by a late-night broadcast of Guillermo Del Toro's Spanish Civil War ghost story *The Devil's Backbone*.

THE YELLOW WALLPAPER

Drama | TV | 75 mins

TX: 02/01/1992, BBC2

Charlotte Perkins Gilman's harrowing tale of delusion and mental collapse is brought to life in this lush, flute-haunted adaptation that builds to a conclusion combining horror, alienation and tragedy.

The story's protagonist is a woman whose physician husband responds to what he perceives as her hysteria by imposing 'rest' upon her. When the escalating conditions of this rest increasingly deprive her of stimulation, her mind turns inwards, and she develops an obsession with the sulphurous yellow wallpaper lining her room. Soon she begins to have visions of a strange woman in a yellow dress who creeps on all fours through the woodland; perhaps, though - as is often the way in ghost stories - this vision is more specular than spectre.

With its unsettling but deeply mournful climax, this drama is all the more disturbing because while it is usually seen as a tale of the supernatural or the uncanny, it can simply be taken as a tale of mental breakdown resulting from isolation – perhaps Gilman's tale is a direct ancestor of Polanski's *Repulsion*, or even Peter Strickland's *Berberian Sound Studios* (*The Giallo Wallpaper*?). Either way, the author stated the tale to be semi-autobiographical and on those terms the sadness and terror of this story acquire an edge that is all the keener.

YESTERDAY – ONCE MORE

Drama | Radio | 4 x 30 mins

TX: 21/12/1993 – 24/12/1993, Radio 5

Moir Leslie returns as Christine, in this sequel to Eric Pringle's earlier series, **Is Anybody There** (broadcast over Christmas 1990-91).

Christine discovers there are spirits other than Kirsty's trapped at Angel Court, and that the past tragedy in which they were involved is threatening to repeat itself in the present.

YOU THE JURY: "Today's proposition: Ghosts Exist"

Documentary | Radio | 45 mins

TX: 23/12/1978, Radio 4
27/12/1978, Radio 4

A long-running show using the format of a debate to address controversial issues of the day. When it finally vacated the airwaves in 1987, it was replaced only a few years later by the conceptually similar *The Moral Maze*, a pit from the fires of which leapt such imps and goblins as David Starkey, Claire Fox, and Michael Gove.

Anyway, there would be no reason at all to mention this show, except that in 1978 the edition broadcast over Christmas addressed the pressing concern (apparently in recognition of the season) of whether or not ghosts exist. Proof, if it were needed, that in Britain even serious conversations veer toward the ghostly when the Christmas decorations go up.

Afterword: Some Deep, Organising Power

"...he has no other name. His past is a mystery, but his work is already a legend..."

Actually, while Mark Gatiss differs in several ways from Swan, the Phil Spectorish record producer in Brian De Palma's *The Phantom of the Paradise*, I do increasingly harbour the suspicion that he's made some sort of pact with the devil.

(This is not an attempt at libel. I feel that in a book about Christmas Ghost Stories, Mark Gatiss has earned a special mention - I'm just being florid about it.)

If it's said that Robert Johnson made a deal with Lucifer to achieve musical greatness, then it's easy to imagine that a teenaged Mark Gatiss once stood at a crossroads (probably in East Anglian fenland, with a vandalised telephone box and an old bus shelter in the background) and made a deal to achieve every single one of those creative ambitions fostered by a childhood illuminated by the light that only a television could produce.

The devil, looking very much like Alfred Burke in an old raincoat, would have emerged from the mists, to be handed a scrap of notepaper with a long list on it. He'd scrutinise it with a heavily furrowed brow, before raising his eyebrows in perplexity. "Well, if you're sure," he'd probably say.

In his career so far, Mr Gatiss has made creative contributions to various incarnations in various media of Doctor Who, Sherlock Holmes, James Bond, Quatermass, Hammer Horror films, Thunderbirds, Frankenstein, Dr Jekyll & Mr Hyde, Dracula, and adaptations of the work of M.R. James, Nigel Kneale, Terry Pratchett, Neil Gaiman, Douglas Adams, H.G. Wells, John Le Carre, and Agatha Christie.

This is just scratching the surface, really. At one time Mr Gatiss was a regular contributor to Radio 4's *The Film Programme*, where he would select forgotten character actors of British cinema and highlight them for contemporary appreciation. I find it quite believable that Mr Gatiss may one day be held up among that same company, an ever-reliable actor whose work has varied from the raucous and funny to the subtle and disturbing; he plays heartless villains quite as effectively as he does harmless eccentrics and decent chaps.

The sheer ubiquity of Gatiss's work, especially in the horror genre, has led some to opine that they'd like to see somebody else tackle these things for a change. While that's perfectly understandable – and, I suspect, something with which Mr Gatiss would very likely agree – it does overlook the possibility that (for example) without his efforts to get new Ghost Stories for Christmas made, they would not be on television at all.

Mark Gatiss is probably the one living person whose name appears most frequently in this book, and it is undeniable that British Christmases would have been considerably less haunted over the last twenty-five years without him.

I feel that speaks for itself, and so Mr. Gatiss surely merits this specific and appreciative acknowledgement.

mysteriousmagpie@outlook.com

ALSO AVAILABLE:

TARGET BOOKS: ADVENTURES WITHOUT THE DOCTOR

A survey of 200 books from the popular children's publisher of the 1970s and 80s that *didn't* involve Doctor Who.

Printed in Great Britain
by Amazon